OPTION LOCK

JUSTIN RICHARDS

BBC BOOKS

Other BBC DOCTOR WHO books include:

THE EIGHT DOCTORS *by Terrance Dicks*

THE BODYSNATCHERS *by Mark Morris*

GENOCIDE *by Paul Leonard*

WAR OF THE DALEKS *by John Peel*

ALIEN BODIES *by Lawrence Miles*

THE DEVIL GOBLINS FROM NEPTUNE *by Keith Topping and Martin Day*

THE MURDER GAME *by Steve Lyons*

THE ULTIMATE TREASURE *by Christopher Bulis*

BUSINESS UNUSUAL *by Gary Russell*

ILLEGAL ALIEN *by Mike Tucker and Robert Perry*

THE ROUNDHEADS *by Mark Gatiss*

THE FACE OF THE ENEMY *by David A. McIntee*

EYE OF HEAVEN *by Jim Mortimore*

THE BOOK OF LISTS *by Justin Richards and Andrew Martin*

A BOOK OF MONSTERS *by David J Howe*

DOCTOR WHO titles on BBC Video include:

THE HAPPINESS PATROL *starring Sylvester McCoy*	BBCV 6183
TIMELASH *starring Colin Baker*	BBCV 6329
THE E-SPACE TRILOGY BOXED SET *starring Tom Baker*	BBCV 6229

Published by BBC Books
an imprint of BBC Worldwide Publishing
BBC Worldwide Ltd, Woodlands, 80 Wood Lane
London W12 0TT

First published 1998
Copyright © Justin Richards 1998
The moral right of the author has been asserted.

Original series broadcast on the BBC
Format © BBC 1963
Doctor Who and TARDIS are trademarks of the BBC

ISBN 0 563 40583 X
Imaging by Black Sheep, copyright © BBC 1998
Front cover claw illustration by Colin Howard

Printed and bound in Great Britain by Mackays of Chatham
Cover printed by Belmont Press Ltd, Northampton

Contents

For Alison, Julian, and the Other One – with love

Dark Ripples

The Khameirian cruiser was already beyond its tolerances when the Yogloth Slayer brought it down. They had been playing cat and mouse across half the galaxy, twisting, turning, running. And the cruiser was the mouse. Rounding Rigellis III, it ran out of space, time, and luck.

The self-targeting torpedo must have torn through the drive section of the cruiser like a wolf through a rabbit. Life support would have escaped the worst of it, but the main computer and navigation systems were taken out along with communications. Perhaps some of them died in the blast, it hardly matters. The Stone knew them.

The systems limped on for a while, unwilling or unable to give up the fight. Some residual energy in the drive systems, maybe. But the end was inevitable. It is said that the Khameirian will to survive is unparalleled. But they had to make planetfall to have any hope at all. And there are no planets to be fallen to in the Rigellis systems. They burned across the cosmos, leaving legends and prophecies in their wake. The Slayer probably broke off after the initial hit. They're great ones for economy of effort, the Yogloths. I have seen one of their assassins turn and leave the seedy bar where he had cornered his target before the bolt was halfway down the guidance beam. Lucky for me.

They had met before. Many times. Though tonight, their leader told them, tonight would be different. But then he always told them that. And they always believed him. But this time he was right. He may have visited each in turn, the lamplight flickering across his face as their wives, their daughters, their consciences, looked away sharply in embarrassment. Or perhaps he told only the first of his followers, and the message was whispered to the others in hushed, reverent, believing tones.

Imagine the cloaked figures making their way through the dying thunderstorm. See them silhouetted against the full moon, glimpsed in the moments when the dark clouds were driven from its glow by the same winds as whipped their hoods around their faces. Dark figures approaching the dark ruins atop the windswept hill. The fallen stonework as stark and black in the night as their unspoken purpose. And all the while, one star in the cloud-hidden heavens was flashing ever closer to their destiny.

Who knows what those men thought as they stood in the dark? See them, cloaked and hooded like extras in a third-rate opera. Imagine with me that you see them as they stand in their circle, toes to the chalk. See the candlelight guttering on their faces and hear the wind howling through the ruined stone. But they don't hear it, lost as they are in their stentorian chant. Arms raised to heaven, voices raised to hell.

And for what? An impossible dream, a mystery, a myth. A hope almost against hope that the new science and the old magic can combine, meld, merge into something wonderful. But tonight the impossible fantasy of the alchemists will become an impossible reality. The dream takes form, becomes a nightmare. Here, in this ruined chapel on this windswept hill beneath this stormy sky.

Imagine their leader standing beneath the ravaged roof of the chapel, transfixed by a sudden shaft of moonlight. Then the light grows, as if in answer to the chant. A vast fireball blurs across the horizon and screams its way down towards them. They must have thought that all hell was breaking loose at their command. I think they still believed that to the days they died. And perhaps they were right. Who knows what power, what will-power, the Khameirian preservation systems responded to, what faint final option they locked on to across the darkness of space? Six lonely men brought together by their crazy aspirations and lazy philosophy. And after that night, that visitation, living out their lives curled around the loneliness of their nightmares, the blackness of the thoughts that were no longer their own.

After the doom-crack of the cruiser furrowing its way across the field outside and cratering the landscape, they stand still. Awed. Believing and not believing that all is as they intended, expected, and hoped. Then the ship wrenches its last few inches of life into the side of the shattered chapel, sends masonry and stonework crashing through the heavy air. They duck and scurry, searching out shelter in the darkness, thinking their lives are in their own hands. The candles dip and waver before flaring in the sudden stillness. And as dawn edges uneasily across the edge of their world, the rotten wood of the door cracks open like an egg.

Imagine you see through their eyes, through their fear, as the creature lurches into the gloom. It probably paused on the threshold, eyes glinting as it struggled to make out the forms of things unknown. Then as their imaginations bodied forth, it may have stumbled down the steps to the end of its life. The stuttering light lost itself in the leathery folds of its wings, in the darkness of its skin. But the face – the pinched, wrinkled features and the short, curled horns – probably made the most impression on the already impressionable men gathered that night.

It's incredible that it managed to get out of the ship, let alone seek out salvation in the dark. But now at last it can give up the ghost, letting it slip from the leathery claw that gripped so tight. It rolls across the cracked, uneven

3

stonework of the floor. The only sound is the rattle of it like a marble as it leaves the creature's hand and curls its way to the leader of the ceremony. A gift to him from the gods. Or devils.

He lifts it up, allows the first hints of light to merge with the reflected candle flames on its surface. Perhaps he can already see the pale inner glow, but if not he imagines it. And then he turns to his comrades and they make the pact. Their first non-decision.

After that, they laugh nervously. They agree to meet again, to share their thoughts and track their progress against an unspoken agenda. Every night they watch the darkening skies, and every day their thoughts, their wills, their selves ebb a little further from the shore. And all the time the light inside the Philosopher's Stone glows slightly stronger as the point of focus sharpens just a little more. Glowing towards fruition; towards life; towards oblivion.

1
Towards Oblivion

The air was heavy with latent thunder. A storm had been gathering for a long while, yet it refused to break. The humidity was so intense you could taste it, and the clouds hung heavy and low in the autumn sky. Captain William Pickering looked out of the dusty window towards the remains of the old manor house on the hill. If he glimpsed a flash among the ruins, then perhaps it was lightning; if he heard a low rumble disturb the afternoon, then it must be thunder. But through the bottle glass of the small panes it was difficult to be sure of things.

Quite what it was, Henry Tanner could not tell. He heard the grating, metallic crescendo of sound as he pushed his wheelbarrow along the cinder path. He caught a glimpse of what might have been a flashlight shone from behind the remains of a wall. He paused, waiting to see if the light came again, pushing a tangle of stray grey hair up from his weathered forehead.

But before it did, his mind cracked open and he sank to his knees in sudden unexpected agony.

The pain seared through Colonel Roskov's brain like a branding iron. One moment he was standing by the relief map on his office wall pointing out the new defensive positions to Lieutenant Ivigan, the next he was on his knees doubled up in agony. A tortured rip down the centre of Krejikistan marked the path of his fall.

Then suddenly the pain was gone. There was just a

realisation, an understanding in its place. Ivigan grabbed Roskov's elbow, reacting too late to prevent his fall.

'Are you all right?'

Roskov looked up surprised. For a second there had been nothing in his mind but purpose, mission. Destiny. No context.

Ivigan helped Roskov back to his feet. 'Are you all right, sir?' he said again.

Pete Kellerman picked himself up, clutching at the lectern for support. 'Yes.' But he wasn't at all sure. 'Yes, I'm fine. Thank you.' He took a sip of water, amazed at how steady his hand was, at how clear his thoughts were, at the enormity of what he had to do. 'Let's call it a day, shall we?' he said to his students, his voice husky with anticipation of the next phase. 'Tomorrow we'll talk about the importance of deploying a coherent strategy across the world.'

Right round the world, time slipped out of phase for a handful of people. Their minds burned with sudden brilliant purpose, reeled under the realisation of who and what they were. And at Abbots Siolfor, Norton Silver stood beside William Pickering, looking out over his estate through distorting glass. 'There's going to be a storm,' he said quietly.

The flames of the everlasting candles guttered and shook as if caught in a storm. Shadows darkened and shifted, the spotlit swirl of the Prydonian Seal seemed to fade in and out of existence as the light flickered. Blackness stabbed through the chamber, darkening the cobwebbed bookshelves and accumulated bric-a-brac. Inverse lightning in a space that did not exist, a time that never happened. A concerto of chiaroscuro.

The howl of the impossible wind mixed with the slurring

strains of Bach as an antiquated vinyl record ground to a halt on its turntable. An old street lamp regained its composure and luminance, lights glowed back into existence on the various panels of the central control console. Above the console a deceptively ancient television monitor went through a retuning cycle of snowstorm patterns and static crackles before settling on a single line of white text against a black background.

The wind dropped, the noise died, the light returned. Samantha Jones pushed her blonde hair back out of her face. It was something of a novelty to have hair long enough to get blown there in the first place. She was not sure it was worth the hassle, but she was getting to like the way it framed her face and hid her ears. The last few weeks had been relatively relaxed. Since they had left Kursaal, the Doctor had taken them to a couple of sunny paradise resorts, on a tour of the monuments of Marsuum, and (accidentally, he claimed) mountain climbing in the Vasterial Wastes of Julana. During this time, Sam had tried to grow her hair (successfully) and quit biting her nails (less so).

And now this. She noted with amusement that the Doctor seemed to have had no problem with his own long hair. He was slumped in an armchair, feet up, reading. The drawing room incongruously joined the console area of the TARDIS.

'So what gives?' she asked him. 'Windswept in the TARDIS – not an everyday fashion hazard, I would guess.'

'I guess not.' The Doctor tossed aside his copy of *The Strange Case of Dr Jekyll and Mr Hyde* and swung his feet off the footstool. His eyes were intensely alive as he strode across to the console. 'Why does this always happen when I'm reading?'

'I think the TARDIS gets bored when you're reading,' Sam told him. 'You know, perhaps she likes to be a bit more involved in what's going on. Maybe chat a little. Social pleasantries. Stuff.' She shrugged and wandered over to join him by the screen.

CRITICAL ARTRON ENERGY DRAIN

The words flashed across the monitor.
'What does that mean?'
The Doctor took a deep breath. 'Who knows?'
Then as they watched the message changed:

COMPENSATING FOR POWER LOSS

'Well, there you are.' The Doctor smiled brightly and made his way back to his armchair. 'Nothing at all to worry about.' He scooped up his book and was immediately engrossed.

Sam was not so sure. There was a sudden calm after the storm that she found unsettling. She looked round, and it occurred to her why it seemed so still. 'The rotor's stopped,' she said. 'We've landed.'

The Doctor turned a page. 'The power drain pulled us out of the vortex,' he said without looking up. 'Or it's something local that happened as we materialised. Doesn't matter. The power's building nicely again now as the Eye of Harmony absorbs background energy from the world outside.' The book lowered slightly and the Doctor's eyebrows became visible above it. 'We'll be stuck here for a bit till everything's charged up again, but that's hardly an inconvenience.' Another page turned. 'We've plenty to read.'

Sam watched him for a few moments. He seemed prepared to sit for eternity with his nose in a book. She grimaced, hands on hips. 'So where are we, then?'

'Earth.'

'Earth?'

The Doctor lowered his book with the slow movement of forced patience. 'Earth. 1998. Or thereabouts.' He raised the book again.

'So why don't we go outside and see what's going on?'

No answer. Sam went over to the Doctor and knelt in front of his armchair. She reached out and pulled the book down from his face. His eyes were already focused on her own as she said again. 'So why don't we go outside and see what's going on?'

For a split second his eyes were hard, his face set. Then he grinned suddenly and broadly. 'Why not?' he said. 'I think it's going to be a lovely day.'

It was a lovely day. A few clouds wandered lazily cross a deep-blue sky and the trees shimmered in the autumn heat and the light breeze. Henry Tanner stared up, aware of the slight damp of the grass beneath his head. Calm. Peaceful. At ease.

So what was he doing lying on the ground?

Tanner struggled to his feet, his elderly joints protesting and his knees cracking as he put weight on them. He blinked several times. A blackout of some sort? He had never had one before. He looked round, hoping for some clue in the landscape – a rock he might have tripped on, a slippery patch of mud. There was neither. Just a toppled wheelbarrow beside the track, the stark ruins of the old manor house on the brow of the hill, and two people hurrying down the slope towards him. As he watched, they passed the fallen remains of a statue, the taller figure pausing for a moment to inspect the grotesque features. Then he was off again, hurrying down the slope after his companion.

Two people. He frowned. Tanner knew he was the only person working in the garden today. It was a Saturday, and the rest of the staff took the weekend off. But the grounds were Tanner's life. He accepted only grudgingly that he needed any help at all, and the weekends were precious short days of peace. Time to plan and to refine. Time to take stock, to enjoy.

'Are you all right?'

The two figures had almost reached Tanner now. The young woman with blonde hair was slightly out of breath, but the older man was not even breathing heavily. He looked to be in his thirties, though his eyes seemed somehow older, deeper. Despite the warmth of the autumn afternoon, the man was wearing a long, heavy coat over a formal shirt and paisley waistcoat. A grey-green cravat added to the formality. Yet the off-centre tiepin, the ragged velvet cuffs of the dark coat, and the wildness of his long hair suggested a lack of interest in his appearance.

'You looked as if you'd fallen,' the man said. His voice was soft but had a powerful edge to it. An indeterminable trace of accent. Northern perhaps. Not local, anyhow. He reached out and dusted a blade of grass from Tanner's shoulder. 'Are you all right?' he repeated.

Tanner nodded. 'I'm fine,' he said, rolling his shoulder where the stranger had touched it.

The man smiled. 'Good.'

Tanner glared at them, trying to hide his embarrassment, and made towards the wheelbarrow.

The girl got there first. 'Let me,' she said, as she uprighted the barrow. Her voice was friendly, with a hint of the town in it.

'I can manage.' Tanner pushed the wheelbarrow slightly off the track, and turned back to the strangers. 'Now who are you? What are you doing here?'

The man considered, hands clasped in front of him. 'Well. . .'

'This is private property, you know,' Tanner prompted.

'We know,' the girl said. 'Don't we?' Her companion did not

answer. 'Don't we?'

'Yes, yes, yes. Of course we do. Absolutely.' He looked round. 'Private property. Indeed. And very nicely kept too.' He leaned forward with a grin. 'You do it all yourself?'

Tanner found himself answering without even thinking. 'The important things, most of them anyway. Of course I need more help these days than when I was younger. I used to help my dad when he was head groundsman, and just the two of us could cope for the most part. But with the new machinery to help. And Mr Silver is more particular about appearances than his father was. Quite rightly so, too, in my opinion. Not that we were ever lax, you understand. Never.'

The man nodded in complete understanding and agreement. 'And the ruins would be, what, fourteenth century perhaps? Thirteenth at a pinch?'

Tanner frowned. Suddenly he seemed to have accepted these two strangers, although he wasn't sure how or why. 'That what you're here for, is it? The ruins?'

'Might be,' the girl said.

Tanner nodded thoughtfully. That would explain things. 'You'd best see Mr Silver if you're wanting to research them,' he said. 'Mr Silver does a lot of researching of these things himself. Very interesting it is to him.'

'I'm sure.'

'Experts, are you? Historians?'

The man grabbed Tanner's hand and shook it with ruthless enthusiasm. 'I'm the Doctor,' he said as if this explained everything. 'And this is my research assistant, Miss Jones.'

'Sam,' the girl added, taking her turn shaking Tanner's hand.

Tanner fumbled in his pocket and pulled out his mobile phone. He stared at it for a moment. He rarely used it, and nearly always to answer calls from his gardeners, usually asking dumb-fool questions they should know the answers to.

The Doctor gently took it from him, turned it over, and flipped open the cover. Then he handed it back.

'Mr Silver expecting you, is he?'

'He will be.'

The girl – Sam – smiled, tossing her head so that her hair swung away from her face. 'We're here to make an appointment, actually.'

Behind them the ruins of the old manor house stood, dark and impassive, against the deep sky.

Norton Silver stood straight and still on the driveway as he waited for them to join him. As they approached, Sam could see that he was a big man, broad and tall. He looked as though he was in his fifties, with steel-grey hair and the first few lines of age on his tanned face. He wore a suit that was slightly darker than his hair, and he looked like a businessman. Behind him was the modern house, as Tanner had described it, although even to Sam's untrained eye it looked ancient.

'The ruins are definitely thirteenth century in origin,' the Doctor said quietly as they crunched up the driveway. 'This house appears to be part sixteenth century and part later, right up to that Victorian wing.' He leaned round Sam to point, his other hand on her shoulder, warm and reassuring.

As they came within earshot, Silver called out to them. His voice was powerful and deep. A voice used to speaking with authority. Used to getting its own way. 'My ancestors had trespassers shot.'

The Doctor and Sam exchanged worried glances.

But then Silver smiled, and strode towards them. 'Thankfully we live in more enlightened times. You must be Miss Jones,' he said to Sam. Then he turned to the Doctor. 'I'm afraid Tanner was rather vague about your name, as he was about your business here.'

'Oh let's not be formal.' The Doctor was grinning, his head bobbing from side to side in jovial amusement. 'This is Sam, and I'm the Doctor.' He took Silver by the arm, swung him round and led him back towards his house. 'We're absolutely fascinated by the history of this place. Old house, big terraced gardens. Ruins. Fascinating.' He stopped suddenly so that Silver was forced to turn round again. 'You weren't expecting us?'

Silver frowned. 'Perhaps,' he said slowly.

'We wrote. Well, I think we wrote. You wrote, didn't you, Sam?'

'Yes,' Sam answered, just too quickly. 'Definitely,' she added with a half-smile.

The Doctor smiled. 'There. You see.'

Silver laughed. 'Oh, that doesn't mean anything. Post's awful round here. Probably arrive next week. E-mail, that's the thing. When it works, of course.' He called back to Tanner, who was lagging behind like a forgotten puppy. 'Thank you, Tanner.'

Tanner nodded to Silver, acknowledging his dismissal.

Silver watched Tanner turn and start back towards the hill. 'He's nearer God's heart in a garden than anywhere else on earth.'

'Kipling,' Sam said knowingly. Silver raised an eyebrow, but said nothing.

'You're too kind,' the Doctor told him, and turned to Sam. 'It's Mrs Dorothy Frances Gurney.'

'You know everything,' Sam said.

'Eighteen fifty-eight to nineteen thirty-two. She had the most wonderful begonias, you know.'

Silver shook his head and continued along the drive. 'Actually, I think she's right, Doctor.'

'That it's Kipling?

'That you know everything.'

The main entrance to the house was through a large

panelled and studded oak door set within a tall archway. Above it a rectangular window was split by stone mullions into tall narrow panes. Above that, the stonework was crenellated into battlements.

'Welcome to Abbots Siolfor.'

'Very impressive,' the Doctor admitted. 'Early sixteenth century, for the most part, I think. Though the battlements look more recent.'

'Definitely,' Sam agreed.

Silver opened the door and waved them through. 'You're right, of course. The window was added later, in about 1620. The battlements are early Victorian.'

'There is one thing I don't know,' the Doctor admitted, pausing on the threshold. He pointed up at a carving in the arch above the doorway. It was a figure, short and squat. Despite the weathering, Sam could see that webbed wings sprouted from its shoulders, and short horns from its forehead. It's hand – more like a curled claw – was held out, as if in offering. The face was a grotesque gargoyle. 'These carvings are all over the old ruins too. I even noticed a fallen statue that might once have been in the same form.'

'It's a recurring motif,' Silver agreed. 'It seems to have been widely used in the original manor house, then picked up and copied here. Nobody is quite sure of its significance.' He leaned closer to the Doctor suddenly, as if struck by a thought. 'Unless you can enlighten us.'

The Doctor considered. 'We'll have a go,' he said.

Silver blinked, then laughed. 'Good,' he said. 'Jolly good. Now, come and meet my wife.'

Penelope Silver was tall and slim. Whereas Silver was dressed in a grey suit as if he were about to attend a board meeting, Penelope was dressed as if she had just ducked out of a cocktail party. Her long auburn hair was tied up and pulled away from her face, emphasising her classical, almost aquiline features. Apart from her obvious beauty, two things were immediately apparent to Sam as Penelope leaned forward and let her husband kiss her cheek: she was about twenty years younger than him, and she adored him.

Silver seemed to be completely at ease now with the idea that the Doctor and Sam were historians who had arrived to delve into the mysteries of the ruined manor house. He introduced them to his wife as if they were old friends and colleagues. 'Let's have some tea, then I'll get Sargent to show you the library,' he said, rubbing his hands together with enthusiasm. 'He's a real boffin when it comes to local history. Knows even more than I do. I think you'll be impressed with my library too – lots of source materials relating to the original house as well as to this one.'

Penelope gestured for Sam to sit next to her on the sofa. 'Once Norton and Sargent get going,' she said quietly, 'there's no stopping them. They're like a couple of kids with new toys.' She reached behind and pulled a thin braided rope on the wall. Far away somewhere a bell rang.

Sam smiled. 'I think there may be three kids now. The Doctor's probably twice as bad.'

Tea was brought by Miss Allworthy, a greying lady of uncertain age and considerable bulk who acted as housekeeper for the Silvers. She exuded an air of quiet efficiency and experience, and was dressed in a white blouse and a dark skirt like a waitress in a tea shop.

Miss Allworthy poured, and Penelope Silver took the first cup and handed it to the Doctor. 'Where are you staying?' she asked him. 'I presume this research of yours will take a while.'

'Yes. Several days.' The Doctor made to take the tea, but Penelope held on to the saucer, determined to get an answer. 'We're staying, er, locally,' the Doctor eventually admitted.

She was scandalised. 'Oh, not at that awful place in the village?' She shook her head in sympathy. 'I suppose Mrs Thompson means well and I gather she's a competent cook, but...' She shook her head again, looking first to Miss Allworthy, who remained impassive, then to her husband. He shrugged, and she took this as agreement. 'You must stay here, with us. We've plenty of room. I won't take no for an answer.'

'Thank you,' the Doctor said at once. He raised his cup in salute. 'We'll collect our things after tea.'

'But won't we get in the way?' Sam asked. 'And think of the extra work.'

'Extra work? Of course not. And I shall be glad of the company – Norton's so tied up with his research. I'm sure Miss Allworthy can cope.' She glanced across for acknowledgement, and seemed to get no response. After a moment, Miss Allworthy left the room.

'She's thrilled really,' Penelope stage-whispered when Miss Allworthy had gone. 'I think she gets bored without a little variation now and again.'

'We've got Pickering staying anyway,' Silver added. 'Another couple of bodies won't make much odds.'

'Pickering?' the Doctor asked, in a voice that suggested he enjoyed a good picker when he got the chance.

'That's me,' said a voice from the door. Standing on the threshold was a tall slim man with short dark hair. He was standing straight and still, hands behind his back, almost to attention. Sam wondered how long he had been there. 'Miss Allworthy hinted there might be some tea if I hurried.' He walked purposely across to help himself to a cup. 'And who are you, then?' he asked.

Again Silver made the introductions, showering accolades on the Doctor and describing him as a noted and widely published academic. Sam was curious to know what the

Doctor had told him while she had been speaking to Penelope. When he had finished singing the Doctor's praises, Silver stood by the window looking out over the grounds. The shadows were beginning to lengthen as the day drew in.

'And you're Pickering?' the Doctor asked.

Pickering poured himself a cup of tea and sat down. 'William Pickering.'

'Military or police?' When he looked startled the Doctor explained, 'Your bearing suggests one or the other. If not both.'

'I'm a captain in the army.'

'And you're here on business?' Sam asked.

Pickering hesitated, and Silver answered for him. 'I do some consulting for the Ministry of Defence, amongst other organisations. Training, personal skills, that sort of thing. Captain Pickering is here to take advantage of some one-to-one education in lateral-thinking techniques and forms of strategy development.'

The Doctor leaned forward, enthralled. 'Really? How fascinating. Perhaps I could join in, offer some advice?'

'I don't think so, thank you, Doctor.' There was an edge to Pickering's voice. Then he seemed to realise he was being too serious, and he added with a smile, 'Not unless you've signed the Official Secrets Act.'

The Doctor smiled too. 'Several times, though usually against my better judgement. It's always amazed me that you can make something officially secret. That rather suggests you have to tell a lot of people, who then decide that it's official that you can't tell them. But I'm happy to leave you and Mr Silver to your lateral-thinking techniques and strategy development.'

'That's probably very wise, Doctor,' Silver told him, turning from his inspection of the gardens. 'After all, history is so much more interesting, don't you think?'

* * *

A shadow fell across Alan Ferrer's face as the car turned on to Rogers Street. The sun had been bright, even through the tinted, bulletproof glass, so Ferrer was glad of the shade provided by the Cambridge Side Galleria across the street. They were almost there now, a couple of blocks at most. Then another round of meetings with a large software company about the tough, and probably irrelevant, export controls on strong encryption technology.

Boston and the surrounding area was home to several of the major players in encryption and secure communications. President Dering had sent Ferrer, as his National Security Adviser, to find out more about the subject before deciding how to tackle the increasing pressure to change the law that classified encryption software as munitions. Ferrer had started with the main players. He had been out at Bedford with representatives from RCA and its parent company, SDI, that morning. Next on the agenda was the Lotus Corporation, the application-software arm of IBM.

Ferrer yawned, knowing that all his meetings would be similar in tone to the one that morning. Experts and businessmen would tell him that the law was crazy, and lawyers would tell him it was impossible to enforce or to police. As if he didn't know. Code that you couldn't legally compile and export on a diskette you could print out and publish in the *New York Times* or any other journal protected by the First Amendment. Crazy. What nobody would tell him was how the President could gracefully climb down and explain his change in policy to Congress without looking like a dork.

A large red-brick building was coming up on the left, opposite a similar complex on the other side of the road. The large black Lincoln started to slow. The engine was powerful enough for it to travel at great speed, but the weight of the armour-plated sides meant that it took a while to stop. In theory that momentum could be a life-saver. In practice it meant than under normal circumstances the car kept its speed low and the driver kept one foot on the brake.

Beside Ferrer, a Secret Service agent pulled mirrored sunglasses from the top pocket of his unbuttoned jacket and slipped them on. Shades on, he turned his attention to the few people on the street, the windows overlooking it, any hint or sign of possible trouble. In the front passenger seat, another agent went through a similar procedure.

'Ready, sir?'

Ferrer nodded. 'Yes, thank you.'

His finger tightened on the trigger as he applied first pressure. The open window was angled so that the sun reflected off it, hiding the muzzle of the rifle. He was on the third floor of the Royal Sonesta hotel adjoining the office block, and had an excellent view of the car as it drew up outside. He sighted on the rear, nearside door.

The door opened and a Secret Service agent got out. He looked round once, slowly, then opened the rear door with his left hand. His right hand stayed in front of his body, never far from the shoulder holster concealed beneath his jacket. He stepped back, looking round yet again, as his colleague got out of the back seat, his head emerging first from the car.

The figure was wearing a dark suit, and the back of his head was framed in the sniper sight. The cross-hairs centred on the area where the short dark hair was thinning slightly round the crown. He exhaled, and squeezed the trigger.

The bullet hit the agent in the top of the head, tore through his brain and exploded out beneath his chin. His colleague, still holding the car-door handle, reacted immediately. Spattered with blood, he whirled round, handgun already drawn. Crouched in the shadow of the Lincoln, he swept the windows above with his eyes, gun held two-handed as he scanned.

Nothing.

Still holding the gun pointing up at the hotel windows with his right hand, the agent dragged the lifeless body from the back of the car.

'You – drive,' he shouted through the door at the driver. 'And you – lie down,' to Ferrer. Then he slammed the door shut and dived for the cover of the low wall in front of the hotel. The Lincoln was already pulling away before the door had closed, the engine roaring and the tyres screeching along the kerb.

On the sidewalk, the dead man's jacket flapped open. His white shirt was soaked in his blood, and his shoulder holster was clearly visible.

The assassin swore, dropped the rifle, and stood up. On a tripod beside him a Russian Ruchnoy Protivotankovy Granatomet – an RPG – stood prepared. He swung it round to follow the Lincoln.

The car was picking up speed. Ferrer crouched down on the back seat, despite the bulletproof glass

The surviving agent peered over the wall and up at the hotel cautiously. He was looking for the tell-tale sight of a rifle barrel or a muzzle flash from the hotel.

What he actually saw was the whole of one of the third-floor windows explode outward in a shower of glass. Instinctively he knew what that meant, and ducked. He screamed a hopeless warning at the car, but it was lost in the deafening roar of the explosion.

The shell ripped into the road ahead of the vehicle, showering it in chunks of pavement and concrete and tearing a wide hole in Rogers Street. The driver wrenched at the steering wheel as he slammed his foot down on the brake. The Lincoln swerved, teetered on the edge of the hole, and shuddered to a halt. The wheels spun noisily as the driver slammed the car into reverse. After what seemed like an eternity, they gained a purchase on the fractured surface and the car started backwards with a lurch. As it gathered speed, the limo weaved from side to side, catching the kerb and juddering back into the centre of the carriageway.

Behind the wall, the agent was shouting into his radio. In the limo, the driver was struggling to control the rapidly reversing weight of the car. Ferrer was curled up on the back seat thinking of his wife and daughters. Then the second shell struck.

The second shell, like the first, was a shaped charge. It impacted on the side of the Lincoln, and exploded. The charge was packed into a hollow cone lined with metal. Because of the cone, the explosion actually took place a few inches from the side of the vehicle. The heat of the detonation melted the metal in the cone, and the force of the charge produced a jet of white-hot gas. In a fraction of a second, the gas jet forced the molten mass of metal through the armour plating of the limo and the bulk of the explosion expended itself inside the car. The strength of the impact knocked the heavy vehicle across the road and turned it on to its side.

The occupants were already dead by the time, a split second later, that the force of the blast ruptured the gas tank. With a thunderous roar the limousine exploded in a black and orange ball of smoke and flame. Debris rained down on Rogers Street.

The Secret Service agent felt drops of molten metal sting his face, smelled them burn tiny holes in his jacket as he raced for the main entrance to the hotel. But he knew he was too late.

The assassin threw himself through the door at the bottom of the stairwell, and charged across the foyer. He heard a shout from behind, and ignored it. He was nearly there now. Through the back doors of the hotel, and across the narrow street outside.

He heard the doors slam open again behind him, another shout, the report of a gunshot and a bullet whistled past him.

Just beyond the street was the Charles river. And tied up at its edge was a motor launch. He leapt the short distance to the boat, and threw off the rope. The engine was already idling and he pushed the throttle forward, feeling the surge of power as the craft leapt forward in the water. Only then did he look back.

On the bank, he could see the Secret Service man standing legs apart, gun held two-handed as he aimed. The figure was receding rapidly as the man's hands jumped slightly. Then the assassin felt a sudden flash of pain in his left thigh, and heard the sound of the shot.

The launch passed under Longfellow bridge and out of sight of the hotel. He could see the rising cloud of oily black smoke in the distance, and feel the blood trickling down his left leg to form a sticky pool on the wet floor. He gritted his teeth and steered the boat towards the nearest bank. He still had much to do.

The Doctor seemed to be wallowing in the local history, the books and documents in Silver's library, and the learned company. Sam found the history boring, and tended to spend most of the day with Penelope Silver. Penelope's husband and Captain Pickering spent most of their time locked away in

Silver's offices in the basement and cellars of the house. And this was a shame, Sam reflected, since Silver seemed quite charming and Pickering was witty, handsome, and always had time to talk to her.

In fact, they spent a lot of time together. The first morning of their visit, Sam had set off almost before dawn to jog a couple of miles round the grounds. She started along a gravelled path that led from the terrace through the rose gardens and out towards a small wooded area. The route she took was a little hilly at times, but pleasant and attractive. From the hill behind the house she had a good view of almost the whole estate. She paused, not so much to catch her breath as to admire the view.

'Come on, slacker. No time to dawdle.'

Sam whirled round, startled by the shout. Pickering ran past her, in the opposite direction to the way she had been going. He turned, jogging easily backwards and waving cheerily to her as he went. She watched him until he turned round again and ran off into the distance.

The second morning, Pickering was waiting for her on the forecourt outside the front door. He was stretching and limbering up, but she knew he was waiting. She set off at a brisk pace without acknowledging his presence. A few moments later he caught her up.

'Good morning.'

'Hi there.'

They jogged a short way in silence. Then he said, 'I knew you weren't slacking, actually. That view is fantastic, isn't it? There's some great scenery round here. Makes a change from pounding the pavements.'

'How far do you go?' she asked him, without thinking.

He answered at once, and without undue humour. 'A couple of miles. Three maybe. Depends how I feel. You?'

'About the same.'

'Every day?'

'When I'm not saving the world.'

He laughed, obviously taking it as a joke. But his answer was in a more serious tone. 'I know the feeling.' After another hundred yards he said, 'Let me show you a good route. Very pretty. Not too steep.'

'OK.'

'Do you know the grounds very well?'

'Assume I'm ignorant,' she said. The effort of running was just beginning to tell, and her voice was low and lacking in tone as a result.

He took it for a lack of enthusiasm. 'Do you mean ignorant, or indifferent?'

Sam caught her breath. 'I don't know,' she said, 'and I don't care.' And they both laughed. A happy, joyful sound in the dew-drenched still of the early morning.

The morning run became a habit after that. Sam found herself looking forward to the refreshing ritual, enjoying the quiet company of Captain William Pickering. She thought he appreciated it as well.

The Doctor spent most of his time lecturing Paul Sargent in the library. Sargent was Silver's part-time archivist and lived in the nearby village of Abbots Clinton.

Sargent was, Sam thought, young for a historian. She had expected somehow that history was the province of the old, being so old itself. Yet Sargent was probably in his early forties. His blond hair was thinning from the front, and there was a touch of grey around the temples, but he seemed otherwise to be in good physical shape. His main problem, Sam thought, was that he seemed to have no topics of conversation other than books, documents, and history, and no discernible sense of humour whatsoever.

The library reminded Sam of the TARDIS, only rather better organised. She actually quite liked it, though the research the Doctor seemed to be doing – initially as a part of his 'cover' for Silver, but now out of passionate curiosity – held little interest for her. She'd had enough of local-history projects and dusty books at school.

That said, there were three things in the library in which she and the Doctor shared a fascination. The first was the recurring gargoyle motif. The bookcases, all custom-built for the oak-panelled room, had the gargoyle's grotesque face carved into their upper frames. The stone fireplace had gargoyle figures either side of the mantelpiece. Even the upper centre panel of the heavy wooden door was adorned with the bizarre image. Sam shuddered whenever she saw it, yet like the Doctor she was intrigued to know its meaning.

The second fascination was a series of nineteenth-century paintings. In fact, they were not limited to the library. Throughout the house were hung identically mounted and framed oil paintings by the same artist in the same style. They all depicted aspects of the house and the surrounding grounds. There were even several of the ruins of the original manor house where the TARDIS had materialised, and these showed how little the ruins had altered over the last century. They were startling in their attention to detail, the perspective was exact. They gave a real feeling for the timeless nature of the gardens and the architecture. Among them, in appropriately lighter frames, were some of the pencil sketches and working drawings from which the paintings themselves had been executed.

Sam was not quite sure what her fascination with the pictures was. She had been staring again at one of them in the library when the Doctor had joined her. Together they looked at the painting, and admired the brushwork and the detail. It was a view over the ruins, from the top of the hill almost where the TARDIS had landed. In the middle-ground, on the brow of the next hill, was a small copse of trees. It was called Lord Meacher's Clump according to Sargent, who saw nothing funny in the name. Two trees at the front were slightly forward of the rest and a little taller, the others evenly spread behind them.

'You sense it too, don't you?' the Doctor said quietly to Sam, obviously not wanting Sargent to hear across the room.

'Sense what?'

'You know,' he said. Then he seemed to realise that she did not. 'There's something unsettling about these pictures. Something not quite right.' The Doctor shook his head and drew in a frustrated breath. 'Don't you feel it?'

Sam turned back to the picture. He was right, of course. She hadn't consciously realised, but there was something unsettling – disturbing even – about the painting. Something, as the Doctor had said, not quite right.

After that she spent an afternoon examining all the paintings she could find, as well as the working drawings. Some of them left her with no feeling of unease at all. But others seemed to send a chill down her spine as far as her boots. In one it might be the way the light fell, in another the detail in a cloud. But whatever the apparent cause, when Sam looked closer, tried to analyse it, there was really nothing wrong. The light source was perfect, the execution of the cloud exemplary. Whatever was wrong with them was not in the detail.

She cornered the Doctor that evening and asked him what it was. 'What is it about them? Why do they seem so… I don't know – so wrong? The perspective's right, the detail's there, the colours are vivid. What is it?'

The Doctor sucked in his cheeks and raised his eyebrows. 'I

wish I knew,' he said. 'It's intriguing, isn't it?'

It was intriguing enough for Sam to ask Penelope about the paintings as they walked along the terrace one breezy afternoon.

'They're by Raymond Coulter, and quite valuable I think. They were painted between about 1820 and 1830.' She smiled, her long auburn hair blown back by the breeze. 'Some say they were the death of him.'

'What do you mean?'

They were passing the French windows into the library, and at that moment they suddenly burst open and the Doctor came running out to join them. 'Glorious!' he exclaimed loudly. Then immediately added, 'Sorry, don't let me interrupt you.'

'We won't,' Sam told him.

'I was telling Sam about the paintings.'

The Doctor nodded. 'Coulter, I believe. I'd guess about 1820 or soon after.'

Penelope laughed. 'You never cease to surprise me. You're right, of course.'

'Of course.'

'I was about to tell Sam,' Penelope continued, 'that Coulter was commissioned to deliver twenty paintings in all.'

'Really?' the Doctor held his hands up and wiggled each finger in turn, as if counting rapidly on them. 'I've only seen nineteen.'

'Then you can't count,' Sam said.

'There *are* only nineteen,' Penelope told them. 'Coulter died before he finished the final painting.'

The Doctor was immediately mortified, stopping abruptly in his tracks and wringing his hands. 'How *sad*.'

'How did he die?' Sam asked.

'He stabbed himself,' Penelope said matter-of-factly. 'With his penknife.'

Sam's lips pulled back over her teeth as she drew a sharp breath in shocked surprise. 'Why?'

'Nobody really knows. He went quite mad apparently. Had some sort of fit, or something.'

'And the final painting?'

'Burned, I believe. Along with all the working sketches for it.'

'Good gracious. Why?'

Penelope shrugged. 'I think he stipulated in his will that all unfinished work be destroyed. They stretched a point with the other drawings, but at least they were for completed oils.'

The Doctor stared off into the distance. Sam followed his gaze. He was looking towards the trees of Lord Meacher's Clump, the distinctive pair of oaks slightly to the front standing upright and still. It seemed to be the only thing not swayed and ruffled by the breeze.

'I wonder what he was painting when he went mad,' the Doctor murmured.

The third thing in which Sam and Doctor shared a fascination was the Philosopher's Stone. Silver had pointed it out proudly when he showed them round and introduced them to Sargent. It was the size and shape of an egg. It sat in a gold cradle inside a polished wooden display case hanging on the wall between the library's main door and the French windows. The stone was pale, with thin red veins running across its surface. It seemed to be made of marble, though it looked fragile and delicate like porcelain. A small halogen spotlight set into the ceiling illuminated the case, so that the stone seemed to glow slightly from within. Sam had seem a similar effect achieved by shining a bright light into an alabaster bowl in a museum. The light seemed almost to seep out through the sides of the bowl, so that the whole thing emitted a warm glow.

'Where did it come from?' Sam asked Silver as she and the Doctor peered into the display case.

'Oh, I don't know. Been in the family for centuries. There are references right back to the fifteenth century and beyond.'

'Was it ever actually connected with alchemy?' the Doctor asked.

Silver snorted. 'I doubt it. Just a romantic name for the thing.'

'Alchemy?' Sam asked. 'Why alchemy?'

'The Philosopher's Stone was a substance produced during, or discovered and then used in, the process of the Great Work of alchemy,' Silver said. 'It's the ingredient that catalyses the base metal, that transmutes it into gold.'

'You mean alchemy can really work?'

Silver shook his head. 'No, of course not. But the so-called science was well understood, if obscurely documented.'

'Jung maintained it was actually metaphorical,' the Doctor chipped in, 'that it was a psychological process of the man becoming whole, rather than a chemical reaction.' He pointed to the glowing stone. 'He saw the Philosopher's Stone as symbolic of a fragmented psyche. He called it the "Dark Night of the Soul".' The Doctor grinned suddenly. 'He was always so melodramatic, dear Carl.'

Within the display case, the stone shone like pale translucent ivory in the harsh light.

2
Melodrama in the Night

Sam's sleep was full of madness and death. She was sitting on a tall seat, like a bar stool, in the midst of the ruins on the hill. The wind was blowing through her hair and pulling at the long T-shirt she slept in, but the trees nearby did not move. It was night, a full moon shining down at Sam, yet the painter in front of her was illuminated by glorious sunshine. He looked up from his work, holding his paintbrush upright and sighting past it to check the angle. Then he disappeared behind his easel again.

Sam frowned. She had seen his spattered smock, his beret, his brush held out. Why had she not seen the painter's face? He held out the brush again, and a large drop of paint fell from it and splashed on to his chest. Red paint. And Sam saw that, although he was sitting directly in the sun, his face was in shadow.

They continued in silence for a while. Sam sitting; the artist painting. Then, the artist leaned back, and swung the easel round so that Sam could see the finished work. He stood beside it, wiping the crimson from his palette knife on to his chest.

Sam examined the painting. The figure it depicted was not seated on the stool, but standing in front of the ruins – colourful and vivid against the grey, cloud-skittered sky and the stark black outline of the toppled walls and jagged uprights. He had reclothed her in an old-fashioned formal dress, perhaps from the early nineteenth century. But despite the fact that she was not wearing her T-shirt or seated on the stool, she recognised herself. She recognised the shape of her body, the line of her breasts, the way her hands were clasped together holding each other as if for comfort and reassurance.

Then, and only then, did she look at the painted face. And screamed.

It was the hideous, stone-carved face of the gargoyle. And as she looked at her distorted, ugly, pinched features, as she saw the short horns sprouting from the hairless head and noticed the shape along the back of the dress where the leathery wings were folded away, the mouth twisted slightly into a ghastly parody of a smile.

She was still screaming as the painter kicked over the easel and the grotesque figure fell face forward to the ground. She was still screaming as he stamped down hard on the canvas, as if to crush the shape squirming beneath it, as it tried to pull free. She was still screaming as the painter turned to her, and she saw his face – saw that it was a half-finished pencil sketch of humanity. The features were thin lines, the mouth a lipless scratch, the eyes hollow smudges of charcoal.

His voice was a hiss of rancid air as he spoke: 'Anything unfinished must be destroyed.' Sam pulled away, swaying, unbalanced, on the stool. She screamed again, and the painter plunged the palette knife deep into his chest. The blood bubbled and foamed as it spewed out and splashed on to the writhing canvas. But as she fell backwards, Sam could see that it was not really blood, but paint. Red paint. The sound she heard might have been the artist crashing to the ground. Or it might have been herself, fallen among the ruins.

The sound had come from just outside her door. Sam was immediately awake, the soundless scream of her nightmare still breaking at her lips. She sat up, feeling tiny drops of sweat running down her spine inside her T-shirt. Her hair was matted and damp, sticking to her forehead as she listened intently.

There – just outside. A footfall in the corridor. Sam slipped out of bed, pulling her T-shirt down as she tiptoed to the door. She leaned her head sideways towards the door, the silence of the night an audible rushing in her ears. And in the distance the retreat of quiet footsteps. She opened the door gently, wincing as it creaked slightly, and slowly peered round the frame. She was just in time to see a figure rounding the corner and starting down the stairs.

Probably it was nothing. Someone after a cold drink, or a midnight snack. An insomniac looking for something to read. A student of the Open University desperate to catch Unit Seven of the flower-arranging course as delivered by a wide-lapelled trendy recorded in the seventies and embarrassed at regular intervals on the BBC ever since. The sensible thing to do was to go back to bed and forget about it.

So Sam set off quietly along the corridor, following the shadowy figure. It was halfway down the main staircase by the time Sam crept close enough to see that the figure was Captain Pickering. Had it been anyone else, with the possible exception of the Doctor, Sam would probably have gone back to bed happy to have secretly identified the figure. But she had been getting on well with Pickering during the few days at Abbots Siolfor, and somehow he seemed the least likely person to wander about at dead of night.

He was also about the one person that Sam felt comfortable going up to and asking why he was wandering about at this hour wearing only a pair of paisley pyjamas. Sam hurried down the stairs after Pickering, and called out, 'Hey – couldn't you sleep either?'

Pickering was at the bottom of the stairs now, in the main hallway. He gave no indication that he had heard her, and made for one of the doors.

Sam frowned. He must have heard. But before she could call out again, Pickering unbolted the door and went through. Sam stood for a moment, mouth hanging open. Then she followed.

The house was built as an open square, so that in its centre was an outside courtyard. The courtyard was paved over and had large wooden tubs of flowers and herbs dotted about it. In the centre was a large ornamental fountain. It had a round shallow pool, and above it on a plinth a stone gargoyle spat water into the air. Sam had remarked to the Doctor how gross the thing looked when they had first seen it. The Doctor had smiled and told her she was lucky it wasn't worse. It had taken Sam a few moments and a further clue about garden water features involving small cherubic boys to work out what he meant.

The door that Pickering had opened led into this courtyard. As Sam reached the bottom of the stairs she could already feel the cold breeze. She shook her head and ran to the door.

'You're crazy,' she was about to cry. 'It's freezing out there. What the hell are you up to?'

But the words stuck in her throat.

The moon was practically full, shining down from a cloudless sky and illuminating the courtyard. Sam flinched as unwelcome half-memories crowded in on her. The water splashed into the base of the fountain, catching the moonlight and splashing silver in the night air. Somewhere in the distance an owl hooted and a dog barked. But Sam noticed none of it.

She watched Pickering, silent and aghast. He was on the far side of the fountain. His eyes were wide open, but glazed and empty. He seemed not to see her standing in the doorway. The night breeze tugged at his pyjamas, blowing the jacket back against his chest. And as she watched, he stepped forward, carefully, deliberately. Into the fountain.

Sam and Pickering both stood unmoving for almost a minute. At the end of it, Sam was nearly frozen. Pickering was drenched. He was right beneath the shower of water cascading from the gargoyle's upturned mouth. Sam watched, unable to speak, just as rooted to the spot as Pickering seemed to be. Then as she watched, he waded forward, through the pool, and stepped out the other side. His feet slapped wetly on the flagstones as he walked back towards the house leaving a trail of dark dampness dripping behind him in the moonlight.

She thought he had seen her and was coming over to say something, to explain. But despite the fact that there was hardly room, he pushed past her and through the door. She felt the water seeping through her T-shirt as she turned to watch him, contrasting with the fleeting warmth of his wet body. She was aware that she too was now soaked to the skin all down her front as she watched him make his purposeful way across the hall. She felt the increased cold of the breeze against her sodden body as she watched Pickering start up the stairs.

Then she heard the laughter. It snapped her back to reality, and she turned to face the sound, looked up towards the source. It was coming from an open window above the courtyard. Standing framed, the light from the room shining round him so he seemed almost to glow, stood Norton Silver. He was looking down into the courtyard, not at Sam but at the gargoyle spewing water. He was laughing so hard that Sam could almost imagine the tears running down his cheeks and splashing into the fountain below. As she watched, he rubbed his hands together in glee, and then threw his head back and laughed all the harder.

Sam watched Silver for a moment, puzzled, unsettled and unnerved. Then she shivered, looked down at her clinging wet shirt, and darted back inside. As she ran, a shape detached itself from the shadows at the foot of the stairs. She tried to stop, to change direction, but managed neither. The shape was the Doctor, and she cannoned straight into him.

'Strange,' he said as he helped her up off the floor. 'I wonder what's going on.'

Sam clapped an arm across her chest. But if she was trying to hide the fact that she was standing in front of him dressed in nothing more than a wet T-shirt, the gesture had the opposite effect.

'You're all wet.' The Doctor stepped back and looked at her. Sam looked away. He snapped his fingers and grinned. 'Of course, Pickering pushed past you as he came back in. I'll bet he didn't notice you watching him any more than he noticed me. Or Silver come to that.' The Doctor frowned, as if puzzled that Sam had said nothing. 'Are you all right?'

'Am *I* all right?' she said loudly. 'We watch a man walk into a fountain in his pyjamas and you ask me if *I'm* all right?'

The Doctor's frown deepened, as if he watched people walk into fountains every day but spoke to girls in nightwear only on rare and unavoidable occasions. 'Well, are you?'

Sam made for the stairs with as much dignity as she could muster. 'Ask me later when I've woken up,' she told him.

'You told me that these are the only documents that relate to alchemy.' The Doctor gestured to two of the shelves.

Sargent nodded. 'That's all we have, yes. When you expressed interest in following up the background of the Philosopher's Stone, I checked back through my catalogues to be certain.' He placed a hand on the lower shelf. 'These are all there are.'

'I've read them,' the Doctor said.

'All of them?'

The Doctor nodded. 'Yes. There's some fascinating stuff in there, as I'm sure you're aware.'

'Indeed.'

'But there are some fascinating gaps too. Something's missing.'

The Doctor, Sargent, and Silver had spent the previous afternoon talking through the connections between Abbots Siolfor and alchemy. While it was not clear exactly when or how the Philosopher's Stone had been acquired by Silver's family, it was well documented that they had an interest in alchemy which dated back to at least the twelfth century.

'Matthew Siolfor,' Silver had explained, 'organised a group of like-minded and learned locals in the early thirteenth century. They met regularly to perform the Art, presumably to little or no effect. Since the Philosopher's Stone is mentioned in an inventory taken after Matthew's death, it may well be that it was he who first came into possession of the stone.'

Silver had shown the Doctor the documents that related to Siolfor, and then excused himself to continue his work with Pickering. The Doctor had spent the rest of the previous evening, and much of the night, examining the documents. Now he was ready to discuss them with Sargent.

'Tell me about the chapel,' he said.

Sargent blinked, perhaps surprised at the sudden change of subject. 'Well, er, there's not much to tell, really,' he said. 'There isn't one.'

The Doctor nodded. 'I know. No mention in the deeds, unreliable and incomplete records from the Domesday Book of 1086. No sign of a chapel among the ruins on the hill, at least not according to any of the surveys.'

'Oh there's nothing there remotely resembling a chapel, believe me.'

'I do. I've looked myself and you're absolutely right.'

'Well,' Sargent said with a smile, 'there you are then.'

The Doctor sat at the reading table and pulled a leather-bound book towards him. 'Not quite,' he said. 'You see, there are too many references to it in among these documents for it to be a mistake. Here, for instance.' He opened the ancient volume and thumbed through it until he came to the page he was looking for. 'Read this.'

Sargent glanced at the passage the Doctor indicated. 'Siolfor's diary,' he said quietly. 'It's his account of the Visitation as he called it.'

'Yes.' The Doctor pulled the book back towards himself and leafed through. 'It's a strange entry in any case. And it's one of several that mention that they met and performed their rituals on the site – in the ruins even – of the old chapel.'

'Well, it's long gone now. And we've no idea really where it was. Siolfor's rather disproportionate in his descriptions. He'll spend for ever describing the weather, and then gloss over his ceremony in a couple of lines.'

The Doctor had found the text he was looking for. 'Yes, I'd noticed that. I think he was torn between documenting what he thought was important, and keeping it secret. I suspect he kept track of the things he might forget in his diary, like the weather on a particular day if that was important to his alchemical process. But other things which were so important they were ingrained in his memory, he had no need to write down.'

'Like the Visitation, you mean? Whatever it really was.' Sargent could see the section the Doctor was looking at.

'Yes, exactly. It obviously had a profound effect on him and his followers, yet he throws away a mention in a few words. I wonder what really happened.'

'You think the chapel might be important.'

The Doctor shrugged. 'Who can say? Perhaps the geographical location was important in some way, or maybe the fact that it was consecrated ground. But I think the missing documents might well be important. To someone.'

'But I don't know of any missing documents,' Sargent pleaded. 'What missing documents?'

'Missing or destroyed. Possibly lost. There are various mentions and references throughout those –' he gestured back at the shelves – 'to "the list". That seems to be the key, and it's referred to right up until the early twentieth century.'

'We know that alchemy was still practised locally right up till the last century. A list of ingredients, or processes perhaps?'

The Doctor shook his head. 'No, I don't think so. It seems to have been a list of people. A list of people currently involved in the secret group still striving for the Great Secret, still trying to solve the riddle of the Philosopher's Stone.'

'Perhaps they got rid of it when they gave up the alchemy.' Sargent turned away. 'I doubt if it's important.'

'If it's not important,' the Doctor said quietly, 'then why isn't it here?' He looked down at the book in front of him. His forefinger was resting on a single line in the diary, a complete entry in itself. There was no date, no further explanation. Siolfor's usually neat and studied handwriting was suddenly ragged and rushed.

'The Visitation.' The words were underlined at the start of the short sentence. Then the entry itself: 'Tonight the Devil came to us.'

There was nothing out of the ordinary in Pickering's behaviour, as far as Sam could tell. They had jogged together as usual the next morning, and it was as if nothing had happened. It was not until after lunch that she was able to summon up courage to speak with him. He had been closeted with Silver all morning.

Pickering still seemed his usual calm, collected and witty self, and he still made no mention of the events of the previous night. So neither did Sam. Instead she suggested they take advantage of the good weather and go for a walk. It turned out that Pickering's jogging routes had not taken in the ruins of the old house, so Sam offered to show him.

It was a bright, fairly warm day but there was a hint of rain in the air. Pickering stoically refused to acknowledge the cold breeze, while Sam pulled her coat tight about her as they trudged up the path that led to the ruins. They talked about the weather, about the Doctor's latest comments on the history of Silver's house and family, and about nothing that really interested either of them.

It was not so much that Sam had forgotten that the TARDIS was parked in the middle of the ruins as that it had simply not occurred to her. It took her a while to calm Pickering's curiosity by suggesting that perhaps it was a convenient place for Tanner to keep his tools and gardening equipment.

'Weird, though,' Pickering said as he walked round the TARDIS for the third time. 'Damned weird.'

'Not as weird as splashing about in fountains at two o'clock in the morning,' Sam told him in exasperation.

'What?' He seemed genuinely bemused. 'I mean,' he went on, 'don't you think it's a bit of an odd thing?'

'No more odd than a lot of things round here.'

Pickering looked round at the fallen walls and the scattered stones. A statue lay on its side a short way down the hill. Its features were weathered and cracked but the stumps of the horns that rose from the forehead were still discernible, and the remains of the wings lay crumbling beside its body. For a moment Sam had an impression of an easel falling on top of the statue, the stone creature writhing beneath it. Then the nightmare image was gone.

'Gargoyles aplenty up here too,' Pickering said. 'It must mean something. Carvings, images, statues.'

'Fountains?' Sam suggested.

Pickering rounded on her. 'What is all this about fountains?'

Sam stood in a shattered doorway that had no wall, hands on hips. 'You really don't remember, do you?'

Pickering sat down on a huge chunk on stone that lay like an altar in the centre of the forest of fallen masonry. 'Obviously not.'

Sam was silent for several moments. 'Let's get back,' she said at last, and set off down the path.

'I'm not sure I understand you,' Pickering said when he caught her up.

'You don't understand me?' She didn't slacken her pace or look round. 'That's a bit rich, isn't it?'

'Oh?'

They continued most of the rest of the way without speaking. Then, as they came within sight of the house, Pickering stopped dead in his tracks. He waited for Sam to stop, too. 'So what's the problem?' he asked when she finally turned and walked back to him. She said nothing. 'Something to do with the fountain in the courtyard?'

'You know it is.'

He laughed – nervous and self-righteous. 'I don't know anything of the sort.'

'Fine. Just fine. And you don't know anything about standing under a fountain at two o'clock in the morning, I suppose.'

Pickering considered. 'Actually, no. Is this something I'm supposed to have done?'

'Not *supposed* to have – you did. I saw you.'

'Ah.' He did not seem surprised.

'And you just ignored me. Just pushed past and went back indoors.'

'Ah. And you're more worried about my ignoring you than about my standing in a freezing fountain in the middle of the night?' He waited for a reaction, but Sam kept her expression stone-blank. He half smiled. 'Joke,' he explained. 'Ha ha.'

'You don't remember?' Sam asked him once more as they started walking again.

'No. But that's hardly surprising.'

'You think I'm making this up? Come on – at the very least you must have wondered why your bed was soaked. Or do you have some other embarrassing behavioural problems you're not letting on about?'

'Oh no. No, I believe you.' He laughed. 'I did wonder why the towel was still wet in the morning, if that makes you feel any better. It's typical of Silver, really. I'll have a word with him.'

'Silver? He saw you too, you know.' They were almost at the hedge round the rose garden now. Away across the terrace, twin gargoyle statues guarded the entrance to a large formal maze.

'I bet he did. He wouldn't have missed it, the old goat.' He laughed again.

'Are you calling my husband an old goat?' Penelope Silver's head appeared above the hedge beside them. A moment later she stepped out on to the driveway. She was wearing a Barbour jacket and gardening gloves, and held a pair of secateurs.

'I beg your pardon, Mrs Silver. Sam here was telling me that I spent last night standing in the fountain.'

Penelope Silver laughed, and Sam was about to explain. But then she said, 'Then he is an old goat. You poor thing, you could have caught the most awful cold.'

Sam looked from one to the other in amazement. After a few seconds, Penelope noticed her bemused expression.

'Hasn't Captain Pickering explained?' she asked. 'Of course he hasn't.'

'Mrs Silver, I think –'

Penelope cut him off. 'Really, have some consideration for the poor girl. Never mind all that Official Secrets rot. Tell her.' She gave Pickering just long enough to open his mouth, then went on: 'My dear, my husband used to be a hypnotist. Still is, really, though he gave up the stage long ago. Now he gives his performances to much smaller but higher-paying audiences, and calls it consultancy.' She turned back to Pickering. 'I really don't think you should pay him to make you stand in the fountain, though.' She shook her head and laughed again.

Sam thought about this. 'What do you pay him for?' she asked. 'The MOD, I mean.'

Pickering looked as though he wasn't going to reply. Then he caught sight of Penelope Silver's glare, and relented. 'Mr Silver offers us advice on a range of things. I'm having some in-depth education about how to resist interrogation techniques that involve the use of mind control. Usually through drugs rather than hypnosis as such, but there's a lot of similarity in the way the brain is stimulated, apparently.'

'How are you doing?' Sam asked. She couldn't think of anything else to say.

'Not very well, I would guess. Not if I still get caught out by the old go-stand-in-a-fountain trick.' They all laughed again, and Penelope went back to her pruning.

'I'm sorry, Sam,' Pickering said as they reached the main entrance to the house. He held the door open for her. 'What can you have thought when you saw me?'

'Nice pyjamas,' Sam said.

'Good work,' the President said.

'Thank you, sir.' Special Agent Don Hallett had not expected praise. Quite the opposite, in fact. 'It's basic forensics, though.'

'And it still doesn't get us closer to the assassin,' Neil Ansty, Director of the FBI, added. He didn't say it explicitly, but it was obvious he was cautioning the President not to expect an early arrest.

'But we've learned a lot. It's a start,' the President told them. 'It gets us a step closer to catching the people responsible for Alan Ferrer's death.' He leaned across his desk, the sunlight streaming through the bulletproof glass behind him. His voice was quiet and stern. There was certainly no mistaking his determination and sincerity. 'And I want them caught,' he said. 'Alan's wife and daughters were here this morning. My God, I want whoever did this caught.'

'It could be just one man, sir.' Hallett counted off on his fingers what they knew. He wasn't sure if he was trying to make the point that they really knew so little, or to make it sound like a lot. 'Agent Reese is sure it was a single man. He thinks he may have nicked him with a shot, but there's no evidence for that as the boat he escaped in has disappeared. The lack of fingerprints suggests he wore gloves, probably surgical ones, to fire the rifle. He guaranteed the room with a credit card stolen that morning, and was so nondescript and ordinary that the check-in clerk doesn't recall him at all. He made no phone calls, didn't use the mini-bar, and arrived only a couple of hours before he made the hit.'

Ansty chimed in. 'The rifle could have come from anywhere – it's as untraceable as they come. As much as anything, that's because it's so old. The RPG we have traced, but that doesn't help much. It was part of a small consignment of weapons that the Russians admit went missing a while back en route to one of the new ex-Soviet states.'

'Krejikistan,' Hallett added. 'Ammunition came from the same source. And it was probably bought on the black market and sold on several times before reaching our man.' Even as he was speaking, Hallett exchanged a quick glance with Ansty. It was enough to tell him his superior had come to the same conclusion. There were no loose ends left to unravel, no hint of a slip-up to exploit.

The Doctor was beginning to think he had discovered as much as he ever would. He had spent an hour with Sam that evening going over what little they knew about the Philosopher's Stone and his suspicions that the list of members of a secret group of alchemists had been hidden or destroyed. Sam had immediately concluded that the alchemists were still active, keeping hidden, and up to no good.

However, the Doctor was not convinced of any of these things. In fact, he was forced to admit, the whole enterprise was really rather boring in comparison with his usual investigations. If it weren't for the fact that the TARDIS was still grounded, he wouldn't be bothering. Even Silver's training in antihypnosis, or whatever it really was, didn't seem that riveting when Sam had told him about it. But then the Doctor was rarely interested in the same things as the military.

And the fact remained that the TARDIS *was* grounded. Something had drained her Artron energy. And then there were the paintings. They still worried him, and he was annoyed that he couldn't put his finger on quite why they had such an unsettling effect.

Everyone else was asleep, of course. And, short of another nocturnal hypnotic excursion by Pickering, the Doctor had the house to himself.

He stood in the library. Alone in the half-light. The only illumination came from the full moon shining in through the open curtains, and from the faint glow of the Philosopher's Stone in its display case. At first the Doctor had thought it was lit from behind. But on examination he had decided that it must somehow retain some of the light from the halogen bulb shining at it, rather like a luminous watch dial. It would be interesting to analyse its composition, although he doubted Silver would ever allow that.

He sat at the reading table, letting the moonlight spill on to Matthew Siolfor's diary and play across the bookcases. He watched the patterns of light scatter over the paintings as clouds skittered across the face of the moon. High on a hill outside, he could see the silhouette of Lord Meacher's Clump, its distinctive shape mirrored in each of the paintings in which it featured. And again, he was unsettled.

Why? That was the real question. What was it that was so worrying about a series of paintings? What could they possibly have about them that could unnerve a Time Lord? He had stood at and looked out from several of the same points as the painter had. In his mind's eye, the Doctor called up his memories of the views, and compared each of the landscapes to the actual terrain as he had seen it. Apart from the expected differences – the length of the grass, the surface of the driveway, the change in the plants and garden layout – they matched exactly. It was not some deviation from actuality that set the paintings apart.

He looked round the library again, examining each of the pictures in turn. Nothing.

But then, as his gaze wandered lazily over the bookcase where the alchemy documents were kept, something tugged at his subconscious – an inconsistency of shadow, an impossibility of refraction. And he realised that it was not in a painting that he had noticed it, but on the bookcase itself.

At once the Doctor was on his feet and across the room. He reached into the shadow that should not be, felt under the small concealed ledge, pulled at the tiny lever his fingers discovered. With a quiet click that seemed deafening in the stillness of the room, a hidden drawer sprang open. The

Doctor smiled, and reached inside.

He took the two rolls, one of canvas and the other of cartridge paper, to the table. He untied the faded ribbon that held the canvas and opened it out. He nodded in satisfaction as he looked down at the heavy blocks of colour, the charcoal and pencil marks on the white painted background. The subject matter was easily discernible: a view from the main entrance to the house up towards the old ruins and the other nearby hills. The final painting in the series, and almost complete. Only one hill remained completely unpainted, the rest blocked out and ready for the detail to be added and refined.

The second roll was a pencil sketch. The style was recognisably the same as the other working drawings that were framed and hung about the house. Unlike the painting, the sketch was complete. The hill that was unpainted in the final picture was sketched in as much detail as the rest of the drawing, the distinctive shape of the group of trees pencilled in against a cloudy sky.

But then someone had scored out the hill, scraping thick, heavy scars of black charcoal across the sketch. The centre of the clump of trees had been ripped through with some sharp instrument, probably a knife, so that it looked as though a wild beast had clawed at it in a sudden frenzy. And there was a streak of reddish brown smeared over the centre of the drawing.

For a moment the Doctor could imagine the artist's blood dripping from the knife on to the paper, smearing across as he fell against his work. For a moment he could imagine the knife slashing through the paper, through the trees, through the painter's heart. Then he felt the light touch of a hand on his shoulder, sudden in the darkness as the moon ducked behind a cloud.

3
Sudden Darkness

'Do you ever sleep?'

'Rarely.' The Doctor turned to Sam, aware that her hand was still on his shoulder. 'Do you?'

Unlike the previous night, she was fully clothed. The moon re-emerged from behind the cloud and illuminated Sam's smile. 'After last night's goings-on I thought I'd have a mooch round and see what's happening.'

'Very wise. And what is?'

She nodded at the canvas and roll of paper lying on the reading table. 'You tell me.'

'All right. Put the light on and I'll show you what I've found.'

The room seemed to get smaller in the sudden light. The glow of the Philosopher's Stone seemed to intensify when the halogen spotlight above it came on.

'So what do you think happened?' Sam asked when the Doctor had shown her the unfinished picture and the scored drawing. 'Why were they hidden?'

He considered. 'I think those may be two quite distinct and separate questions.' He pointed to the canvas. 'It looks as though he stopped work on this at the point when he got to blocking in Lord Meacher's Clump. And as you can see from this drawing –' he rolled out the paper and weighed down the corners with small books from the nearest shelf – 'it's that copse that gave him – or someone – a problem.'

'You think it was something to do with the Clump that drove him mad?'

'Quite possibly. Coulter was about to paint it. And it's hacked through on the working drawing. From the state of it, I think he probably died while working on it.' The Doctor waved a hand over the bloodstains on the drawing without elaborating further.

'And then someone else hid the painting and this drawing.'

The Doctor nodded. 'For whatever reason, they did not want to destroy them. That may not be important. What is important is that there's something here, some clue, that somebody wanted hidden.'

Sam pulled the canvas across the table towards her and studied it for several moments. 'Well, I can't see anything.' She looked up at him. 'OK, I give up. What am I looking for?'

The Doctor smiled back at her. 'I wish I knew.' Out of the corner of his eye he caught sight of movement. The door was swinging open slightly. Probably a draught from somewhere. 'No, I'm afraid that like you I'm completely in the dark.'

At which point the lights went out.

'Hey!' Sam's cry was more than just surprise. She cannoned into the Doctor, and they both went sprawling against a bookcase.

The Doctor lifted her straight on to her feet, already making back towards the table and the dark figure that had pushed Sam roughly aside. But despite his speed, he was too late. The figure scooped up the pictures, sending the books that had held down the drawing skidding across the table. Their assailant was barely more than a shadow as it ran across the room ahead of the Doctor. For a stark moment the shape was silhouetted against the French windows as it leapt towards them. A trick of the light or of the imagination caused it to grow short, stubby horns from its head; transformed the flapping canvas into leathery wings.

Then the windows crashed open under the impact. Fragments of glass showered down on the paved path outside as the figure stumbled to its feet and set off at a run across the terrace. The slivers of broken glass were still rattling on the flagstones as the Doctor followed, Sam close on his heels.

The pale moonlight washed the grounds with thin light, so that colours seemed muted and distances magnified. Away in the distance, a shadowy form ran past the beds set into the rose terrace. The autumn roses were thin, fleshless fingers pointing up at the glowing sky.

Sam's foot splashed into a puddle, shattering a reflected moon as she raced after the Doctor. He was already halfway down the terrace, the dark shape in front of him starting down the steps from the terrace to the croquet lawn. Sam quickened her pace, breath already tight through her clenched teeth. She caught up with the Doctor as he sped across the lawn.

'Which way now?' she managed to ask between deep breaths. The figure they were pursuing was no longer visible.

The Doctor pointed ahead as he ran. 'The North Garden.'

The entrance to the North Garden was through a short tunnel of laburnum. The ground was slippery wet where the excluded sun was unable to dry the rain that dripped from the arched roof of the tunnel. The moonlight speckled through in scattered patterns of light on the muddy ground. The whole of the tunnel roof was illuminated, the light seeming to drip down the laburnum as it hung from the trellis covering, a green cascade of pale colour in the night.

Ahead of them, a shadow flitted past the moonlight that streamed in through the opening at the end of the tunnel. A slap of feet sounded in the shallow puddles as the figure ran onward into the garden. Sam and the Doctor ran after the shape, muddy water splattering up their legs as they splashed through the puddles.

The gardens seemed even paler as they emerged from the glowing green of the laburnum. The North Garden stretched out ahead of them, and there was a hedge along the left beside them. There was no sign of the figure they had been chasing. Sam followed the Doctor as he moved into the garden, cautious and looking round for where the shadowy figure might have hidden or escaped. But despite his caution, the Doctor took a step backward as a shape loomed up at them from a gap in the high hedge. Sam yelled out in surprise.

Immediately she felt stupid. 'Sorry.'

The Doctor shrugged without comment. The figure was a huge stone gargoyle, set on a large plinth. Its twin crouched just ahead of them. The two grotesque figures guarded a way through the hedge. Or rather, an entrance.

'What do you think?' the Doctor asked quietly.

Sam looked round. 'I don't see where else he could have gone,' she said.

They looked at each other for a moment, the light making the Doctor's face seem pale and nervous. As pale and nervous as Sam was sure her own face seemed. As pale and nervous as she felt.

She took a deep breath. 'Come on, then,' she said. And they stepped between the two stone guardians and entered the maze.

President Dering rubbed his eyes with the heels of his hands, and looked again at the list. Even for a relatively non-political appointment, the gaze of the world – and, with an election looming, the opposition – would be upon him. The names were blurring before his tired eyes, and suddenly he didn't feel he could distinguish between the candidates either. There was nobody he knew personally. All his friends with any ability already had posts in his government, or if they did not it was because they didn't want them.

His thoughts drifted as he mentally went through his friends and colleagues who might be able to offer advice. Sensible, impartial advice rather than political opinion. And Andrew Price was the obvious choice.

Dering had known Price from their days at Harvard when they had lodged together in Cambridge. Ironic that it was in the same city that Ferrer had been so brutally killed. Now Price owned and ran one of the most successful financial institutions on Wall Street. When Dering had asked him if he wanted to run the US Treasury instead, Price had been unable to control his mirth. The idea of leaving a financial body with a multi-million-dollar profit line for one that was in effect in debt for multiple billions had struck him as absurd, and Dering didn't bother trying to talk him into it. Instead they each had a Jack Daniel's, and talked about the old days and how they had both come on. One of them had just been elected President of the most powerful nation on the planet, but neither of them had any illusions about who was the better off.

Dering smiled at the thought, and reached for the phone.

Andrew Price had been worried that Dering might not call, though all the indications were that he would. There were contingency plans, of course, though Price would not realise what they were until he needed them.

'Tom, what a pleasant surprise… Advice? Of course, always happy to serve my country. And my friend, of course.' He listened for a while, commenting briefly when appropriate. Eventually, Dering fell quiet, waiting for his response. He said, 'Well, Tom, there's only one man for the job in my opinion. He's completely apolitical, an academic rather than a statesman, but I think that's all to the good. What's more, practically nobody will have heard of him, and those who have will endorse the decision.' He waited a moment to let

Dering express interest. 'Kellerman. Pete Kellerman. He's chief lecturer in Strategic Studies at CIPA. Top-class mind, brilliant brain. Just the man, in my opinion.'

They ended the call with the usual and necessary pleasantries. Dering promised to consider Kellerman, obviously trying not to sound too enthusiastic. 'He'd make you a good NSA. The best,' Price concluded. 'He's got what it takes, and he'd give it everything he's got.'

'Give me everything you've got,' the President said, 'on Pete Kellerman. He's a lecturer at the California Institute of Political Affairs.'

'In what context, Mr President?'

'I'm considering him for the post of National Security Adviser.' The President put down the phone and leaned back in his Kevlar-lined chair. There was something reassuring about following Andrew Price's advice. Somehow, he knew everything would be all right, that this was the right option.

The Doctor took the left turn without hesitation, Sam close on his heels. It was a dead end, a wall of box thick with tiny green leaves glistening with moisture in the moonlight. The Doctor stopped short, and Sam crashed into his back, sending him reeling forward into the hedge.

He turned and glared at her, brushing droplets of dew from his waistcoat. 'Let's try the other way,' he said and pushed past her. He paused at the entrance to the short corridor of greenery, finger held up as if testing the direction of the night breeze which ruffled through his hair. From somewhere in the distance came the noise of a hedge being disturbed, the brush of body against maze wall. The Doctor turned towards the noise, waited a moment, then set off in the opposite direction.

Sam was not convinced he had any idea of the layout of the

maze, but she followed him anyway. They might as well get lost together. She caught sight of him rounding the next corner of the maze as she turned out of the cul-de-sac. His heel kicked up as he flew after the shadowy figure they could hear ahead of them. She paused for a moment to catch her breath. Then she dashed after him, rounding the same corner at a sprint, and skidded in the mud, arms thrashing to preserve her balance.

Ahead of her was a blank wall of greenery. She stood for a long moment, mouth open, lungs pulling in huge gulps of air. She spun round, hand out, brushing against the hedges, testing for an opening. But there was none. She looked down towards the ground in case there was a low archway through the hedge. There was nothing.

She could hear the Doctor's footsteps receding into the distance, his feet slapping into the mud as he ran. A pause. 'Sam?' a voice called in the distance. 'Keep up.' Then the feet were off again, their pace undiminished even as the sound faded.

'Sure,' she called back, looking round again. She jumped as high as she could, but it was nowhere near high enough to see over the wall. She retraced her steps, to check she had not missed a turning. But there was nothing that looked the least bit promising. Sam had visions of being trapped within the maze until the Doctor or Tanner found her, days later. She shook the idea from her head, and grabbed at the strongest-looking branch in the hedge in front of her. She tried to pull herself up, her feet scrabbling for something solid in the hedge to push against. The green wall gave under the pressure, bending away from her wherever she tried to gain a purchase. It was like trying to climb the walls of a padded cell. After her third failed attempt, she grunted in frustration and launched herself at the hedge. She thrust her hands through the tiny leaves, and tried to feel her way through the thin branches inside, putting her head down and forcing it through the opening she had made. The wood caught at her hair, scratched her hands and face. Water ran down her cheeks as dew and tears of frustration mixed.

She had got to the point of hoping she could get her head back out again without too much damage when she heard something behind her. She ran out of the dead end back into the corridor of greenery outside. Her sudden movement sent the reflected moon scattering to the sides of a puddle as she splashed through.

'Doctor,' she said in exhausted relief. 'Thank g –'

Whoever it was, it was not the Doctor. A blur of movement as the dark figure shouldered her aside, a scrabble of fingers and nails as she tried to grab him. A roll of canvas dropped to the ground and spun to the shadows at the bottom of a hedge. Sam hung on to the man's arm, but he swung it violently, trying to throw her off. She put her head down and tried to push him into the hedge wall. The impact sent them both tumbling to the ground as their legs slipped away from them. Then the figure was on his feet again and running back towards the entrance of the maze. In a moment he was lost from Sam's sight.

Beside her, the Doctor stepped out of the shadow of the maze wall and retrieved the roll of canvas. It was smeared with mud, one end crumpled in on itself. He held it up and watched a few drops of water slide down its length and drip to the floor. Then he looked up at Sam, his smile broad and relieved in the moonlight. 'Are you OK?' he asked. 'You look like you've been pulled through a hedge forwards.'

'Just about.' She ignored the joke. 'Who was he?'

The Doctor shrugged. 'Didn't get round to the introductions, I'm afraid.'

'Nor me.'

The Doctor led the way back to the entrance to the maze. 'Should have guessed he'd double back. Easier to get out that way than trying to make it all the way through.' He reached up and patted a stone gargoyle on the cheek as they left the maze. Ahead of them, the house seemed to draw the moonlight towards itself. Lights were shining through several of the ground-floor windows. There was no sign of the figure they had been pursuing.

'So what was he after, whoever he was?'

The Doctor brandished the rolled painting like a club, smacking it into his palm. 'Something to do with this. There's obviously something we're missing.' Suddenly he stopped and crouched down beside a flower bed. 'As it is, we don't even know the context. Without any idea of what's going on, it's hard to interpret a particular incident.' He reached out, fumbling within a dense clump of small blue flowers. 'And context is around eighty per cent of how we communicate.'

He stood up, a small flower between his fingers. He held it out to Sam, twirling it round by the stem held between forefinger and thumb. 'You know what this is?' he demanded.

She peered at the tiny flower. It had five overlapping petals. Each was a deep cobalt in the centre, the colour bleeding away to a pale blue at the ragged edges. The stem was bright orange, and a leaf emerged just below the flower. The leaf was dark red. 'No,' Sam replied. 'I'm not very good on flowers.'

'Really?' He seemed surprised. 'Well, I am.' He took a slim leather-bound book from his coat pocket, opening it at a ribbon bookmark in the centre.

'So, what is it?'

He carefully placed the small flower between the folds of the pages. 'I have no idea.' He snapped the book shut and returned it to his pocket. 'I've never seen anything like it before.' He set off along the terrace. 'Now then, let's see who has returned to the scene of the crime, shall we?'

The library lights were on, shining through the shattered casement and spilling over jagged shadows on to the terrace, where a thousand shards of glass reflected it back at the heavens. Inside, Sam could see Miss Allworthy on her knees with a dustpan and brush. As always, she was dressed in a dark skirt and white top. Sitting on the reading table behind her, watching, was Pickering.

The Doctor paused for a moment on the edge of the light spilling out of the house, and stuffed the roll of canvas inside his coat. He pulled the coat tighter round him, buttoning it to the collar so as to hide the painting. Then he stepped out into the light.

Sam followed the Doctor into the library, stepping carefully over the remains of the lower edge of the French windows. Sam was acutely aware of Pickering watching her as she came in. He smiled.

'I prefer a shower in a fountain to a mud bath,' he said, swinging his legs.

Sam glared at him. 'At least I'm responsible for my own actions.'

Pickering laughed. 'Are you sure that's something to boast about under the circumstances?'

Sam opened her mouth to reply, but the Doctor waved a finger at them both. 'Children,' he chided gently.

Before either of them could respond to this, the main door opened and Silver came in. 'Ah, there you are, Doctor, Sam. Perhaps you can explain what the deuce is going on here.'

'I rather think we disturbed an intruder,' the Doctor told him. 'I came down to check on a few things we had been discussing, and Sam joined me. When we came in, somebody left.'

Silver nodded, seemingly satisfied with this explanation. 'And in something of a hurry by the look of it.'

'Indeed.'

'And you gave chase?' Pickering asked.

The Doctor nodded. 'We did.'

'Who do you think it was? Anyone you recognised?'

The Doctor and Sam both shook their heads.

'Probably just a burglar trying his luck,' Pickering said. 'Anything been taken?'

Miss Allworthy abandoned her attempts to sweep up the broken glass. 'There appears to be nothing missing, sir,' she told Silver. 'Shall I telephone the police?'

Silver considered, chewing at his bottom lip. 'What do you think, Doctor?' he asked at last.

'I doubt they'd be able to tell us much. And I think the intruder is long gone.'

Silver nodded. 'I agree.' He stood in front of the Philosopher's Stone, hands clasped behind his back as he gazed at the illusion of its inner light. 'At least this is safe.' Without turning from the display case, he went on, 'Leave that now, Miss Allworthy. Get Tanner to help you clear up in the morning.' He turned abruptly. 'Thank you all for your help and concern. I suggest we make use of what night remains, and get some sleep.' He nodded to emphasise his advice, and turned to leave.

Pickering slid off the table and followed Silver. As he passed Sam, he winked. 'And a shower,' he said quietly, putting his hand on her shoulder. He squeezed slightly, smiled at her, and left.

'Yes, I think sleep is in order,' the Doctor said. Sam was still looking after Pickering as the Doctor stepped in front of her. He stretched and yawned theatrically, then made for the door. 'See you in the morning, Sam,' he called back as he went. It sounded suspiciously like an afterthought.

'There's lots to be done. But at least you'll have an idea where to start.'

Pete Kellerman nodded. 'Oh yes, Mr President. I've already been briefed by Mr Ferrer's staff. Everyone is being very helpful.'

The President stood up and walked round behind his chair. He stood looking out of the window of the Oval Office and out across the White House lawn. 'I'd expect no less,' he said. 'Ferrer was a good man. It will be tough for you to follow him.' He turned and looked across the large desk at Kellerman. 'You think you can do it?'

Kellerman's voice was level. 'I believe so, Mr President.'

'Good.' He sat down again, and drew a thick folder across the surface of the desk towards him. It was a good signal that the meeting was at an end. The Secret Service agent was already moving to open the heavy door. He stood constantly in the room whenever anyone other than immediate friends and family was with the President. 'If there's anything else you need, Pete, just let me know.' The words were a polite formality. The folder was already open in front of him.

But formality or not, it gave Kellerman the opening. He looked down at his feet for a moment, made no move towards the door. Then he cleared his throat.

The President looked up. The agent by the door hesitated. 'Yes, Pete?'

'There is one thing I'd like to ask, sir. If I may?'

The President closed the folder and pushed it slightly away from him. He leaned back, hands clasped together in his lap as he nodded to Kellerman to continue.

'Station Nine, Mr President.'

The President's eyes narrowed. 'You're not serious?'

Kellerman was looking at his feet again, unsure quite how to play it. 'There are rumours in the press, sir. Rumblings.'

The President snorted with laughter. 'There are always rumours, Pete. And Station Nine has been a fantasy of the press for longer than I've been in this office.'

'All the same, sir, the question may well come up.'

'And if it does?'

'I'd like to be able to categorically deny that Station Nine exists. And when I do, I'd like to know that I'm telling the truth.'

The President of the United States rocked slightly in his chair, swinging it slowly from side to side. 'A man of integrity and conscience.' He smiled for a moment. Then he leaned forward over the desk. 'I don't believe that Station Nine exists, Pete. To the best of my knowledge, it has never been mentioned, even as a joke, in this room before. But I have to confess I've never asked. You really think there's a chance it might not be the product of overactive imaginations and Cold War paranoia?'

Kellerman swallowed. 'No, Mr President. I don't believe it exists either. But there have been rumours for a long time. And the premise does have more than an ounce of plausibility.'

President Dering counted off on his fingers: 'The SAC Underground Command Post at Offcutt, the NORAD Combat Operation Center under Cheyenne Mountain, the National Military Command Center at the Pentagon, the PAVE PAWS, DEW and BMEWS early-warning installations. That's six. Add in the Nightwatch plane and that makes seven. Looking Glass takes it to eight.' He was looking Kellerman straight in the eye. 'The eight installations from which we would run the offensive and defensive operations of a nuclear war. I think that is more than enough.'

President Dering pushed his chair back as he stood up. He

walked round to the front of the desk and sat back on it, perching on the edge so his eyes were level with Kellerman's. 'But there are those that would have the people believe that sometime during the latter days of the Cold War Reagan or maybe even Carter –' He broke off. 'Carter, for God's sake,' he muttered, then continued: 'One of the two secretly assembled Station Nine. It would have to be the most important, the most protected, and the most hidden asset we have, Pete.' He sat back in his seat again and smiled. 'I ain't never heard of it.'

'Yes, sir.' He wasn't sure what else to say.

'But,' Dering said, stabbing an index finger at him, 'let's just make sure. For your conscience's sake.' He reached for one of the phones on the desk. 'For both of our consciences' sakes.' He pressed a button on the handset. 'Get me General Kane.'

General Howard Kane was at his desk when the call came through. He raised an eyebrow and reached for the secure phone. As Chairman of the Joint Chiefs of Staff he was the senior ranking member of the United States Armed Forces, and principal military adviser to the President, as well as to the Secretary of Defense, and the National Security Council. That advisory role took precedence over his military commitments, whether he liked it or not.

He listened for a moment, his hand growing cold against the receiver. His face was impassive, his jaw set. 'Why do you ask, Mr President?' He forced a hint of humour into his voice at the reply. 'I see, sir.' So, it had come to this. A simple yes or no to his superior. A time for truth or for… discretion.

A tiny droplet of sweat rolled down Kane's dark temple. 'No, Mr President, Station Nine does not and has never existed. There is no such installation.'

He replaced the handset and sat silent and almost motionless for a while. His fingers drummed a thoughtful rhythm on the desk. Then they itched towards the phone and tapped on it instead. With a sudden movement he scooped up the receiver again. His mouth was dry and his voice stuck in his throat for a moment. 'Get me as many of the Joint Chiefs of Staff as you can. I want a conference call now. Tell them –' He considered a moment. 'Tell them we may have a problem.'

The Doctor was pacing round the room. Occasionally he pulled a book from a shelf, flicked through it, grunted in frustration, and then thrust it back where it had come from. He seemed not to notice Sam.

'Doctor?'

He did not answer. So she intercepted him en route to a bookcase, and stood directly in front of him. He leaned to one side to reach round her, and she leaned with him. His hand stopped just shy of her arm. His mouth twitched in annoyance, and he reached out with both hands, took her by the shoulders and moved her gently aside. Still he said nothing.

The book the Doctor took down was a thick, heavy volume. He carried it to the reading table and started turning the pages. Sam joined him, looking down at the book. It was an encyclopedia of plants and flowers. On each spread of pages, one side was taken up with small textual descriptions while the facing page showed delicate hand-drawn representations of the flora.

After a while, the Doctor closed the book. He reached into his pocket and took out the slim leather-bound volume into which he had placed the tiny blue flower he had found the night before. He removed the flattened flower and laid it down on top of the encyclopedia. 'I can't find it,' he said, as if seeing Sam beside him for the first time. He gestured round the room.

He took the tiny blue-petalled plant and held it up. They both examined it as he slowly turned it round. 'This flower,' he said, 'so abundant in the grounds of this house, so well established in this area, is not local.'

Sam frowned. 'You mean it came from another country?' she asked. Behind the flower she could see the faint glow of the Philosopher's Stone, a blurred backlight silhouetting the tiny shape.

'I mean,' said the Doctor in a petal-soft whisper, 'that it came from another planet.'

4
Quiet Whispers

At first the sound was a background hum, almost like the buzzing of a wasp. It was faint behind the pounding of the rain. Sam, Bill Pickering, and Penelope Silver were taking tea in the drawing room when they heard it. But as the volume increased they could tell that the noise was mechanical, made by a powerful engine. They hurried to the window, and Pickering pointed to the tiny black dot over the distant horizon.

'Norton didn't mention he was expecting anyone,' Penelope said. 'But then he rarely does. I think he doesn't want to burden me with irrelevant information.'

Pickering smiled, but did not look away from the approaching speck of darkness. 'Very likely.'

'I'm never quite sure,' Penelope went on, the speck slowly swelling in size as it quickly closed the distance between them, 'whether it comes from the nature of his work. First there were the secrets and devices of the theatre, now the need-to-know mentality of the military.' She moved closer to Sam and lowered her voice slightly. 'Or does it come from the age difference, do you think?'

Sam was taken aback for a moment, not sure what she was being asked, or why. She glanced at Pickering, but he was standing apart from them and seemed not to have heard.

Penelope shrugged. 'I thought perhaps you might suffer the same problem. I've noticed the Doctor is rather secretive in nature, although the age gap between you two is rather less than between my husband and myself.'

Sam smiled tightly. 'You have no idea.'

Penelope turned back to the window. 'There's no need to be tactful or diplomatic, Sam.'

Sam gulped. 'No, no – I meant –'

'I'm quite happy to admit that my husband is old enough to be my father. In fact,' she went on, 'he is a distant cousin, but that's by the way.'

The noise was louder now, a rhythmic drone. The black shape was much larger, as big as Sam's thumbnail. It was almost close enough to make out its features. Almost.

'But there are advantages, as you know,' Penelope was saying. 'With greater age comes more experience, variety of conversation, a depth of learning and insight that the young are so cruelly denied when it would be most useful to them.' She laughed, a short but sincere burst of noise above the increasing sound of the engines. 'They say that men fall in love through their eyes, and women through their ears. I think that gives us a double advantage, don't you? Not that it matters, of course. I *do* love him. That's all that counts.'

Sam opened her mouth, unsure what she was going to say to that. But before she could say anything, Pickering pointed up at the skyline.

'Russian,' he said. Whether he had heard any of Penelope's words, Sam could not tell. But Pickering's attention was directed completely at the dark shape heading towards them out of the sun.

It was like a matt-black spider hanging hunched above them. The rain bounced off its chipped paint. The noise from the blurred rotors was deafening as the helicopter lowered itself slowly towards the croquet lawn outside. Sam knew little about helicopters, but she could tell that this was a military model. Missiles and guns spiked out from pods on the landing legs and the underbelly. Its wheels bounced slightly on the turf as it settled, giving just a hint of the immense weight of the craft. The rhythmic pulse of the engines slowed with the rotor blades as they spun slowly to a stop, lazily completing their last few revolutions as they dipped lower and lower over the main cabin.

Before the rotors were completely still, the door opened and a man leapt out. Sam could see the pilot behind him, still seated in the cabin. The pilot stared forward, unmoving, his face a mask of goggles and flight helmet. The man who ducked under the rotors as he approached the house was wearing a long grey trench coat. He seemed oblivious to the heavy rain. As Sam watched, he pulled a cap from a pocket and pulled it into exact position as he stood upright at last and saluted. An exact, snapped gesture. A dribble of water trickled over the peak of his cap, distracting from the precision.

The man was tall, in his mid-forties, and displayed a military bearing.

Norton Silver crossed the driveway towards him. He was carrying a large charcoal-grey umbrella, his free arm already extended in greeting. He held the umbrella out over the new arrival as they met. They shook hands, and together headed for the front porch.

'Who is he?' Sam asked.

'I really have no idea,' Penelope said. 'Captain Pickering?'

Pickering shook his head. 'Not one of ours. The helicopter is Russian – a Hind – but that could mean anything these days. The style of the salute suggests Eastern Bloc, though.'

'Russia?'

'Not necessarily. There are more ex-Soviet countries out there than you can shake a tomahawk at. I wouldn't like to hazard a guess at any particular one.'

Behind them, the door shut suddenly, making them all turn to look. It was the Doctor. He strode over to the tray and helped himself to a cup. 'I see we have a new guest,' he said lightly as he poured himself some tea. He waved the teapot dangerously. 'Anyone else for a cup? I'll be mother.'

'Captain Pickering thinks he might be Russian,' Sam said as she dashed to remove the teapot from the Doctor's wavering grasp.

'Could be,' the Doctor said as he slumped down in an armchair. 'His name's Anatoli Roskov. Certainly sounds Russian.'

Pickering sat in the chair opposite the Doctor, his eyes narrowed. '*Colonel* Anatoli Roskov?' he asked.

The Doctor nodded between sips. 'That's right. How clever of you to guess. Silver introduced us in the hall just now. He didn't say much, but apparently Roskov runs some sort of military base in a place called –'

Pickering cut him off. 'Krejikistan,' he said.

'I thought,' said Sam, 'that you didn't know anything about ex-Soviet states. I take it this place is ex-Soviet.'

Pickering nodded. 'Not terribly well known. But after the break-up of the Soviet Union it found itself left with a few nuclear weapons.'

'And it's your job to know about such things?' the Doctor asked, setting down his empty cup.

'Part of it, yes.'

The Doctor considered. 'I assume that it isn't part of your job to recognise the name, rank, and serial number of every base commander in the ex-Soviet Union, though. Which suggests to me…' He let the suggestion hang in the air, his eyes locked with Pickering's across the dead teacups and the silverware. Sam looked from one to the other, trying to work out what the Doctor was implying.

At length, Pickering sat back in his armchair. 'You're right, Doctor. I don't know why he's here, but I do know that

Krejikistan is looking to join NATO. As well as drawing on Mr Silver's own skills, the MOD uses this house as a conference centre for, shall we say, "sensitive" meetings. They might be setting up some secret NATO session. Colonel Anatoli Roskov is quite high up in their military. He commands the Nevchenka Nuclear Missile Installation in southern Krejikistan.' He looked round at Sam and Penelope. 'In terms of raw megatonnage under the trigger finger, he's about ninth in the world ranking of nuclear commanders. In this brave new world, we're very polite and accommodating to people like that.'

Pete Kellerman, National Security Adviser to the President of the United States, was lying on his back with his pants off. His left leg was still painful when he put weight on it, and the doctor was feeling carefully round the exit wound.

'Hurt, does it?' the doctor asked for the third time as Kellerman winced in agony, then nodded thoughtfully without waiting for a reply. 'Stupid occupation in my opinion.' He straightened up. 'What were you hunting anyway?'

Kellerman smiled. 'Big game.'

'Yeah. Sure.' The doctor washed his hands thoroughly in a small stainless-steel washbasin in the corner of the room. 'I'll put on a new dressing. It should be pretty much healed in a couple of weeks.' He started sorting through a drawer of sealed bandages and dressings. 'I should think twice before you go out with the same gang of maniacs again, though, or your hunting days will be over.'

Kellerman lay back and stared at the bleached ceiling. 'Too busy now, I guess.' He smiled. In a couple of weeks his hunting days would be over. It would all be over.

They were enjoying an indifferent lunch at the pub in Abbots

Clinton. The White Lion was about thirty minutes' walk from Abbots Siolfor, and Pickering had suggested they take advantage of what was becoming a fine autumn day now that the heavy rain had stopped. Sam had found it difficult to refuse the offer, though she had worried she might see posters of herself pinned up outside the local police station. Just what she needed to impress Pickering: 'Have you seen this girl?' Fortunately, Abbots Clinton did not seem to run to a police station, a pub perhaps being a more important institution for a small rural community.

Pickering insisted that, while the White Lion's food wasn't up to much, the beer – in particular Nick's Fourpenny Ale – was excellent. She took his word for it, and sipped at a slimline tonic. A thin slice of lemon curled at the edges as it floated indifferently beside the bobbing remains of a single small ice cube. She drank the slimline variety, she had explained to Pickering, because the bottle was bigger. Pickering had insisted on paying. He had a handful of loose change which he referred to as shrapnel he was keen to lose.

The pub itself was an honest, old-fashioned establishment which had been recently spoiled by progress. In particular Sam noted the new upholstery, new wooden panelling, brass fittings, and queuing system for food, which relied on numbers stamped into the top of each table in the eating area. If Pickering's assessment of its worth was half right, then the beer was an obvious aberration.

'So who's this Russian guy?' Sam asked during a lull in the otherwise safe conversation. 'Why's he here?'

'You're right, he is Russian by birth. Though his family originated in Western Europe way back, so far as I remember.' Pickering took a swig of beer. 'Look at the way that cleans the glass as it goes down,' he marvelled.

Sam waited.

'I don't know for sure why he's here,' Pickering said at last, 'but there are two possibilities. One, as I said, is to set up a meeting of some sort. Probably with NATO officials.'

'And the other is training, right?'

'Right. His military has a deal with Silver and he trains them too.' He straightened his pint glass on its drip mat. 'Hell, we're all friends together these days.'

Sam laughed. 'Really?'

Pickering laughed, too. 'No,' he said. 'Not really. I doubt if Silver's giving their lot the same level of training as we get. Still, I'll have to check into it when I go back. Just in case.'

'Which is in a couple of days, right?'

'Right.'

'And where,' asked Sam casually, 'do you go back to?'

'London. I have a flat there, and I've got some leave due.' He grinned. 'Now that we're all friends together, there's less call for my particular talents and expertise.'

Sam leaned across the table. 'Which are?'

'Which are…' He smiled. 'Classified.'

'Hmm.' Sam sat back again. 'Fair enough.' She endeavoured to sound as if she was trying not to sound disappointed. 'I'm from London,' she said after a decent pause. 'Shoreditch, or near enough.'

'Not that far away from my place.'

'Really?'

Pickering nodded and then drained his glass. 'Really. Here.' He picked up a drip mat and peeled off the printed outer layer of cardboard, leaving a rough white square. 'Give me a call next time you're in town. I may be around, if not leave me a message.' He pulled a pen from his jacket pocket and scribbled down an address and phone number.

'Thanks, I will.' Sam took the mat from him, glanced at it and put it in her pocket.

* * *

'Are you sure you won't have a drink?' Silver asked.

Roskov declined. 'It would seem, I think, out of place,' he explained in hesitant English.

'You feel like you're on duty, eh?'

Roskov looked around the huge basement area in which they stood. 'It would be hard not to feel that. Yes.'

'You're impressed, then.' Silver smiled. 'Good.' He leaned on one of the control consoles and put his whisky down next to the flat colour display panel set into the top of the desk. The ice chinked and bobbed in the glass, catching and reflecting the light of an incongruous black candle. 'It took a lot of time and money to set this up. Subterfuge, too, of course. But soon it will be rewarded.' He breathed heavily, leaning his full weight on the console. 'Soon.'

'You have the information?' Roskov still stood stiffly to attention. Despite the accent there was no mistaking the relief in his voice.

Silver straightened up. 'Alas, no. Our primary source, shall we say, has been unable to discover anything at all of substance. So, it is up to you.'

There was a tension now in Roskov that Silver could sense. 'You are sure there is no other way?'

'None. We must resort to desperate measures, I'm afraid.'

Roskov sighed. 'The most desperate.' Suddenly he turned and slumped down into one of the operators' chairs at an adjacent console. 'And what if we are wrong? What then? What a stain there will be on our consciences, on all our consciences.' He looked up at Silver, his eyes wide, pleading for reassurance. 'What if, after all, Station Nine really does not exist?' he asked.

Silver stood up and walked round the console. 'We are not wrong,' he said emphatically. 'And the timing is such that it must be now. We can't hesitate, can't wait for the prick of conscience to become dulled by time.' He took Roskov by the shoulders are looked deep into his eyes. 'The readiness is all,' he hissed.

For a moment Roskov seemed to resist. But then his pupils dilated under Silver's intense stare. Silver continued to murmur reassurances until Roskov's eyes were completely glazed over. Then all at once he straightened up and snapped his fingers.

The pistol-crack of sound jolted Roskov out of the mild hypnotic trance and he leapt to his feet, coming at once to attention again. 'The readiness is all,' he barked. 'You have the computer disks?'

Silver went to a safe set into the wall of the chamber. Beside it was a small opening, just wide enough to take his hand. He reached in, palm uppermost, and watched the light scan over it like a photocopier. With a dull click the safe door sprang open. He reached inside and lifted out a metal briefcase with combination locks. He held it out to Roskov. 'The Zero Simulation,' he said quietly. 'Our option lock on the Americans.'

Roskov took the case from Silver, then stepped back and saluted smartly. 'We shall not meet again,' he said emotionlessly.

The Doctor sat at the reading table, thinking through the events of the last few days. There had to be some sort of pattern that he was missing. The table was spread with books and manuscripts, and as the Doctor stared at the piles of information in front of him, Sargent dumped another collection of books next to them.

The librarian struggled to prevent the topmost volume from slipping off as he eased his fingers out from underneath. 'I think that's the lot, Doctor.'

The Doctor nodded slowly. His point of focus did not change. 'Good,' he murmured. 'Very good.' Then he broke into a huge smile and slapped his hands together in delight. 'Now we can really get started. It must be in here somewhere.' He reached for a book, apparently at random, and flicked through it. 'Mind you, this one's a bit boring,' he said a few seconds later.

'Oh?' Sargent lifted the book from the Doctor's hands and opened it in the middle. 'There's some stuff here about Matthew Siolfor,' he said as he leafed slowly through. 'Might be relevant.'

The Doctor was already flicking through his fourth volume. 'Not really. There's some background detail on his family on page ninety-seven, and a contemporary engraving a couple of pages later.' He waited for Sargent to find the right page. 'There you are, it's by Crozier.'

The engraving showed a middle-aged man with a heavily lined face and long straggly hair. Sargent skimmed through the accompanying text. 'Have you read this before?' he asked. 'There's no mention of Crozier that I can see, it just says "a contemporary artist".'

'I'm a fast reader,' the Doctor admitted, setting aside another dusty book. The pile of volumes he had read was growing rapidly. 'And Crozier's work is unmistakable. Look for the slightly ragged edges to the cuts that are angled from left to right at about sixty-three degrees to the horizontal.'

Sargent frowned and held the book in the light from the halogen spot that shone on the Philosopher's Stone. The Stone was briefly in shadow as he stared at the page, though it seemed now to glow just as brightly as when fully lit. Sargent laughed, closed the book and put it down on the table. 'I'll take your word for it.'

Without answering or looking up from his reading, the Doctor lifted the book Sargent had set down and moved it over to his read pile. Sargent watched him for a moment, then sat down opposite the Doctor. He reached for a yellowing manuscript and settled back in the chair. Within seconds the room was silent save for the rustle of turning paper and the low moan of the wind outside.

This was how Sam found them when she came in two hours later. The Doctor's pile of things he had already read had been transferred from the table to the floor and was tottering dangerously. Sargent was halfway through his third manuscript.

'Can I help?' Sam asked after they had both ignored her for a full minute.

Neither looked up, but the Doctor said, 'Catch that, will you?'

Sam looked round, wondering what he was referring to. She was in time to see the pile of books and papers by the Doctor's chair topple into an untidy heap on the floor. The Doctor looked up at last, glaring at Sam in annoyance.

'Sorry,' she said before she could stop herself. 'Actually,' she said quickly, 'I'm not sorry. Now, what are you doing?'

The Doctor finished leafing through a large leather-bound volume that looked suspiciously as though it had been written in Latin by a spider who was short of a few legs and a lot of artistic sensibilities. Then he closed it carefully and dropped it heavily on top of the mess of information on the floor. He reached out for the next book, but Sam put her hand on it first, holding it down on the table.

'What are you doing?' she asked again.

The Doctor waved a hand over the mass of literature on and around the table. 'There's something here, some clue we're missing. I'm sure of it.'

'So what is all this stuff?'

It was Sargent who answered. 'This is everything we have that refers or relates to Matthew Siolfor, would-be alchemist of days long gone.'

'Him together with his troupe of followers,' the Doctor added. 'There were six of them initially in the group. But as far as I can tell, the numbers kept growing. There are thinly veiled references to a secret society during the sixteenth century, and it still gets the odd mention right up until the late nineteenth.'

'So who were they, and what did they do?'

'The sixty-four-million-dollar question,' Sargent said. 'Though I'm not sure what good it would do us to know. They just knocked about trying to turn lead into gold, so far as I can tell. Arcane rituals, secret handshakes, the lot.'

'No.' The Doctor stood up and stretched. 'No, there's more to it than that.' He made a tour of the table, stepping carefully over discarded books and strewn manuscripts. He stopped in front of the display case and pointed at the Philosopher's Stone. 'That stone –' he swung round and pointed next to the carvings on the door – 'the gargoyles –' he waved a hand over the reading table – 'all this, even the paintings.' He shook his head and sat down again. 'They're all somehow related. All pieces in the same puzzle.'

'And you want to find the edge pieces?' Sam asked with a smile.

'Oh no. I want to find the picture on the front of the box.'

Sam rummaged through some of the books and papers on the table. 'And you hope it might be in this lot?'

'What I hope,' the Doctor told her as he picked up the next book and started in, 'is that I'll know it when I see it.'

Sam watched the two of them read for a few moments. She wandered round the room for several minutes, ending up by one of the paintings. 'Could the clue be something in the paintings?' she asked. 'Is that why they're important?'

The Doctor did not look round. 'If they are important.'

'If they're not, why did he kill himself?' Sam said. 'And why hide the final painting? And why go to the trouble of trying to get it back after we unearthed it?'

Sargent looked up at this, frowning. But before he could say anything the Doctor leapt to his feet.

'Of course, Sam, at times you're a genius.'

Sam grinned. 'So, there is something in the pictures.'

'No no no.' The Doctor shook his head sadly. 'Those times don't seem to last very long, sadly.'

'Well what, then?'

The Doctor was already rushing over to the bookcase where he had found the secret drawer the previous night. 'We're looking for something that is probably more important than the final painting,' he said feeling for the mechanism to open the drawer.

'Important enough that it might be hidden in the same place?'

The drawer clicked open and the Doctor reached eagerly inside.

'Hey,' Sargent said in surprise. 'I didn't know that was there.' He went over to join the Doctor. Sam was already peering over his shoulder.

The Doctor sighed. 'Nothing,' he said in disappointment as he withdrew his hand. 'Empty.' He brightened. 'Quite a good idea, though, Sam. Good idea.' He was halfway back to the table when he swung round and retraced his steps. 'A very good idea, Doctor,' he said quietly as he busied himself about the adjacent bookcase. Sure enough, another hidden drawer sprang open after a few seconds' fumbling. Inside lay a large folded sheet of thick, yellowed parchment. Sam and Sargent followed the Doctor back to the reading table and helped him clear a space to unfold the parchment.

The document was old and discoloured. It was a single folded sheet, but when unfolded it more than covered the top of the large table, one end hanging over the edge. It showed a hierarchical diagram, text connected by lines. It seemed to have been written and drawn by various different hands, and the lower down the single large page the darker the ink became as if the diagram had been added to over a period of many years.

'It looks like a sort of family tree.'

'Indeed it does, Sam. Certainly there are names and connections of some sort. Relationships.' The Doctor traced his finger down the page, walking along the side of the table as he read quickly through.

'So what is it?' Sargent asked. 'Something important?'

'Oh yes. Very important, I think.' The Doctor pointed to the top of the document. 'Up there we have the original members of the group. See, there's Matthew Siolfor himself.' He traced his finger down the page. 'The rest of the document lists the various members of the group, the society, over the many years. It was kept up to date by each generation of the society, though at some point in the seventeenth century, about here, they started using initials rather than full names. Saving space, perhaps. Or preserving their anonymity. They recorded the dates of the deaths of members, and of the admission of new members. Thousands of them over the centuries, though only a few tens at any given point in time. So we get some idea of the timescales. Right up to... let's see.' He peered at the last entries almost at the bottom of the document. 'Good gracious.' He straightened up. 'This goes right up to the nineteen thirties.'

Sam was amazed. 'You mean this society, whatever it is, whatever it does, existed right up until then?'

'No, Sam. I mean this document was kept up to date until then.' The Doctor broke off from his examination of the diagram and turned to Sam and Sargent. 'I think the society still exists today, though the interesting question is why?

What's its purpose?'

'What makes you think that it's still around, Doctor?' Sargent asked.

'Circumstantial evidence, if you like.' The Doctor pointed to the last sets of initials. 'There are too many members by this point for them all to give up and go home overnight. It might have petered out over the years since, but I doubt it. It survived for centuries, so what's a few more decades. And someone,' he pointed out, 'hid this from us.'

'It could have been hidden years ago.'

'Yes. But when I found the painting last night, someone – someone in this house – cared enough to snatch it from us. Someone who must have been watching me in here, who knew I'd found the hidden drawer.'

Sargent laughed. 'You're taking a risk, then, aren't you, Doctor? On that basis I could be head of this society by now.'

The Doctor shook his head. 'No. You weren't here last night. You could hardly have guessed I'd find the painting exactly at that moment and hurry back from the village.'

'True.'

'Then who?' Sam asked. 'Silver?'

'Or his wife. Or Miss Allworthy the housekeeper. Tanner at a pinch – his lodge is close by. Or Captain Pickering.'

'Hardly likely,' Sam said. 'He's just visiting, like us.'

'Hmmm.' The Doctor did not sound convinced. 'Well, whoever it is, we may be one step ahead of them now. Mr Sargent and I need to glean as much information as possible from this document.'

Sam put her hands on her hips, her head slightly to one side. 'I notice you pointedly didn't include me in that.'

The Doctor smiled. 'That's because you're going to interview the suspects and see if you can find out who might be our mystery alchemist.'

'Fair enough. If I learn anything useful, I know where to find you.' She paused at the door. Her fingers grazed the polished wood of the carved creature on the central panel as she tried to order her thoughts and decide how to play things.

'Sam,' came the Doctor's voice from behind her, 'be just a little discreet, won't you.'

Sam's idea of being discreet was to talk to Bill Pickering. Despite the Doctor's misgivings, she was certain that Pickering was not involved in whatever was going on. But he had been at the house for longer than they had, and it seemed he knew Silver and his wife quite well. By talking to Pickering she could learn about them without alerting them to the fact that anyone was prying. She found him reading a cheap novel in the drawing room, while waiting for one of his final training sessions with Silver.

'Mindless,' he explained as he closed the book. 'A good way to clear the brain ahead of a session.'

It did not take Sam long to realise that in fact Pickering knew very little about the Silvers that she had not already discovered. Norton Silver had started off doing some sort of stage hypnotism act, and progressed into the training consultancy he now ran. His wife was much younger than he was. They had been married for about seven years and had no children. Penelope Silver was a distant cousin of some sort, and Silver had known her since she was a child. Abbots Siolfor was Silver's ancestral home, which he had inherited from his parents.

Sam decided to try a different approach. There seemed to be no new information to be easily gleaned about Silver's background or personal history, so instead she started asking Pickering about the training he was going through. It might, she knew, be more fruitful to tackle Penelope Silver, but Sam enjoyed Pickering's company and he seemed happy to chat to her. In fact, he was generally more at ease and outgoing, and had become quite chatty on their morning jog.

They had hardly begun. Pickering was talking in general terms about the use of self-hypnosis and how to focus the will-power to block pain and combat various interrogation techniques, when Silver joined them.

'Ah, there you are,' he said to Pickering. 'All set?'

Pickering got to his feet. 'Yes, sir. Though I think you may have a rival soon.'

'Oh?'

'Miss Jones here is very keen to find out about your techniques and mystiques.'

Silver raised an eyebrow. 'Is she indeed?'

Sam tried to sound noncommittal. 'Oh, just curious. You know, making conversation.'

Silver held the door open and gestured for them both to leave. 'Well, then,' he said, 'we must satisfy your curiosity a little. Why don't you join us for a while and see exactly what horrors I'm inflicting on your dear Captain Pickering?'

'Well…' Sam wasn't certain about this. 'If you're both sure I won't be in the way…'

'I never remember anything much about these sessions anyway,' Pickering told her, 'so it's no skin off my nose.'

Silver rubbed his hands together in delight. 'Splendid,' he said. 'Then that's settled.'

Sam was bored. Pickering seemed to be in a trance and Silver was once more rubbing his hands together with delight.

They were in the ballroom, Silver having explained that he liked to vary the location of his training sessions so that the immediate surroundings offered no established or continuous point of reference. The room was huge, with a minstrels' gallery at one end and a stage at the other. Silver apparently hosted diplomatic and political conferences at the house from time to time and the ballroom was pressed into service on such occasions as the main conference hall.

At the moment, about twenty large circular tables were positioned around the room. Without tablecloths, they revealed their stained, unpolished, wooden surfaces, which brought to the room a hint of squalor which embarrassed its otherwise magnificent decor. Pickering and Silver sat at one of the tables. Sam had pushed her chair away slightly and was tilting it on its back legs as she watched the proceedings.

On balance, Sam thought, it would probably have been slightly less boring to have stayed with the Doctor and Sargent in the library. Her mind was drifting, wondering if she should phone home while she had the chance. But what would she say? 'Hi there, it's Sam. I'm fine, can't stop – got to whiz off into infinity and beyond for a bit. Catch you later.' And what if it were she herself who answered the phone at the other end? Some future or past self, depending on which trick Time had decided to play on her today…

Having put Pickering into a waking sleep with a long stare and a few murmured words, Silver then asked him to respond to various words and phrases. He noted down the answers Pickering gave, and occasionally nodded or tutted depending on the result. One phrase cropped up repeatedly, in different contexts but always with the same response. The phrase was 'the lambs to the slaughter'. And invariably, in reply, Pickering would stand up and raise his right hand. It reminded Sam of cross between a word-association game and the ritualistic greetings of spies in a second-rate Cold War movie. During the many pauses, she would occasionally ask Silver a question. Sometimes he would answer it.

'So when's the next conference you've got lined up?' she

ventured as Silver paused yet again to scribble notes. 'Second strike,' Silver had said to Pickering. And Pickering had immediately replied, 'Retaliatory response.'

For a change, Silver looked up at Sam's words. 'I'm hoping to set something up quite soon, actually.'

'Something interesting?'

Silver nodded, and carried on writing. 'Friends of the captain's in fact.'

'Americans?'

Silver stopped writing and frowned. 'Ministry of Defence. But with some international implications, certainly. Why do you assume Americans?'

Sam shrugged. 'He's in an intelligence unit that has something to do with our relationship with the Americans.'

'He told you that?' Silver was suddenly intent, leaning forward, hands clasped on the table top. Pickering sat impassive and silent opposite him.

'Well, yes.'

Silver's hand slapped down hard on the table top. The sound ricocheted round the walls, making Sam flinch. Pickering was unmoved, staring ahead with glassy eyes. 'They never tell me anything useful.' He shook his head. ' "Need to know", indeed.'

'You didn't know?'

Silver had calmed slightly. 'No, indeed. They tell me only as much as I need to know – the exact parameters of the inducement or mental blockages they want. But it's my own fault – I should have asked.' There was a furious intensity behind his eyes now. 'What else do you know about the captain's work?'

'Is it important? To the training?'

'The training?' Silver stopped, considered. Then he smiled. 'I'm sorry, I get carried away sometimes. Of course, it is not important. Not important at all. Though it might help me now if I knew what aspect of UK–US relations is Pickering involved in. Do you know?'

'He didn't say.' Sam thought back over her conversation with Pickering in the pub. Then she remembered Colonel Roskov. 'I think it's something to do with nuclear bases,' she hazarded.

Silver said nothing for several seconds. His eyes were bright with interest as he turned back to Pickering. He leaned across the table, every inch of him exuding a suppressed excitement. He cleared his throat, an almost theatrical gesture. 'Captain Pickering,' he said quietly, 'are you listening?'

'Yes.' There was no emotion in Pickering's voice, and his eyes were still moist, glassy and unseeing.

Silver licked his lips. 'Where is Station Nine?' he asked slowly and clearly.

And for the first time in response to one of Silver's strange questions, Pickering did not respond at all. He sat completely still, and said nothing.

Silver sat back, the tension gone from him. 'I think perhaps I have trained you too well,' he said quietly. 'If only I had thought to ask before the inhibitors were in place we might perhaps have saved ourselves a lot of trouble.'

'I hate to ask,' Sam said, 'but what exactly is Station Nine?'

Silver started, as if a gun had gone off close to his ear. He looked at Sam as if he had completely forgotten her presence. But his apparent surprise lasted only a few seconds. Then he smiled and turned in his chair so that he faced her. His pupils were deep wells of blackness as he gazed into Sam's eyes. His face filled her field of vision, her awareness, her being.

'I think it's time I explained everything to you, my dear Miss Jones,' Silver said. His voice was a receding echo, soft in the rushing approach of darkness.

5
Approaching Darkness

Sam waited in the drawing room while Pickering packed. Out
of nervousness as much as habit, she straightened ornaments
and tidied up generally as she waited, restless. She sorted the
newspapers and magazines in the overflowing rack into date
order, knowing that nobody but herself would ever know or
care. She heard him at last on the stairs, and wandered out to
meet him casually, as if by accident, in the hall. If he was
surprised to see her when he came down, he did not show it.

'Is that all you brought?' Sam asked, pointing to his large
kitbag.

He laughed. 'It's all I ever take. Anyway, I've not really been
here very long.'

'And now you're leaving so suddenly.'

'Not really. My training's finished.'

Sam almost said something. But she wasn't sure what. There
was something in the back of her mind, an inkling no more. A
thought that it had not been meant to end just yet, that there
should be at least one more session for Pickering with Silver.
But she could not think why she had that impression. So she
said nothing, and opened the front door for Pickering.

His car was already outside. It was an old MG – red, of course,
Sam noted. Despite its age, it seemed in immaculate condition.
Pickering threw open the boot and heaved his bag into it. He
slammed the lid down, pulled at it to check it had latched, then
opened the driver's door. He looked across the roof of the car
at Sam as she stood in the doorway. For a moment she thought
he would wave, get into the car and drive away.

Instead he walked back round the car and stood close in front of her. 'Goodbye, Sam,' he said. 'It's been fun.'

'Yes,' she said quietly. 'Yes, I suppose it has.'

Suddenly he leaned forward and kissed her gently on the cheek. Then he straightened up and said, 'If you're in town, do give me a call.'

She nodded. 'I will.'

This time he did wave – a brief throw of the hand. Then he clambered into the car, slamming the door, and started it up.

The gravel skidded away from the spinning tyres as the MG roared off down the drive. Sam stood in the doorway and watched until it was out of sight. She still had a brief impression that she had forgotten something, something important. Then the fragile fleeting moment was gone, and she was aware of her eyes stinging slightly in the autumn breeze.

She closed the door behind her and headed for the library.

The place was in turmoil. There were books and papers spread over very available surface, including the floor. Odd documents and pages of handwritten notes were taped to the walls and hung from shelves. Interspersed between the papers were occasional glimpses of a painting, the door, and the Philosopher's Stone, which seemed to reflect the clean whiteness of the paper beside it.

There were several stepping-stone islands of spaces visible through the carpet of documentation. Two of the larger spaces were occupied. Sargent stood in one of them, looking around with an expression that mixed awe, horror, and shellshock in roughly equal measures. In the other space, the Doctor sat cross-legged, staring down at the list of members of the secret alchemical society which lay spread across a large part of the floor in front of him and up the side of the reading table.

This, then, was what Sam found when she entered the room. She looked round for a while, trying to work out a safe path to the single chair that did not seem to be quite so densely stacked with books. She gave up, and tiptoed through the sea of information, aware that the Doctor and Sargent were watching her every step. When she reached the chair, she scooped up the books, and turned to place them on top of the detritus on the reading table. She caught sight of the Doctor's horrified expression before she did, and froze.

He leapt to his feet and was across the room in a couple of well-aimed bounds. Without a word, he lifted the pile of books from Sam's arms and nodded for her to go and sit in the space he had just vacated. Sam shrugged and picked her way to the space. The Doctor waited till she was sitting in his place, then deposited his armful of books and papers back on the chair exactly as they had been. Then he turned the chair slightly so it faced both Sam and Sargent, and sat down on top of the books.

'So,' he said from his elevated position behind the table, 'what have we learned?'

'Always put things away when you've finished with them,' Sam suggested. 'Otherwise it soon gets out of hand.'

Sargent smiled back at her.

The Doctor sniffed. 'I will,' he said.

Sam nodded and chewed at her bottom lip. 'Pickering's gone,' she offered. 'Just seen him off.'

The Doctor frowned. 'Already? I thought he still had a couple of sessions with Silver.'

'Apparently not. I tried to gatecrash his last session, but Silver insisted I keep out. Trade secrets I guess.' She shuffled her position, trying to get comfortable. 'You found anything useful among this lot?'

'Well –' the Doctor took a deep breath – 'the secret society is still very much in existence, though its aims are not clear. There's plenty of corroborating evidence, but most of it is rather vague and unspecific when it comes to details.' He waved towards a group of cascading piles of books and documents in one corner of the room. 'You're welcome to go through it if you like, and see if you can come up with anything more concrete.' He broke into a sudden grin. 'Fresh pair of eyes, new point of view. Might help.'

'Thanks,' Sam said, 'but I'm more than happy to take your word for it. I'm sure you've got it covered.'

'There's actually quite a bit of detail up until the nineteen thirties,' Sargent said. 'Not about aims and intentions, but appointments, dates for meetings, lists of members and so on. Administrative stuff if you like.'

'Yes,' the Doctor went on, 'the most peculiar thing perhaps, and it may be a clue to the society's *raison d'être*, is the composition of the membership.'

Sam looked from the Doctor to Sargent and back again. 'Meaning what, exactly? They start off as lead and turn into gold?'

The Doctor laughed, sudden and genuine. 'That's good, Sam.' Then just as suddenly he was serious again. 'Very good. But no. It's more a question of genetics.' He leaned forward from his precarious perch, and for a moment Sam thought he was about to topple over on to the reading table like an overstacked pile of books. 'We've managed to decipher many of the sets of initials and shorthand versions of names on there.' The Doctor was pointing to the large document that showed the members of the society. 'And the peculiar thing, the odd thing, the thing that seems more extraordinary is –' He broke off as if considering how best to phrase the information.

Sam was leaning forward, eyes wide, breath held. 'Yes?' she

asked at last.

The word seemed to wake the Doctor from his reverie. 'They all belong to the same families,' he said.

Sam sat back, holding her crossed feet and rocking slightly. 'I said it looked like a family tree.'

'So you did. And so it is. All the members of our group are descended from the same six people who formed the initial society under Matthew Siolfor back in the thirteenth century. Not so many people as you might think, actually, as they've intermarried quite a bit, it seems. But still they are split now across continents, their names and nationalities changed down the centuries. But all stemming from a common root.'

'I guess then,' Sam said after a suitable pause, 'that, apart from their purpose in life, that only leaves us with one outstanding question.'

The Doctor nodded.

'What's that?' Sargent asked.

Sam looked at the Doctor as she answered. 'Why?' she said.

The Doctor nodded again. 'It's difficult to say,' he admitted. 'We haven't much to go on, but we have to make do with what we have.'

The Mi-24 helicopter was far from ideal for Roskov's mission to Britain. It was primarily intended for providing support to ground troops, and its range was only 750 kilometres, so they had to stop several times to refuel on their return to Krejikistan. Fortunately in these post-Cold War years, with NATO expanding eastwards, it was straightforward if not simple to fly a Soviet-made helicopter from a former Eastern Bloc state across Europe without raising too many eyebrows.

NATO had called the Mi-24 the Hind and for much of the inbound flight they had been shadowed by fighters. The Hind was in effect a flying tank which would have played a key role in the typical Warsaw Pact offensive, which called for a massive and swift frontal attack. But with most of its weapons removed, it became an inefficient and noisy means of transport.

The Hind bumped slightly on the concrete as it settled back on to the main pad at the Nevchenka Military Installation. A figure wrapped in an army greatcoat braved the gale, holding his hat on, as the rotors slowed and dipped. Lieutenant Ivigan saluted Roskov and made to take his briefcase from him. But the colonel held on to it and waved Ivigan back towards the main base.

'How was your mother, sir?' Ivigan asked as soon as the noise had died down sufficiently. 'We were worried for her – for you – when you were gone so long.'

'She is much improved, thank you,' Roskov said without emotion. 'The information I received was exaggerated, thankfully. But St Petersburg is not a place to hurry back from.'

Ivigan grinned. 'And Nevchenka is not a place to hurry back to.'

'Indeed.'

They had reached the main building now, a low, windowless, concrete bunker. The lieutenant held the heavy steel door open for his commander.

'I wish to see my nephews,' Roskov told Ivigan as he set the briefcase down carefully on his desk. 'They will be concerned for their great-aunt, and I must set their minds at rest.'

Ivigan nodded. 'Of course. I shall send them to you, sir.' He saluted crisply, and closed the door behind him.

Roskov waited a moment, the fingers of one hand drumming on the metal of the briefcase. Then he thumbed the combination dials to the correct settings and opened the case. From inside he removed two CD jewel cases. He opened each in turn and inspected the CD-ROM inside. He was still holding the cases several minutes later when there was a knock at the door.

'Come.'

Two young soldiers, Sergeant Gregor Roskov and Private Ivan Roskov, entered the office and drew themselves up to attention in front of Roskov's desk. Gregor was twenty-two, the older of the brothers by three years. He was also taller by an inch, and heavier by almost three stones. His face was impassive granite. Ivan, by contrast, had a less weathered complexion. The hint of a smile curled his thin lips.

Colonel Roskov stood, holding the compact discs so they could see them. 'Gregor, Ivan. It seems we are all present,' Roskov said.

'When do you think it all began?' Sam asked him.

'The night the Devil came to Matthew Siolfor.' The Doctor lifted a book from the table in front of him – Siolfor's diary. 'Siolfor is suitably cryptic about what, if anything, actually happened. But we can find out who was with him at other ceremonies. And the names match the top line of the family tree.'

'Anyone of interest?'

'There were six of them.' The Doctor counted the names off on his fingers as Sam tried to read the upside-down scrawl of a thirteenth-century quill pen from the parchment on the floor in front of her. 'Thomas Kilner, St John Ross, Henry Tannian, William Wyrpe, Tobias Pryce. And of course Matthew Siolfor himself.'

'Have we no way of tracing where their descendants are now?' Sargent asked. 'There must be some records, birth certificates and so forth.'

'I'm sure there are. But that could take for ever, even assuming the descendants stayed in Britain.'

'Is there anywhere local we could look?' Sam asked. 'Records offices, church registers, whatever?' A thought came to her and she jabbed her finger at the Doctor. 'Hey, what about the chapel where they met?'

'Well, that's another odd thing,' Sargent replied.

'What is?'

'It doesn't exist,' he told her simply. 'No record of such a place other than in Siolfor's diary.'

'It was a ruin even then,' the Doctor pointed out. 'But you would expect some sort of reference, even the odd mention of the ruins of the ruins, as it were.'

'There's nothing?'

'Not so much as a dicky bird. Siolfor indicates that it was connected to the old manor house.'

'Then perhaps it's lost among the ruins there,' Sam suggested.

Sargent shook his head. 'No. No, those ruins have been thoroughly surveyed. They even did one of those TV excavations – *The Past is with Us,* or whatever it's called – up there. Computer graphics to re-create the original site and everything. No evidence of any chapel. It was one of the things they remarked on as being unusual, I remember.'

'Unusual,' the Doctor repeated quietly. 'There's a bit too much going on here that's unusual in my opinion. Some of them we haven't even considered yet. Like the Philosopher's Stone up there, the gargoyle images, the flowers.'

Sargent frowned. 'The flowers?' he asked puzzled.

The Doctor waved a hand in dismissal. 'Don't worry for now.'

Sam stood up. She was getting pins and needles sitting on the floor. But she decided almost immediately that there was nowhere else to go, so she stretched, stamped her sleepy foot, and sat down again. 'So, we're a bit stuck then.'

'Not at all.' The Doctor grinned. 'At least one family stayed in this immediate area. The records might not trace the lineage right up to the present day, but they give us an excellent start. The family remained influential, even gained in reputation and power over the years. Their name changed over the course of the centuries, of course, but they're still here.' He stood up sharply, sending the books he had been sitting on skidding and sliding into a muddled heap on the floor. 'But it's somewhere to start,' he cried enthusiastically as he rubbed his hands together.

Sargent and Sam exchanged glances. 'Where is?' Sam asked.

The Doctor stared at her as if he could not believe she had just asked him such a question. 'Here of course.' He spread his arms and turned a full circle on his heels. '*Siolfor*,' he said as his face spun back into view, 'is an Old English form of *Silver*.' His turn stopped as suddenly as it had started, his expression frozen on his face as he gazed past Sam.

Sam saw Sargent's frown deepen, and realised that he too was looking past her. She turned as quickly as she could from her cramped position on the floor. Behind her, Norton Silver was standing framed in the doorway. And he was holding a gun.

For a moment there was complete silence. Then Silver said quietly, 'It seems there is much you still don't know, Doctor. And that is probably for the best.'

'Perhaps,' the Doctor hazarded. 'I wouldn't know, of course. Maybe you should tell me, and then I could judge for myself.' He was picking his way across the room towards Silver. Silver's pistol tracked his every careful step. 'After all,' the Doctor continued, as he approached the door, 'I'd hate to die in ignorance.'

Silver's expression did not change. 'Nevertheless, that is how you must die, I'm afraid.'

Sam saw Silver's knuckles whiten slightly as his grip on the pistol increased. She looked round, searching for something to do. But she was sitting on the floor, unable to move fast enough to help. Sargent was too far away and probably scared out of his mind. The Doctor was making his painfully slow way across the room towards the gun that was even now levelled at his hearts.

'Goodbye, Doctor.' Silver's voice was quiet and calm. Like his expression, it lacked emotion.

The Doctor slipped slightly on a loose piece of paper. He glanced down at his feet as he regained his balance. 'So soon?' He took another step forwards. 'Well, goodbye, then.' But his last word was transformed into a cry – perhaps of fear, perhaps of surprise, perhaps of triumph – as he slipped again, his foot skidding out from under him, and he pitched suddenly forward. Somehow the fall was transformed into a flying leap, the Doctor's shoulder striking Silver full in the chest. Silver's arm came up in an attempt to ward off the collision. The pistol bucked in his hand as he fired. The gunshot was an explosion of sound in the oak-panelled room. A chunk of plaster fell away in a shower of powder and debris as the bullet embedded itself in the ceiling

Silver flew backward, knocked off his feet by the force of the collision. As he fell to the floor outside the room, Sam caught a glimpse of Miss Allworthy in the corridor behind him. The housekeeper was also holding a pistol. But it was only a glimpse, then the Doctor slammed the door shut and in almost the same motion dragged a chair under the handle.

'That won't hold them for long,' he said. 'Come on.'

The Doctor dragged Sam to her feet and pulled her across the room by the hand. Sargent was close on their heels. The French windows were still a shattered mess, the missing glass replaced with polythene and the broken wooden struts crudely supplanted by rough offcuts of two-by-four. The Doctor barely paused, crashing through the makeshift window and out on to the terrace beyond.

'Oh well,' Sam said as she followed through the torn wreckage, 'here we go again.' She ignored Sargent's quizzical stare.

Roskov ignored Ivigan's quizzical stare as he and his two nephews, Gregor and Ivan, left the office. They made their way through the complex towards the elevators. The main command-and-control centre occupied the deepest level of the facility. Once inside the lift, Ivan punched the lowest button on the panel. After a few moments, the doors slid open again, and Roskov and his nephews stepped out.

The elevators were located at the back of the main control suite, at the rear of the large viewing gallery. The gallery was a glassed-in box looking down on the main control centre where dozens of technicians sat in front of computers and monitors. The whole of the far wall was taken up with a huge illuminated map of the world. Krejikistan was shaded in green, the rest of the world a neutral grey.

Roskov gestured for the two soldiers to remain where they stood, and made his way to an armoured door in the side of the gallery. A flight of metal steps led down from the door to the control-suite floor. As the door closed behind Roskov, the two soldiers watched through the glass side of the gallery as the colonel descended to the huge chamber below.

Behind them, the door of an elevator quietly opened and Lieutenant Ivigan emerged. He stood just outside the lift doors, hands on hips, watching the men silently. After a while, he turned and went back into the elevator. The doors closed almost immediately.

* * *

Almost immediately, the Doctor set off at a run. Sam and Sargent did their best to keep up, but still the Doctor had to pause several times before they were out of sight of the house. Behind them they could hear the shouts from Silver as he organised Miss Allworthy to follow them.

'Is Miss Allworthy in on this too? Or is she just following orders?' Sam asked between taking deep breaths as they paused on the edge of the croquet lawn for Sargent to catch up. He was fumbling in his jacket pocket, probably a nervous reaction, as he reached them.

The Doctor gave Sargent a few moments to catch his breath. The librarian was doubled over, drawing long rasping breaths that made his whole body heave with the effort.

'William Wyrpe,' the Doctor said. 'Remember?'

Sam nodded. 'One of the six. So what?'

'So *Wyrpe* is an antiquated word meaning reputable, honourable.'

'Worthy?'

'Exactly.' He turned to Sargent. 'You up to this?'

Sargent choked a response that could have been anything, but was probably a negative.

'Good,' the Doctor announced, his own demeanour suggesting he had enjoyed a light stroll through the gardens so far. 'Come on, then.'

Behind them a flashlight was shining through the trees and they dashed towards the steps down to the water garden. Clouds skittered across the face of the full moon like smoke from a cauldron.

Ivigan set down the steaming Styrofoam cup on the grubby tabletop. 'May I?'

The pilot waved a hand at the seat opposite. 'Of course, sir.'

They sat in silence for a while. The pilot sipped his black

tea, Ivigan blew on his hot coffee.

'So how was St Petersburg?' Ivigan asked at last. His smile was knowing and conspiratorial.

The pilot grinned. 'How would I know?'

Ivigan's smile grew until it reached his ears. This was going to be easier than he had hoped. The pilot obviously assumed that Ivigan knew where Roskov had really been. Certainly he had not been to see his dying mother. Ivigan pulled a silver hip flask from his coat pocket, unstoppered it, and held it out as an offer. The pilot nodded, surprised at the gesture, and Ivigan poured some of the rough vodka into the man's tea. He poured a rather smaller measure into his own cup.

'So, how did it go?'

'How does the colonel think it went?'

Ivigan raised his cup in a silent toast. 'Oh, you know the colonel. He is not one to share his emotions easily. And he has been busy since his return. So much paperwork for a thing like this.'

The helicopter pilot snorted. 'You're telling me. Organising payment for the refuelling is a nightmare. Have you any idea how to go about finding the common exchange rate between the rouble and the franc?'

Ivigan's cup paused at his lips. Western Europe? He had suspected the Ukraine, possibly Poland. But what the hell was Roskov doing in Western Europe?

'And the weather?' he suggested.

The pilot drained his tea and stood up. He looked round quickly to check there was nobody within earshot. Then he leaned forward. 'They're not joking when they say it is always raining over there.' He shook his head at the memory before straightening and giving the lieutenant a lazy salute.

It was Ivigan's last shot before the man left. Rain, where did it always rain. Something suggested the plains of Spain, but he discounted it. 'So what did you get for the wife from Harrods?' he asked to the man's retreating back. If he had guessed wrong, the pilot might go straight to Roskov. It was a slight risk, but a risk nonetheless.

The pilot paused, turned, grinned. 'Some chance. We didn't get within a hundred miles of London.' He gave a half-wave, and left the canteen.

Ivigan sat back in his chair. He stared at the steam still rising from his coffee, watched it wisp its way faintly into the air above the table as he thought through the possibilities. He did not know what was going on. But whatever Colonel Roskov was up to, he didn't like it. He left the vodka-laced coffee cooling on the table and headed back towards the command centre.

Colonel Roskov was seated at the commander's terminal. From here he could monitor any of the other terminals in the centre. Currently it showed the main map display from the huge screen on the back wall of the room. He could also relay instructions to them. From here he could initiate dummy missile runs and simulations that would test the responses of his staff to a possible attack. In effect, he could monitor how they reacted to a recording of a Western nuclear attack relayed to their systems. And to ensure that nobody took things too seriously, the word *Simulation* flashed constantly across the top and bottom of the screen during the exercise.

Roskov slipped the first of the CD-ROMs into the workstation. This would set up the environment. As he watched, the image on the screen in front of him stretched, so that a couple of centimetres at each of the extremes of the picture were lost beneath the plastic edges of the monitor.

Roskov removed the first CD and replaced it with the second. A countdown started on his screen:

He watched it in satisfaction for a few seconds, then turned and looked up at the observation gallery above him. He raised his hand, and Gregor and Ivan nodded their understanding. A moment later the gallery door opened and the two soldiers started down the staircase, their boots clanking on the metal steps.

Their feet rang on the stone steps as they raced down towards the water gardens. The steps were steep, running parallel to a small stream that fed the ponds and water features. The water was running quick and deep after the autumn rain, a constant torrent of sound in the quiet of the night, which Sam hoped would deaden the sound of their footsteps.

'There's still something we're missing,' the Doctor called above the noise of the water. 'Anyone got any ideas?'

'A bulletproof vest?'

'Don't be flippant, Sam,' the Doctor told her in the same tone. 'I mean there's lots of this that we don't understand. Why chase us through the night because we know they're in some sub-Masonic group trying to achieve the impossible with respect to alchemy?'

'Good point, Doctor,' Sargent gasped. 'But right now I'm not sure I care.'

'Reputation?' Sam suggested.

'It's an awful lot of trouble to go to just to save face.'

'What about the alien flowers?'

The Doctor stopped abruptly at the bottom of the steps, and the others cannoned into him. 'Maybe we should ask Tanner.'

'Yes, maybe, Doctor.' Sam pulled herself upright again. 'But one thing at a time, eh?'

'No, no. I mean, ask him now.'

'Now?'

The Doctor pointed into the darkness ahead. 'Why not? He's just over there after –' He broke off as suddenly as he had stopped running. 'You know, I can be incredibly dense sometimes, Sam.'

Sam was still peering into the gloom ahead when Tanner stepped into the moonlight. He was holding a shotgun over the crook of his arm. He raised it to cover them as he approached.

'Another little piggy who stayed at home,' the Doctor said with obvious disappointment. 'A descendant of the long dead Henry Tannian, I presume.'

Tanner said nothing, but gestured with a wave of his shotgun that they should turn round and go back up the steps. Behind him the moonlight shone through scattered clouds on to the uneven surfaces of water whipped up by the increasing wind. Ripples spread outward in the ponds and pools, lapping gently right to the edge.

6
Right to the Edge

Silver and Miss Allworthy were waiting at the top of the steps. They said nothing, Silver gesturing for the Doctor, Sam and Sargent to follow him back towards the house.

They were almost at the house, making their way along a narrow paved path across the lawn, when Sam made her move. A cloud edged over the moon, the light dimming suddenly. She dived off the path, rolling across the grass and behind a tree. Immediately Tanner was after her. But he was slow, and not sure where she had gone. Sam was already running across the lawn, keeping to the shadows, as Tanner edged cautiously round the tree, his shotgun levelled.

Silver kept his gun at the Doctor's throat. 'Tanner,' he called. 'Get back here.' He turned to the Doctor, jamming the gun hard into his chin. 'She's not important. Not now.' Then he pulled the gun away and waved the Doctor forward. 'But you, Doctor, you could be *very* important.'

As they continued on their way towards the house, a shadow skittered across the edge of the lawn. Sam waited until they were inside, then cautiously made her way across the driveway after them, careful not to make any sound on the gravel.

She slipped inside, stopping silently on the threshold. She could just hear Silver's voice coming from along one of the corridors, and picked her way towards it. She had no clear plan, no real idea what she was going to do. But if she could see where they were taking the Doctor she could decide later how to rescue him.

The sounds of the people moving ahead of her faded. There was a bang as a door slammed shut, then silence. Sam paused in mid-step. When it remained silent for several seconds she continued along the passage. There was no light, and she had to feel her way along. The passage turned abruptly to the left. Then it stopped in what felt like a blank wall.

Sam fell furiously round the panelling. Had she missed a turning? Had she followed the wrong route? She was beginning to panic. 'Calm down,' she told herself. 'Think.'

The passage must lead somewhere. Even if she had missed them, this passage was here for a reason. And the reason was so it could lead somewhere. That was what passages did.

She felt her way back along the panelling, more carefully this time. Sure enough, there was a break in the beading. A handle worked into the decoration. She pulled it, cautiously, trying to make no noise, and the heavy door swung slowly open. In front of her, Sam could see a huge room. The door led on to a small landing at the top of a short staircase. Both were made of metal plates with holes punched through in a grid pattern.

The steps led steeply down into a large room. A huge room, in fact. It looked as though it had been fashioned out of cellerage which might run under a good part of the house above. The brick walls had been whitewashed, and the floor was a level expanse of poured concrete. The ceiling, she saw, was high and vaulted, made from whitewashed brickwork.

The metal staircase led down a side wall of the chamber. The Doctor and Sargent were already looking around as they stood at the bottom. Sam dropped silently on to her belly, edging her way forward so she could look down into the room from the edge of the landing area. She hoped the lighting was sufficiently low and the shadows sufficiently deep for nobody to be able to see her.

The large room was dominated by a huge display screen at one end. At the moment it was blank, a grey monotony of liquid crystals waiting for the current to turn them into specks of colour. Lined up in front of the screen were several rows of heavy wooden desks like those found in a modern office. And on each were several smaller screens connected to a workstation under the desk and to a bank of equipment at the end of the row. Cables ran along the floor like arteries carrying current, data, information between the humming machines.

The rear quarter of the room was a separate raised area enclosed in glass or perspex. Sam could see several rows of seats inside, raked like those in a theatre. It was clearly an observation gallery. A short flight of steps led up to a door, also made from the transparent material, although punctuated with visible metal hinges and heavy bolts.

But the most bizarre aspect of the whole place was the lighting. The screens would provide sources of light when they were on. But they were the only modern lighting that Sam could see. The whole chamber was illuminated by the flickering yellow flames of hundreds of thick black candles. Every desk had at least two candles on it beside the high-tech equipment. Every available flat surface was used, a black candle stuck in place by a ragged agglomeration of dripped wax.

Silver was standing in front of the large screen. The candlelight glimmered across his face. He had a small black remote-control box in his hand, and pressed a button. The screen sprang into vivid life behind him, so that he was silhouetted against the sudden riot of colours and visual noise. The candlelight receded into the background as technology took over. Fluorescent lights flared into life in concealed recesses around the walls, and Sam pulled herself back slightly as the shadows in which she was hiding thinned and evaporated. After another second the screen cleared and settled. It showed an outline map of the world, curved lines criss-crossing over it and tiny letters and symbols of identification labelling each curve.

'You're impressed,' Silver said. His voice was powerful, echoing round the chamber so that the candle flames seemed to shy away from it. 'And so you should be.'

The Doctor laughed, and Silver's smile froze. 'Well,' the Doctor said, his voice carrying easily across the room despite his quiet tone, 'when you've seen one dastardly villain's lair you've seen them all.' He wandered over to a screen and blew imaginary dust off the top before polishing the plastic casing with his cuff. He cupped his hand round the flame of the nearest candle, watching it gutter and jump in his faint breath. 'Such fragility,' he murmured.

'You could land men on Mars from here,' Sargent commented.

'Oh I don't know,' the Doctor retorted. 'Most of this is for strictly local monitoring and tracking. Just orbital stuff.' He turned to Silver. 'What's your range? As far as the moon?'

'Far enough,' Silver's reply boomed back.

The Doctor nodded grimly. 'But far enough for what? That's the question.' He picked up a calculator from the desk and turned it over in his hand, weighing it experimentally. Tanner stepped up to him, took the calculator from his hand with a glare, and set it back on the desk.

'You shall have your answer soon enough,' Silver told him. He turned back towards the main screen, working at the remote. The lines faded away, leaving just the map outlined in green against the dark grey background.

'So, you're not interested in the satellites, then.'

'Indeed not.' Silver flicked switches on what seemed to be a main control panel on the middle front desk. 'Monitoring military satellites is a technical challenge, but somewhat boring. I now have a better use for my time.'

As Silver switched them on, the monitor screens around the room flickering into life. Unlike the main screen, they seemed to show views of countryside. Some Sam recognised as places in the immediate area of the house, but others looked to be views of a completely different area. The land was flat but with rocky outcrops. There was some grass stubble and a variety of weeds pushing up through the dry, baked earth, but there were no trees.

'Fascinating,' the Doctor murmured. He walked along one of the rows, inspecting each screen in turn. At the end of the row he turned on his heels to face Silver. 'I bet you can see inside the house as well.'

Silver pressed a button on the remote, and the outline map on the main screen was replaced with dozens of smaller images – the same images as on the monitors. But there were more pictures on the main screen than there were monitors in the room. Added to the views of the countryside were images of the inside of the house above them. They were shot from strange angles, usually high up, and Sam guessed they came from hidden security cameras.

The Doctor walked up to the screen and pointed up at one of the images. It was a shot of the library, taken apparently from above the main entrance to the room looking across at the shattered French windows, the curtains flapping in the wind. At the edge of the frame, the Philosopher's Stone was a glowing egg, as if the camera were somehow enhancing its colour and luminosity.

'So, that's how you knew I'd found the painting.' The Doctor turned back to Silver. 'I assume it was you and not one of your hench-people who tried to repossess it the other night.' When

Silver did not reply, the Doctor turned his attention back to the screen. 'I also assume this was originally a security system, since there is only really coverage for the rooms where valuables are to be found.' He grinned. 'Am I right?'

Silver sighed in mock boredom. 'Doctor, I did not have you brought here to engage in social chitchat.'

The Doctor seemed undeterred, however. 'Is there another view of the library?' he asked. 'I've just had an idea.'

Silver gestured to Miss Allworthy. 'Show him.'

The housekeeper returned her pistol to an incongruous shoulder holster and sat down at one of the monitors. She opened a small hatch beneath the screen, and a keyboard and mouse sprang out.

Sargent hesitated for a moment, still standing at the foot of the stairs.

'I think you should join your friend,' Silver told him, and the librarian crossed to where Miss Allworthy now had two pictures of the library displayed in windows on the screen. As she moved the mouse, the view in the active window panned and tracked in sympathy.

'I see. Very clever.' The Doctor reached out. 'May I?'

Silver nodded, and the woman slid off the seat and allowed the Doctor to take her place. In moments, the Doctor was moving the cameras, panning round as if looking for something. 'And this must be the zoom control.' He punched a key, and the camera zoomed in. Sam squinted, trying to make out the image. It looked as though a painting by the library door now filled the window. A few more moments' work, and the second window now displayed the output from an external camera. It was a close match for the view that the painting represented, as if the camera were seated where the painter had been over a century earlier.

The two windows on the monitor were joined by two more,

tiled so they quartered the screen. A short while later, one of the new camera angles showed another of the paintings; the other soon displayed the equivalent view of the actual grounds. Again, they were a near-perfect match.

Silver laughed. 'I see what you're about, Doctor.' He wagged his finger like an admonishing headmaster. 'It won't help you, though. Take it from me, the paintings match the countryside. They were painted from life, and there's nothing you can learn from comparing art and life except that the one mirrors the other.'

The Doctor swivelled round in his chair. 'But there is something odd about the paintings, isn't there? Something that drove poor old Raymond Coulter to kill himself before he had even finished his work.'

Silver turned back to the main screen. 'Doctor,' he said, 'I tell you you're barking up the wrong tree entirely.'

Sam craned forward, trying to get a better view of the monitor. Both pairs of views showed Lord Meacher's Clump in the background. Its shape was distinctive, with the two trees at the front standing slightly forward of the rest and a little taller, the others evenly spread behind them. A constant silhouette at the back of each of the perspectives.

'Barking up the wrong tree?' the Doctor muttered. 'The wrong tree?' And his face clouded as if he did not understood the phrase.

'But for the moment,' Silver was saying, 'we are not interested in local geography.' The shots of the inside of the house and the grounds disappeared from the main screen, and the images of the barren rocky landscape reflowed and enlarged to fill the space. At the centre there was a single square of blackness, numbers flashing over it in white as they counted down the seconds:

'So where is that?' Sargent asked.

Silver turned to the Doctor. 'Well?' he asked. 'You're the one with the answers.'

'Oh no, I'm the one with the questions. So where is it?'

'Krejikistan,' Silver said. 'A live feed. In fact it came on-line just little while ago. Which means that everything is going well there.'

'And where exactly is *there*? I mean, Krejikistan is not a small place.'

'Indeed not. I understand it is about twice the size of Wales.' Silver smiled. 'I sometimes think that Wales only exists to act as a unit of measurement for other countries. Much its most useful role, I dare say, though I'm sure several thousand sheep would beg to differ.' His smile faded into the lines of his face. 'We are looking at the area immediately surrounding the Nevchenka Military Installation. In fact, we are seeing it through their own security cameras.'

Sam decided she had seen enough for now. The Doctor did not appear to be in immediate danger, but she did not at all like the look of the big countdown on the screen. It was obvious she couldn't rescue the Doctor or stop whatever was going on by taking on three armed people, even with the Doctor's and (perhaps) Sargent's help. So she needed a plan that was clever rather than blunt.

She looked round for inspiration. The most striking thing was the contrast between the candles and the high-tech screen and computer equipment. Whatever Silver was up to, he was reliant on that technology. And that gave her an idea.

'So what are we watching?' The Doctor asked as Sam slid back from the edge of the landing and climbed carefully to her feet. She opened the door just wide enough to squeeze through. Before she closed it behind her, she looked back down into the room.

Silver was at the front of the room, turned to face them. He spread his arms, a crucified silhouette against the pixellated tessellation of landscape behind him. Over his shoulder, the countdown reached zero. 'The end of the world,' he said. 'Perhaps.'

Roskov watched as the countdown on his monitor reached zero. And the siren screamed through the base.

At the same instant, the simulation program on the CD-ROM punched the recorded data and status information through to the main computers. They in turn passed it back to the appropriate workstations. Because they knew it was a dummy run rather than an actual situation, they overprinted *Simulation* on the top and bottom edges of the formatted screen output. They also gave the commander's terminal in the control centre override capability so that he could control events. In effect, this meant that the program running on the CD was in charge of the output fed to every other device. And, since the control screen had been set to overscan the images such that the edges of the information were lost, that setting was passed down to the slave terminals. The result was a slightly enlarged image on each monitor, the *Simulation* warning lost off the edges.

And the result of that was that the operators believed what their systems told them was real.

The main screen flared suddenly in red over the USA. The flashes resolved themselves almost at once into curved lines arching towards Eastern Europe. Dotted lines completed the projected trajectories.

'We have multiple launches from the mainland United States.' The operator was on his feet, one hand cupped to his headset, despite the fact all the data was visual.

A moment later another operator swung round towards Roskov. 'I have it too. Estimate thirty-seven independent launches.'

Roskov leaned forward, apparently appalled. 'My God, that means at least four hundred warheads.' He strode to the front of the control centre. 'Do we have target projections yet?'

'All targets are in the Eastern Bloc zones. Mostly Russia.'

'Confirmation?'

'We have launch confirmation coming through from the satellites now.' There was deathly hush as they waited. 'Confirmed. Thirty-six launches from known nuclear installations in the USA. All missiles running true.'

'Options?' Roskov demanded.

The senior soldier apart from Roskov was Nikita Veyevski, the Weapons Officer. He was seated at a console at the side of the room. 'We should wait for accurate target projections,' Veyevski advised. 'They should be through any moment, and it's possible that we are not targeted.'

'Very well.' Roskov stroked his chin. 'Meanwhile, maintain full alert. And seal this facility.'

'But sir, Lieutenant Ivigan should be here. We need another officer for authentication and concurrence should a launch be required.'

Roskov stared Veyevski down. 'Ivigan could be miles away. Sergeant Gregor Roskov is the senior military officer present after you and me. He can authenticate.'

The Weapons Officer seemed to notice the sergeant for the first time. 'Yes, sir,' he said without enthusiasm. 'Operating shutters now.'

Behind them steel plates started to descend noisily, slowly, over the windows of the observation gallery.

'Targets confirmed,' another terminal operator shouted above the noise. 'Twenty-seven warheads are targeted on locations within Krejikistan. The rest are in the Ukraine and Russia.'

Roskov nodded grimly. 'Hardly a surprise, gentlemen. What response do we have from our allies?'

'Some engine emissions in the Ukraine. Probably they are running rocket motors while they decide. Nothing from Russia.'

Roskov snorted in annoyance. 'Those spineless fools left in the Kremlin probably don't believe their intelligence information. That will be the death of them.' He pointed to the operator responsible, a young woman in her mid-twenties, her brown hair tied back severely. 'Start the motors. I trust our own commanders will be somewhat more decisive.'

'Sir.' She unlocked a protective cover on her console, and raised it. Then she jabbed her thumb hard down on the recessed button beneath. This sent a signal to the control systems to start the motors on twenty-two ballistic missiles fitted with multiple nuclear warheads.

Somewhere at the back of the room, right on cue, a dot-matrix printer clicked into life. Its print head tracked across the paper with a noise like tearing fabric. Immediately one of the technicians was beside the device, reading the text as it scrolled up slowly, line by line. 'Sir,' he called out, 'we have an Emergency Action Command.'

Apart from the staccato sound of the printer, the room was in silence.

Ivigan stared at the blast shutters over the glass. 'What is he playing at?' he wondered out loud. 'It will be eighteen minutes at least before the first missile strikes, even assuming there has been a launch.' His mind was working quickly, fuelled by the abnormal adrenaline flow. Why close the shutters so far ahead of danger? If not to keep a blast out, then perhaps to exclude something else. Something or someone… Himself?

Ivigan shook his head. The siren wail was cutting into his brain. Certainly Colonel Roskov had not been himself recently, not since that fall in his office the other day.

The lift doors opened behind him and a private ran over. 'Sir, the preburners are running,' he reported breathlessly.

'What is he doing?' Ivigan asked quietly. 'Preparing to launch?' He checked a terminal in the corner of the gallery. 'But there have been no incoming communications. No Emergency Action Command, and without that he cannot get the launch codes from the Weapons Operator.'

He turned to the private. 'Find Sergeant Kosimov,' he snapped.

'Sir, he is off duty.'

'I know. So he isn't in there,' Ivigan stabbed his finger at the steel shutter. 'Find him, quickly, and ask him how we can stop the rocket motors manually.'

'But if we have orders to launch, sir –'

'Yes,' Ivigan cut him off. '*If*. But only if.' He jerked his head towards the elevators. 'Move.'

The private saluted and ran back to the lifts.

Ivigan picked up the phone next to the terminal. 'Get me General Orominsk. Urgently.' As he waited for the call to go through, Lieutenant Ivigan held the receiver away from his ear, as if it might burn him.

The operator tore off the printout and carried it to Roskov. He held it carefully between finger and thumb. 'Sir,' he said as he handed it over, 'I have a properly formatted Emergency Action Command.'

Roskov took the flimsy paper and scanned it quickly. 'I concur. Sergeant Roskov?'

The sergeant was already beside them. He took the paper,

read it carefully, and returned it. 'I concur. A properly formatted Emergency Action Command.'

'Authenticate.' Roskov took the message to a console at the side of the room, where the Weapons Officer waited, hand already out to take the paper. He took the message and laid it on his console beside the screen.

'Please check that I type the correct authentication string,' he said as he carefully pecked at the keyboard. A line of numerals and upper-case letters appeared on the screen. It matched the coded sequence labelled MESSAGE IDENT on the printout.

'The identification code is properly entered,' Roskov said as soon as the officer's fingers were still.

'I concur,' the sergeant agreed.

Weapons Officer Veyevski hit the Enter key.

All three of them stared at the screen in silence for several seconds. The room was deathly quiet.

'So now we know,' Roskov said at last. 'Weapons Officer, do you concur that we have a properly formatted and authenticated Emergency Action Command ordering the release and deployment of nuclear weapons against the mainland United States?'

A moment's hesitation. A droplet of sweat edged its way from Veyevski's forehead and trickled down his cheek. 'I do, sir.'

'Sergeant Roskov, as the senior soldier here present besides myself and the Weapons Officer, do you concur that we have a properly formatted and authenticated Emergency Action Command ordering the release and deployment of nuclear weapons against the mainland United States?'

There was no hesitation this time. 'Yes, sir.'

Colonel Roskov turned back to the Weapons Officer. 'Then, in accordance with Directive Five, you will release to me the trigger codes and the firing keys.'

The Weapons Officer slowly pulled a thin chain from around his neck. Hung on it was a key. He fitted the key into a heavy steel drawer in his console. For a second, he let go of the key, then his moist fingers clenched it tightly and turned. From inside the drawer he removed a perspex box. Visible within were two plastic cards, each about the size of a credit card and with a magnetic strip down one side. He handed the box to Roskov.

Roskov took the box to his own terminal. He removed one of the plastic cards and handed it to his nephew, who took it across the room to another terminal. The dual-key system ensured that no one person could authorise a launch alone.

One the main screen at the end of the room, tiny blips of light slowly traced their way across the map towards Eastern Europe.

'Do we have the firing codes yet?'

The Weapons Officer was intent on his monitor. A bar of red was slowly filling a progress indicator as the computer calculated the correct codes using an algorithm from the exact time and date of the Emergency Access Command as defined in its ident code, and a random number based on a predetermined seed.

'In a moment, sir.'

A line of text flashed above the progress indicator, and on every other screen in the room:

Emergency Action Command authenticated. Calculating firing codes...

Ivigan read the text in disbelief. He had stopped in mid-sentence as the information message flashed up on the screen in front of him, just as it had on every screen on the network.

'Sir,' his voice was husky and broken as he spoke into the phone again. 'Whether you appreciate my concerns or not, Colonel Roskov has now authenticated the Emergency Action Command which you have not sent and we have not received.' He paused, partly to swallow and try to get his voice back, partly because he knew that General Orominsk would now be seeing the same message as he was. 'Roskov is accessing the firing codes.'

He continued to watch the screen. Soon the codes would flash up as they were entered into the navigation and targeting systems. When that happened, they would know for sure where the missiles were aimed. And they would also know that it was too late to prevent a launch.

Ivigan was barely aware of the general's voice in his ear, hardly surprised that his superior officer was asking him what he would do rather than giving him direct orders.

'Sergeant Kosimov believes we can cut the engines and disable the launch vehicles from outside the command centre,' Ivigan said quickly. 'But each vehicle must be disabled individually. Assuming Colonel Roskov intends to launch as soon as he has the codes, Kosimov's best estimate for the time he needs would still leave at least seven missiles in a go condition if – when – the colonel launches.'

'Very well.' The general's voice sounded distant and faint. 'Do what you can, Lieutenant. I won't pretend that will alter events significantly, but it will help.'

'What will you do, sir?'

The answer was preceded by a heavy sigh. 'We can pretend no longer. I must tell the Americans what their satellites will already be reporting. President Dering must prepare his country for a nuclear attack the likes of which our world has never seen. Let us hope he can find it in his heart to forgive us. May his people forgive us. May God forgive us.'

The phone went dead.

Ivigan stared at the screen as the red bar edged its way towards the end of the world.

7
The End of the World

The red bar of the progress indicator was a bleeding cut across the huge screen in Silver's basement control room. The Doctor watched in appalled silence while Silver rubbed his hands together in undisguised excitement.

Neither Miss Allworthy nor Tanner made any comment, either verbally or by their expressions. They stood either side of the room, guns held at the ready in case of any trouble from their prisoners. Sargent sat at one of the control stations, his chin in his hands, apparently oblivious to what was happening around him.

'Not long now, Doctor,' Silver said, his attention never straying from the screen. 'Not long and you will begin to understand what we are about.'

'I'm not sure I want to understand,' the Doctor said. 'I'm a firm believer that sometimes ignorance is bliss.'

Around the progress indicator in the centre of the screen, the other images showed the area round the missile base. From several of the rocky outcrops in the wilderness landscapes, white smoke was pouring, erupting, from the gaps between the rocks.

'What on earth is that?' Sargent asked nervously.

'Preburners,' the Doctor said grimly. 'Roskov is preparing to launch his missiles.'

As if to confirm the Doctor's horrifying diagnosis, the various rocky outcrops and piles of stones slowly, mechanically, silently, swung aside so that the steam billowed out in ever-increasing quantities. And between several of the ragged clouds, the cold, hard, stubby nose of a nuclear missile stood proud, enveloped in the smoke.

It took Sam less time than she had feared to find the main fuse box. It was in the first place she looked – the cupboard under the stairs – and was actually pretty hard to miss. There was the usual grey domestic fuse box. Through the transparent cover Sam could discern two rows of switches. Beside these was a single, larger, red switch. White text etched into the barrel of the switch said: ON. But beside this was a smaller box with a hinged transparent lid. Inside Sam could see a single round button, a keyhole in its centre. Across the cover, printed in bold capital letters, were the words: EMERGENCY POWER OFF.

Sam lifted the cover and reached out for the button. But as her fingertip touched it, she hesitated. If she simply cut the power, then the Doctor would be as much in the dark – literally – as Silver and the others. She needed to warn him somehow what she was doing. He needed to be ready. He would not have long to make his getaway, especially with all those candles still burning brightly, oblivious to the loss of power.

So the problem now was how to get the Doctor's attention and pass him a message. Sam stood a while, finger on the red button, and pondered this.

Then she went out of the house, descended the steps from the front door to the forecourt, and knelt down in the gravel.

'Hell.' Jimmy Reading dropped his half-eaten cheese sandwich and ran his fingers along the text on the screen as he read it again. The satellites precoded their own reports according to a pattern analysis of the area they were photographing compared with the previous photos. If there was a dramatic change, they flagged the message as URGENT. If there was a slight change but one that seemed to continue a trend from two previous photographs, that might merit an IMMEDIATE status. Most were ROUTINE.

This batch of photographs was labelled PINNACLE. Reading had never seen a PINNACLE message before, but he recognised the code. The reason he had never seen one was because he had never been in direct receipt of one. And the PINNACLE designation for an incoming message, whoever it was from, meant it was to bypass the local and regional commanders and go straight to the Joint Chiefs of Staff.

Since Reading knew that the satellite had just completed its regular pass over the Nevchenka Military Installation in Krejikistan, he had no illusions about what the satellite's surveillance pictures would show.

'OK, guys,' he called across the room, his cracked voice betraying his nerves and the urgency of his words. 'Round up the JCS – it looks like we've got a preburn in Krejikistan.' He hit the Print key, and the set of photos started emerging almost immediately from a colour laser printer. On the other side of the room, another printer spat out letter-size envelopes with PINNACLE – UMBRA stamped along the top. Each had the name of one of the Joint Chiefs of Staff printed in capitals across it. The first out of the printer bore the name of General Howard Kane, CJCS.

General Howard Kane, Chairman of the Joint Chiefs of Staff, was at dinner with his wife when his pager bleeped. The noise was artificially loud in the quiet restaurant, the low lighting seeming to amplify it further. Kane ignored the turned heads and disapproving mutterings from diners at the surrounding tables, and wiped his mouth with his napkin before turning off the pager.

'Don't worry, it's probably nothing,' he said as he saw his wife try to disguise her disappointment. He pulled the pager into the light, and read off the short sentence scrolling across it.

'I'm sorry,' he said simply as he stood up, tossing the napkin on to the table in front of him.

'So am I.' She made no move to leave with him. She was used to finishing her meals alone. 'Will you be long?'

Kane stooped down beside his wife, surprising her by taking her hand in his own. 'Perhaps,' he said. 'Yes, probably.' He stood up with a sigh. 'You know we talked about you taking a trip. To see Nancy in Kansas, maybe.'

She looked up sharply. Even if she had not already been alerted by his artificially offhand tone, she recalled the ancient conversation he was referring to in vivid, frightening detail. 'Yes?'

He nodded. 'Now might be a good time.' He buttoned his jacket, only to unbutton it again almost immediately. 'I love you, Barbara,' he said suddenly and quickly.

Her lips pursed, the moisture in her eyes enhanced by the glow of the candle in the centre of the table. 'Take care of yourself, Howard.'

He nodded, and kissed her on the cheek. Perhaps, they both knew, for the last time. Then he turned abruptly and headed for the door. They knew where he was, of course. They always knew. The limo was waiting at the kerb. The engine roared as he got in. An officer handed him a sealed envelope as the car lurched and pulled sharply away.

Kane was at the Pentagon just minutes later and made his way immediately to the briefing chamber in the National Military Command Center on the third floor. The Deputy Chairman of the Joint Chiefs of Staff, Harry Pringle from the USAF, was already there. The others arrived within moments. Kane let the muted conversations go on around him as he planned out in his mind where to start and how to proceed.

'Where's Ben?'

'On vacation in Europe. Not due till next week.'

'Do we fly him back?'

'Hell, no. He's better off where he is.'

Around them the maps on the walls showed the current US and foreign troop dispersals and fleet positions together with their states of readiness. A bank of clocks ticked off the seconds in each of the world's major time zones. The Battle Staff were already handing out folders, while below the platform on which the Joint Chiefs were taking their seats, the four Emergency Action Officers hammered away at their keyboards, updating various displays thrown at intervals on to the walls.

'OK, gentlemen,' Kane began, 'it appears we have a situation.' His words brought immediate and utter silence to the room.

Sergeant Kosimov was sweating. He had a code book in one hand, and was punching urgently at a keyboard with the other. In theory, this procedure ought to instruct the missile's control systems to abort the launch and shut down its motors for essential maintenance. In theory.

His finger hovered over the Enter key for a second. He was aware of the others watching him intently. He jabbed at the key, and they all stared at the image on the screen. It showed one of the silos, the disguised hatch pulled back and the nose of the missile poking out through the smoke from the preburner.

'Has it worked?' one of the soldiers asked.

Nobody answered. Nobody knew. They kept watching the screen for the slightest suggestion that the smoke was clearing.

There was a muted cheer as the fog thinned to a mist before blowing away on the breeze until only a few wisps of smoke curled round the rocket's nose. It was muted because they all knew that there was only one console with the right level of security clearance, and each of the missiles had different codes and would have to be disabled uniquely. A long process. Too long. All they could do was to disable as many of the missiles as possible before the firing instructions were sent.

The messages were sent out with UMBRA – ultra-top-secret – coding. That alone was enough to ensure that the Defense Secretary and the new National Security Adviser joined their President in the White House Situation Room within minutes. Tom Dering looked and felt tired. He had been called away from a charity dinner that he had actually been quite enjoying, and given a quick and horrifying briefing over the video link to the Pentagon by General Kane. Now he sat with Harold Horner, his Secretary of Defense – SecDef in the shorthand parlance of the White House – and Pete Kellerman, his new NSA. He missed the quiet confidence that Alan Ferrer had exuded.

The room was about the same size as the Oval Office, and was directly beneath it. But unlike the Oval Office, which commanded a superb view out over the White House lawn, only slightly distorted by the thick bulletproof glass in the bow windows, the Situation Room was a windowless subterranean box. There was a large circular table in the centre of the room, around which the President sat together with his SecDef and NSA. On the wall in front of them was a screen showing the latest situation reports, and another on which was a video link with the Joint Chiefs of Staff in the National Military Command Center on the third floor of the Pentagon. A permanently open telephone line linked the Situation Room to the Alternate National Military Command Center, a backup facility hidden deep inside Raven Rock

Mountain in southern Pennsylvania. Around the President and his immediate team, various staff bustled efficiently and quietly, keying in data and handing out updates printed on flimsy paper. Silent in the background was Andy Summers, the President's Secret Service agent. Two of his colleagues stood guard outside the blastproof doors, suit jackets unbuttoned, earpieces firmly in place.

There was one other man seated at the table. His expression was set and emotionless in a craggy, rugged face that looked like it needed ironing. The lines and crevices contrasted with the crisp neatness of his dark suit. His left hand rested on the top of the table, lying beside the dull metal briefcase to which it was handcuffed. The Bag Man. His official title was Emergency War Officer, and in fact he held the rank of Lieutenant-Colonel, although he wore his uniform rarely. His responsibility was as straightforward as it was awesome. He was the keeper of the briefcase, pure and simple. And the briefcase contained the firing codes with which the President of the United States could unleash the Apocalypse.

Agent Summers put a finger up to his earpiece as he listened intently for a moment. Then he stepped forward a pace and said quietly to President Dering, 'The Vice-President has just arrived at the main entrance, sir. He'll be with us in three minutes.'

Sam picked out a handful of the smallest stones. She stuffed them into her pocket and stood up. Of course, for once she could just give up, go home. But even as the thought occurred to her she knew it was not a realistic option.

She took a deep breath of the cold, autumn night air and went back inside the house.

'Three minutes, sir, then we shall have the firing codes.' Nikita

Veyevski, Duty Weapons Officer, reported to Colonel Roskov.

'And the US strike?'

'Still nine minutes out, sir.'

'Good. Very good.'

Veyevski's eye was caught by a warning message flashing across a window on an adjacent screen. He leaned across to read it. 'Sir, a second missile has aborted the prelaunch sequence.'

'What?' Roskov crossed the room quickly, the heads of the operators turning to follow his movements despite the importance of the data on their own screens. 'Show me.'

Veyevski tapped the screen, and Roskov leaned across the console and swore.

'It is odd, sir, that we have had no further communications from Military Command,' Veyevski said quietly.

Roskov turned, his face was only inches away from Veyevski's. The Weapons Officer was struck by the depth of darkness in his eyes, by the hard edge that the light from the screen lent to his features. That edge was there in his voice, too, when he spoke. 'What are you suggesting?'

'Sir, nothing sir.' Veyevski hesitated. 'Only –'

'Only what?'

Veyevski noticed out of the corner of his eye that Sergeant Roskov had approached and was standing behind his commanding officer. The sergeant's machine pistol was slung loosely over his shoulder. It had been pointing at the floor, but now it seemed to be angled slightly upward. Veyevski swallowed. 'Only, sir, perhaps we have a communications problem. Perhaps the aborts are not mechanical failures but someone trying to alert us to a change in the situation.'

Roskov straightened up abruptly, and Veyevski found himself sitting more upright in sympathy. 'You can see for yourself the situation, Lieutenant Veyevski,' Roskov snarled, his teeth almost clenched in anger as he pointed to the yellow traces arcing across the map on the main screen. 'Our commanders have more on their minds than telling us what we can see for ourselves.'

'Yes, sir. Sorry, sir.'

'And if the failures are a deliberate act, then it is sabotage. Another act of war.' He raised his voice so that everyone in the room could hear him clearly. 'We will launch in two minutes. No mistakes. We cannot delay any longer.'

'We can't delay any longer, Mr President.' General Kane's voice was hard and abrupt.

'Delay what?' Vice-President Jack Michaels asked. He was already leafing rapidly through a folder, getting up to speed with the situation. He was the youngest man in the room apart from Pete Kellerman, a handsome and clean-cut graduate of Harvard Business School and former governor of Iowa. His relative youth and renowned sense of humour coupled with his increasing reputation for common sense and fair play had lent a credibility and humanity to Dering's presidential campaign which had arguably secured his victory the previous year. 'Alert status?' he asked.

Dering nodded. 'Comments?' he asked.

'Best to be on our toes, whatever's going down over there.'

Dering nodded. 'Very well. I agree, General.'

'Thank you, sir.' Kane's face was slightly blurred by the slow frame rate as he turned to give the order to the Pentagon staff. 'Go to DefCon-3.'

Three down now. But more to go. Too many more. Kosimov wiped his forehead with his sleeve, and keyed in the diagnostic access code for the next missile. His fingers on the keyboard were the only sound in the small room. The noise of his typing was like a death rattle as he rapidly entered the code.

* * *

The codes were entered automatically as soon as they were released by the computer. Veyevski turned in his seat and called across to Roskov, 'Sir, the codes have been released. The missiles are now primed and the target package loaded.'

Roskov's cheek twitched slightly, just below his left eye. His hands clenched at his side. 'Begin the firing sequence.'

Sam's first shot missed entirely. She had aimed at the Doctor's head, but the tiny stone had gone wide and landed on the floor somewhere beyond. She had heard it cracking on the ground, bouncing away across the stone floor. But nobody else seemed to notice.

Especially not the Doctor. He was watching the screen, fixated by the events unfolding on it.

Sam tried again. She raised herself up on her elbow and threw the stone hard at him. A direct hit this time, and she clenched her fists in glee. The stone lodged in the Doctor's thick hair. And he ignored it, seemed not to notice.

Sam shook her head in disbelief and annoyance. She felt in her pocket for another stone, drew back her arm ready to fling it. Just as her arm was fully tensed, the Doctor turned and looked straight at her. He winked.

Sam resisted the temptation to wave. Although everyone seemed intent on the screen, a sudden, obvious movement could attract unwanted attention. So she just smiled, knowing the Doctor could not see her where she crouched in the shadows at the top of the stairs.

After a moment, the Doctor stood up, stretched and yawned loudly, and sauntered across the room towards the staircase. Miss Allworthy turned, watching him with gimlet eyes as he made his casual way to the console beneath the landing. She kept her eyes fixed on him as he slumped in the chair beside the console, and leaned back, hands cupped behind his head.

He was staring up at Sam through the metal mesh now. Apparently satisfied that the Doctor was going nowhere further, Miss Allworthy turned back to the main screen.

'They're beginning the firing sequence,' the Doctor said, just loud enough for Sam to hear him.

She was lying on her belly, her chin resting on her hands, her elbows resting on the bare metal floor of the landing. 'Is this... *it*?' she hissed, aware that her mouth was dry and her stomach knotted.

'Perhaps. Yes, perhaps.' The Doctor leaned forward and drummed his fingers on the console for a moment. Then he stopped, raised his hand towards his face and inspected the palm. He clenched it suddenly into a fist and slammed it down on the table. Sam flinched, but nobody else seemed to notice. 'There's something else, though. There must be,' the Doctor whispered. 'We still aren't seeing the whole picture. Something else is going on here. Something big.'

Sam looked sadly down at his grim face. 'Doctor,' she said quietly, 'it's the end of the world. You don't get much bigger than that.' She rubbed her eyes. It was the inaction that was getting to her most, the fact that even if she and the Doctor could somehow overpower Silver, Tanner, and Miss Allworthy, it would make no difference to the events that it seemed were being played out across the globe. She noticed the Doctor's disapproving stare, and realised she was biting a fingernail. Typical, the world was about to explode and he was worried about the state of her nails. 'Give us a break,' she hissed at him. 'I'll get Silver to hypnotise me out of it when this is over. Come to that, you could probably do it.'

The Doctor shook his head, apparently taking her suggestion in all seriousness. 'That's not the way, Sam,' he told her, glancing furtively across the room to make sure nobody was paying him too much attention. 'It's a non-decision. You need to do these things yourself, through self-will and determination.'

'Yeah. Right. Well, through self-will and determination above and beyond the call of duty, I can cut the power down here whenever you're ready to leg it.'

Sam saw the Doctor raise his fist again. He hesitated, as if weighing it, then he lowered it carefully. If this was his way of showing his gratitude, then she was less than impressed. 'I'll tell you when,' he hissed back at her.

'Fine. Just give me two minutes' warning.'

Dering lowered the phone carefully and set it down. 'So, now we know.' The conversation with General Orominsk had been brief and to the point.

'Sir,' Kane's voice was firm and loud. 'They have a rogue nuclear missile commander who now has firing codes. I strongly advise –'

Dering cut him off. 'I know, General. I know.' He sighed. 'And I have no choice. Please advise your forces that we are at DefCon-1.'

The President leaned forward and put his head in his hands, rubbing his tired eyes. Across the video link from the Pentagon he could hear Kane instructing his staff.

'OK, you heard the Supreme Commander. Let's get the message out fast. We are at Cocked Pistol. I want that now in a Flash Override.'

```
FLASH OVERRIDE
FROM:   JCS WASHINGTON DC/ / J3 NMCC/ /
TO:     AIG931
        AIG6861
SECRET
POTUS HAS DECLARED STEP-UP IN DEFENSE
```

READINESS CONDITIONS (DEFCON) FROM HIGH
READINESS (DEFCON-3) TO MAXIMUM FORCE
READINESS (DEFCON-1) AKA 'COCKED PISTOL'.
INTELLIGENCE AND OPERATIONS REPORTS INDICATE
NUCFLASH / NUDET POSSIBLE. COMMANDERS WILL
TAKE APPROPRIATE ACTIONS TO ASSURE MAXIMUM
READINESS.
— ENDS —

Deep inside a mountain near Colorado Springs, the duty officer at NORAD, the North American Aerospace Defense Command, read the message and passed it quickly on. Within seconds, the DefCon-1 alert was passed to the American early-warning sites around the world.

High above the United States' eastern seaboard, Looking Glass received the flash message and varied its holding pattern to a different, more complicated, random course. Looking Glass was the Strategic Air Command Airborne Command Post. A Boeing 767 had replaced its ageing 707 predecessor and been converted into what was in effect the twin of the SAC Underground Command Post at Offcutt Air Force Base in Omaha, Nebraska. Both Looking Glass and Offcutt received the alert at the same moment, and both immediately took stock of the situation. Their main purpose was to monitor the status of US nuclear forces and the progress of SIOP, the Single Integrated Operational Plan, which addressed and brought together all aspects of United States nuclear contingency plans for all branches of the military across all geographical regions.

At the same moment as Looking Glass varied its course, the US Air Force upgraded its own defence warning from Yellow – 'Probable' – to Red – 'An attack by hostile aircraft or missiles is imminent or in progress.'

* * *

'Arming in progress,' Veyevski reported. The codes had been validated and the targets loaded. Now it simply remained to fire the missiles. The *remaining* missiles, since all but a dozen had now aborted their prelaunch sequences.

'Sergeant.' Colonel Roskov called to his nephew across the room.

'Yes, sir.'

'You will operate the secondary launch controls.'

'Sir.'

The sergeant made his way briskly to the secondary launch station across the room from his commander's console. The firing-code sequence had to be entered on both consoles at exactly the same time, as a final fail-safe. That way, Veyevski reminded himself, no one maniac could launch the missiles.

And yet there was something wrong. He watched as another missile aborted. Only eleven now. For a moment he almost called out to Roskov again. But he decided it would do no good, and returned his attention to the screen in front of him. And frowned.

That was odd. He had not noticed before, but the warning message seemed misshapen, as if it had been stretched upwards slightly. The letters were thinner and taller than usual, he was sure of it. He studied the message for a moment, and then examined the rest of the display. Everything, now he looked closely, seemed stretched the same way. Almost as if the screen was overscanning for some reason.

It did not occur to Veyevski that as Weapons Officer his console, like the base commander's, slaved the main screen. So, as he adjusted the vertical alignment of his screen, so the image on the main screen also changed. The picture grew slightly wider as the top and bottom of the screen compressed to make room for the small areas off each vertical edge as Veyevski slid them back into view. He stared in astonishment at his screen for a moment, his fingers already fumbling at the catch on the holster as he tried to draw his handgun.

But he had hesitated too long. For a split second Veyevski thought the someone had dropped something. But even as he realised his mistake, while the single percussive sound was still echoing round the room, he saw the splash of his own blood across the front of his screen.

SIMULATION

was the last thing Veyevski saw, through a reddening haze.

SIMULATION

That for him it was anything but a simulation was Veyevski's final half-formed thought as he slumped forward. What was left of his head slapped into the monitor.

There were only eleven missiles left to disable now. Kosimov was tiring, his forehead a sheen of perspiration as he hammered at the keyboard. But he was making more mistakes now. He cursed as a code was rejected as invalid – a stupid error of transcription. He wiped his face on the back of his sleeve and started again.

Just eleven more to go.

'We have no idea how much time we have left,' the President said.

'All the more reason not to waste time diluting out efforts and lengthening our channels of communication,' the Vice-President said.

Dering shook his head. 'Jack, we have no way of knowing how far or how fast this thing will go. We have to split the command. We need a contingency.'

'Fine, Tom. Then you should go.'

'No, Jack. My place is here, in the White House. But I need you somewhere safe, ready to take over.' He held his hand up to prevent Vice-President Michaels replying. 'No argument, Jack. I need you on Nightwatch.'

Nightwatch, the National Emergency Airborne Command Post, was on standby. She was always on standby, her engines ready to lift her from the runway at less than a minute's notice. Andrews Air Force Base was judged to be just seven minutes from the White House by helicopter. Michaels was rushed there in six. There was no terminal building, no gate from which to board. Instead the Vice-President climbed the steep metal steps that were wheeled alongside the huge bulk of the Boeing 747. The metal hull, painted a glistening white, seemed to shimmer in the cool of the night air.

Michaels settled himself into a large comfortable seat in the forward section of the aircraft. Even before he had fastened his seat belt, the plane was taxiing the short distance to the end of the main runway for takeoff. Behind Michaels, separated from the small lounge and seating area by a thin bulkhead, was the main operations room of the aircraft. Banks of monitors kept Nightwatch in touch with the situation, linking her directly to the White House and the other Incident Control Centers. At the end console sat the man with the metal briefcase, a non-identical twin of the President's Bag Man. Given the theory that any deliberate hostile strike would target the White House and other government centres in Washington, Nightwatch had the facilities to make her chief officer effectively Commander in Chief in waiting.

Without the hundreds of passengers and their baggage that would normally fill the jumbo, Nightwatch was able to cram in far more electronic and 'smart' equipment than her predecessor – a Boeing 707 recently retired from service under the same allocation of funds as had upgraded Looking Glass. She could stay in the air for over fifteen hours without having to take on extra fuel, and even then could be refuelled in flight. The Airborne Launch Control System could use the Presidential Codes duplicated in the Nightwatch Bag Man's briefcase to release and target every nuclear missile controlled by the United States of America. The objective was to make Nightwatch the plane that safeguarded the world. And to do that, she was made potentially the most dangerous aircraft in aviation history.

Vice-President Michaels felt the pressure of his back against the padded seat and the tilt of his body as the aircraft climbed ponderously into the darkening sky.

Sergeant Kosimov closed his eyes, trying not to think about what might happen if he failed in his job. Nine missiles to go. Just nine.

He tried to push aside the tiny voice in his mind that told him that those nine delivery vehicles meant fifty-four nuclear warheads ready to rain down on the United States, blowing it apart.

The sound of gunfire was audible through the heavy shutters. Ivigan had so far avoided any action that might intimidate Roskov into firing the missiles. He had no idea what Roskov was up to, why he had suddenly taken this strange, desperate, and deadly course of action. But so long as the launch sequence remained unactivated, the longer Kosimov had to disable the missiles. So Ivigan had shied away from trying to blow his way into the Control Centre. Until now.

Now he knew that there were still nine missiles to be

disabled, and that Roskov had the launch codes entered. He knew that Roskov could easily launch in the time it would take to blow open the shutters – which were after all designed to withstand a far higher explosive impact than Ivigan could conjure up – and force his way through.

But now there was gunfire from inside the Control Centre. This suggested that events were beyond crisis point. It also provided a distraction for Ivigan to launch his assault with a slightly better chance of success.

The charges were already set. They did have some advantages. The shutters were designed to withstand a heavy blast, but a uniform one. The assumption was that the detonation would be some way away from the Control Centre, since there was no point trying to guard against a direct hit from a nuclear weapon. Even that safe-haven edifice of Cheyenne Mountain, Ivigan knew from US as well as Soviet calculations, could be brought crashing down on its occupants with a single well-aimed warhead. But while they were optimised for a uniform wave of pressure, Ivigan and his team knew where the weak points were – the areas that could be penetrated by the impact of a more focused detonation.

The engineer waved for them to take cover. His hand appeared above the upturned table he was sheltering behind, his fingers counting down the seconds to the explosion. The assault team waited inside the open lifts, guns firmly grasped and safety catches off. They would be running towards the shutters as soon as the explosives were detonated, well before the smoke had cleared.

Even before he sent his Vice-President to Nightwatch, Tom Dering, on the advice of Defense Secretary Horner, had authorised JEEP. The Joint Emergency Evacuation Plan was the means by which key government officials and other personnel vital to running the country during a war were evacuated from the main target areas to safe locations in the USA.

Within twenty-five minutes, forty-four key government officials, scientists, and technical personnel who carried JEEP-1 cards were evacuated. As soon as the crisis had reached DefCon-3, a shoal of helicopters had started arriving at the Pentagon ready for such a contingency. Some of them had waited at the Pentagon heliport, rotors lazily turning as they awaited the probable stand-down. As the situation escalated, more of the huge insect-like creatures arrived, until they were three deep on the paved area between the Pentagon building and the Potomac River behind it.

When JEEP was activated, many of the personnel to be evacuated were already en route to their lift-out points. The rest soon followed. These first evacuees were taken to Site-R, the Alternate National Military Command Center in Raven Rock.

The next wave of JEEP personnel started to include the less vital people. Still essential to keeping the country running during a protracted engagement, they were airlifted to various dispersed locations. Some followed their colleagues to Site-R. Others were taken to the Mount Weather Special Facility. Just four of the several hundred evacuees were designated as FEMA, the Federal Emergency Management Agency. They were flown to a location so secret that despite the many exercises and drills every JEEP-card carrier undergoes, even they did not know where they were headed. In fact, it was at the ultra-secret National Warning Center in Olney, Maryland, that their helicopter touched down.

As the first helicopters touched down at Site-R, Ivigan's engineer folded down the index finger of his raised left hand. At the same moment, the index finger on his right hand pressed home the detonator button.

With the shutters down the observation gallery had become a metal box. The sound of the blast echoed deafeningly round the enclosed space, only slightly muffled by the sudden smoke. Ivigan was first on his feet, already hurling himself through the barely visible gap in the torn metal, aware of the soldiers close behind him.

The smoke curled and drifted across the Control Centre. But this did not obscure the view of what was happening. Ivigan caught a glimpse of movement, heard the crack of gunfire as he fell the ten feet through space from the raised gallery. He rolled as he hit the metal floor, feeling the friction burns on his knees and side. Then he was up, machine pistol raised and scanning for a target. There was a crack and ricochet in front of him as the few remaining technicians sheltered behind their consoles while Roskov and his two nephews fired at them, trying to get across the room to the secondary launch station. The thump and clang behind him were his men landing and rolling into position just as Ivigan had done.

Gregor Roskov was already turning towards Ivigan, his machine gun rising as he hunted out the target in the smoke. Behind him lay the sprawled bodies of several technicians and operators. One girl's cap had come off, allowing her blonde hair to spill out into the pool of blood on the console. The Weapons Officer lay in a crumpled heap across his monitor, his head a bloody mess of shattered bone and brain. Across the room, Colonel Roskov was at the commander's console. The trigger key was clearly visible in the slot, the numeric code on the screen waiting to be keyed in. Ivan Roskov was making his way slowly over to the secondary launch terminal. Gregor had been laying down covering fire while he dashed from one console to the next. He was almost there.

Almost.

Ivigan and his men had only to stop Ivan Roskov from reaching the console, had only to prevent him from keying in the six-digit number in concert with his uncle, had only to keep him from initiating the launch.

But they were too late.

Ivigan could tell. With a sort of fatalistic realisation he knew that they were too late even as he squeezed the trigger. Gregor Roskov was already firing, dispensing death in an arc that curved ever closer to Ivigan as if in slow motion. Ivigan's burst of fire was better aimed, better timed. It ate into the target's chest, stitching a line of black then red across Gregor Roskov's uniform. Gregor was hurled across the room by the force of the impact, crashing into the console behind him and sending a chair skidding across the floor as he collapsed in a heap. His mouth dropped open and his machine pistol fell to the floor with a clatter. It lifted slightly, spun on its end, and crashed back down beside the lifeless body.

Behind him, Ivigan's men had covered the same target. A mistake, as it gave Ivan Roskov the distraction he needed to cover the remaining distance to the secondary launch controls. Already his finger was jabbing down on the firing button, and Ivigan realised with a jolt of horror and a sickening lurch of his stomach that the code had already been entered. They needed only to initiate the launch, to press home the final button at the same moment, and the missiles would be on their terrible way.

On the other side of the room, Colonel Roskov mirrored his young nephew's action. The sequence was complete. In the split-second silence that followed, six thin traces of green started on their courses outward from Krejikistan and inched across the map on the main screen.

In silence, the President of the United States of America and his country's top soldiers and security advisers watched the same trajectories, albeit in red. In each of the linked situation rooms a printer started chattering at the same moment – an initial diagnosis from the smart satellite systems ahead of a full and unequivocal launch confirmation.

```
FLASH OVERRIDE PINNACLE
SATELLITE SURVEILLANCE INITIAL DIAGNOSIS
***UNCONFIRMED***
TO:    POTUS / / JCS WASHINGTON DC/ / J3
       NMCC/ /

SECRET
NUCFLASH PROBABLE. ORIGINATION NEVCHENKA
MILITARY INSTALLATION, KREJIKISTAN.
ASSUME NUDET IMMINENT.
FINAL CONFIRMATION TO FOLLOW...
— ENDS —
```

The President took the flimsy message printout from the white-faced aid. He glanced at it, knowing already what it said. The irony of the satellite software's phraseology – 'FINAL' and 'ENDS' – was not lost on him. But the terrifying implications of the code words bit deeper. He had hoped and expected – prayed – that he would never receive a message including NUCFLASH, the identification of a nuclear launch, and even less NUDET, a nuclear detonation. But he could feel the texture of the thin paper in his hand, see the grim expressions on the blood-drained faces around him, feel the pit of his stomach receding.

'The bombers are already airborne. The defence systems are primed and SIOP is running to schedule, Mr President.' General Kane's voice was calm, almost reasonable. 'Do we respond?'

'No.' His voice was husky, dry. 'This is the work of a maniac, a single madman. We should not attack his whole country, the whole of the Eastern Bloc, out of revenge, however justified we might feel.'

Kane's face was large on the monitor. 'Sir, there are more practical considerations. We have detected only six launches. We know that Nevchenka has three times that many missiles at least.'

'There is no confirmation yet. We don't know for sure they have launched.' This could not be happening. Could not.

'We have to respond, if only to prevent further launches. He *has* launched.'

'No.' Dering was emphatic. 'We don't know for certain yet. We have to get confirmation.'

Kane was shaking his head in exasperation. 'Mr President.'

Dering's response was a shout: '*Not yet!*'

Harold Horner leaned across to his President. 'Then at least put us on a war footing,' he said quietly. 'Prepare for the worst, Tom.'

Dering considered. 'Very well. We go to Death Watch.' In front of him the red lines traced like nerves across the screen.

Across the screen the thin red lines were arcing slowing from Krejikistan towards the USA. Sam lay open-mouthed, unable to move or think as she watched them slowly edge their way across the map.

Below her, the Doctor was silent and still.

Silhouetted against the blood-red map on the screen, Norton Silver rubbed his hands together and chortled with glee as he watched the messengers of mass destruction blaze their fiery trails across the world.

8
Blazing Fire

Colonel Roskov and his nephew Ivan seemed frozen in position. It was as if the enormity of their action had suddenly pressed home. Each mirrored the other, leaning forward over a console, index finger jabbed down on the red button. Still holding it down as if afraid to let go now.

Even when the burst of gunfire hammered into the base commander, driving his body first upright, then down over the control panel, his finger remained firmly in position. Ivan mirrored his uncle even in death, his own body jolted and rocked by the impact of the 9mm shells as they slammed him across the console. His head hit the screen with so much force it cracked the glass.

Ivigan stared in disbelief at the mess of bodies and debris that littered the floor of the room. A narrow river of blood met his left boot and formed a rock pool round the toecap, thickening and becoming viscous.

The staccato echoes of the final shots faded and the smoke from the firefight thinned and drifted away to nothing. The silence was broken only by Ivan Roskov's body slowly sagging and slumping to the floor, his right arm still extended towards the launch button. On the cracked, blood-spattered screen, the red tracer lines continued their slow, significant progress across the world.

Across the world, Norton Silver leaned forward across the desk as he watched the tracer lines intently. 'Any moment now,' he murmured. 'Any moment now and they must respond.'

The Doctor leaned suddenly forward, his face appearing over Silver's shoulder so that the large man flinched. He had been concentrating so much on watching the screen that he had neither seen nor heard the Doctor's approach.

'You actually want the Americans to respond?' The Doctor's voice was also quiet, but there was an edge of steel to it as his hand closed on Silver's shoulder and he turned the man round to face him. 'What exactly is going on?' Their eyes met and locked. 'What are you doing?'

Silver shook himself free, agitated rather than angry. 'They will respond to the attack.' His clenched fist slammed down on the desk in front of him. 'They must respond.'

'We must respond.' Pete Kellerman's words brought silence to the table. It was the first unsolicited comment he had made since arriving in the White House Situation Room. Even the President turned to him, surprised.

'Pete?'

'If we respond immediately, we have a chance of making the strike more significant. More decisive.'

From the main monitor, General Kane coughed. 'We still don't have actual confirmation that a launch has taken place.'

'Oh, come on!' Kellerman pointed to the map display where the tracer lines were slowly following the dotted arcs that projected the paths of the missiles, connecting the dots inexorably as they headed towards the eastern coast of the United States. 'Why don't you wake up and smell the fallout?'

Kane ignored the interruption. 'And even if they have launched, we know it's probably the work of a madman. Who do we retaliate against? It would certainly not, in my opinion, be appropriate to consider a wider response than a defensive strike against Nevchenka. What response can we reasonably make?'

'Reasonably?' Kellerman was leaning across the table in anger. 'If you won't even admit there's been a launch yet, how can you assume that this is the work of an isolated maniac rather than a deliberate, calculated first strike? We only have the word of this General Orominsk about what's really going on over there.'

'So –' the President's voice was quiet, reasonable – 'what exactly do you suggest, Pete?'

'I suggest we strike back now. Hard.'

Kane was shaking his head. 'The bombers are already at their control points, that happened at DefCon-1. We can recall or commit them at a moment's notice. But if we initiate a launch... There's no way we can call back or abort our missiles any more than they can theirs. We would kill many millions of innocent people.'

'So you advise that we do nothing?' Kellerman was on his feet.

'Easy, Pete. Easy.' The Secretary of Defense reached up and tapped him lightly on the shoulder. It was enough to break the spell, and Kellerman sat down again. His hands clenched and unclenched in anger as he seethed. The performance of his life.

'I advise, again, that you evacuate the Situation Room and get airborne in Airforce One.'

Dering nodded. 'Which is fuelled and waiting at Andrews. I know, General, I know.' He sighed and leaned back, the chair springing slightly as he shifted his weight. 'And are you evacuating?'

Kane frowned, surprised by the question. 'I don't believe that would serve any purpose, sir.'

'Don't you have a war to fight, General?'

'If I do, Mr President, my officers can fight it from their command posts once Washington is gone. If there has been a launch, then we're already too late to avoid the strike.'

Dering nodded, satisfied. 'That is exactly the situation here too. Jack Michaels is on Nightwatch, and he can manage quite well without us.' He leaned forward again, hands resting lightly on the table, as if he were addressing a mildly interested television audience. 'I have another consideration, General.'

'Sir?'

'At this time more than any other, our country needs strong leadership. How do you think it would look if I ran for cover right now? Especially as we all know I wouldn't make it.'

'Unless it's a false alarm.'

As if in answer, the printers at both ends of the video link sprang into life.

'If it's a false alarm,' Dering said as he reached for the printout being handed to him, 'then there's no need to evacuate.' He smiled thinly. Then he read the printed sheet. Without comment he handed it to Horner, who skimmed it quickly and passed it on to Kellerman.

Kellerman also read the sheet quickly. Like the others, he already knew what it said. On the screen in front of him, he could see Kane and the other Joint Chiefs huddled in close and quiet discussion. He could guess the subject they were debating.

'Mr President,' Kellerman said, his voice calmer and more reasonable than a few moments previously. Dering looked up and their eyes met. On the monitor, Kane turned from his discussion to listen. The lines on the map started flashing in time to a muted alarm. 'Mr President, we have positive confirmation of a hostile nuclear launch. You have to release the trigger codes now.'

The edge to his voice was so hard that the Bag Man was already pulling the armoured briefcase towards him. The sound of the metal scraping across the polished wooden top of the table was the only sound audible over the quiet hum of the equipment.

'I think Pete's right.' Horner's voice was quiet, almost humble. 'I think we're out of options now.'

'Mr President.' Kane's voice was clear and loud. He was looking directly at the video camera.

'No!' Behind Kane's head, the bulky, grey-haired form of General Liston was rising to his feet. 'We can't!'

Kane turned to face Liston, the back of his head large on the video monitor as his voice came through the speakers slightly muffled. 'We have no choice any more.'

Liston was shaking his head, the motion a blur as the frame rate failed to keep up. 'To reveal our trump card now, when world peace is so delicately balanced – we'll destroy everything we've won over the last few years. It will spark a new arms race as the Russians, the Chinese – God, even the British, probably – try to catch up.'

'General.' Kane's voice was loud and sharp. 'If we have the trump card and never reveal it, we might as well not have it. And if we don't play it now, when this country is about to be cut off at the knees perhaps by a maniac, perhaps as part of an ill-conceived powerplay, then we never will.'

Dering's voice cut across the argument. 'What trump card, General Kane? Whatever it is, I think I should be the one to choose whether or not it is brought into play.'

'I agree, Mr President.' Kane turned back to face the screen. 'You do have one other option. Nuke Kill.'

NUKILL was a message designation that only a handful of people in the US military understood how to handle. Even fewer knew what it meant.

Of the personnel forming the crew of the Looking Glass plane, the second-in-command was the first officer in the chain who even knew there was such a designation. Only the commander had an inkling of what the message might mean. The FLASH was direct from the Joint Chiefs at the Pentagon, and was passed from officer to officer until the second-in-command sent for his superior.

'You know what this means?' Colonel Atkins chewed on the end of an unlit cigar. He waved the message printout almost in Captain Sanders's face. Apart from its NUKILL heading, it consisted of only a series of sets of four-digit numbers.

'No, sir. But I know we have to act as a relay for the codes. I assume you know where to send it.'

Atkins laughed shortly. 'You kidding? Of course I know, though don't ask me to make sense of it.' He pulled the cigar from his mouth and dropped it to the floor, as if forgetting it had never been lit. 'Point the transmitters at quadrant Halo, and set them for maximum strength when you retransmit that message. And don't worry about being overheard – we're way past those problems now.'

'But sir – quadrant Halo?' Sanders was shaking his head. 'But that's –' He broke off and pointed at the ceiling. 'That's above us, sir. Straight up.'

'Indeed it is.' Atkins ground the cigar into the metal floor of the operations centre with the toe of his boot. The tobacco flaked and shredded, fanning out like weed growing through the deck. 'You want to take a guess at who's up there listening out for us?'

The answer came into Sanders's head as if it too had been transmitted. Under any other circumstances he would have rejected the thought as ridiculous, but right now the world was going crazy around him. 'Station Nine?' he breathed incredulously.

Atkins nodded, pulling another cigar from his top pocket. He jammed it between his teeth. 'That's right, it really exists. Station Nine.'

* * *

Station Nine hung like a grotesque insect against the blackness of space. Dark against the dark. The central spike of the slowly revolving structure was adorned with aerials and receiving dishes. The outer sections, radiating from the main spoke, jutted out like rigid limbs. Each seemed to be held in place by an exoskeleton of equipment and scaffolding.

Under several of the outer sections hung clusters of long cylindrical chambers, linked back to the gantries by looping, trailing pipes and tubes: the missile housings and their umbilical support and control systems. And inside these silos, poised above the Earth, pointing downwards in eager anticipation of their launch, were the missiles.

The Nuke Killers.

Who should have military jurisdiction over the base had been a hard-fought argument. Few people knew about it, so the discussions were limited to the highest levels of the military and the Reagan administration. The US Air Force had assumed that, since the station was flown into space and circled several thousand miles above the ground, it should naturally be their responsibility. Their arrogance more than any practical considerations had persuaded both the army and the navy that they should fight this, if only to make a point. But if the future of the art of warfare was in space, then they also wanted a piece of the action.

The solution was born of pragmatism. Since Station Nine needed a dedicated and specially trained crew, it did not really matter to which of the armed services they notionally reported. The team was drawn from all three, and while it worked rotations and its members were allowed leave, once you were assigned to Station Nine, the special security considerations meant that you were never reassigned.

The only remaining question was whether the commanding officer should be drawn from the USAF or one of the other forces. The notion of recruiting a commander from the higher echelons of the CIA or even the FBI was considered only for long enough to be deemed ridiculous. Station Nine was a military base and would have a military commander. Or, rather, three military commanders, rotating in their duties like their crew. So each of the armed forces provided a commanding officer for Station Nine, and each was equally unhappy with the situation. But since almost nobody, including the President once Reagan was gone, knew about Station Nine, there were limited avenues for complaint. And the longer the situation remained unchanged, and the better it worked, the harder it was to complain.

The duty commander when the FLASH NUKILL came in from Looking Glass was Major Susan Rogers. She was from a typical army background, made unusual only by the fact that she was a woman. The armed forces were still predominantly male, especially in the upper ranks. When the message came in, Rogers was on the cramped bridge together with almost all her immediate command team. Several of the officers were standing in a now habitual stance with their heads slightly to one side so as to avoid banging them on the pipework hanging from the low ceiling. Someone had once told Rogers that the station was like a nuclear submarine, only with less space. She had not been on a submarine, and on that sort of recommendation she was in no hurry.

They had received notification of the launch at the same time as the other major US installations and had since been monitoring the progress of the missiles. The only surprising thing about the message that was chattering through the printer was the length of time it had taken their superiors to decide to send it.

'How long do we have?' Rogers asked the tracking officer.

He already had the calculation. 'The missiles are above

seventy degrees north at the moment. We have to wait till they dip down and we can get a direct line of sight. That should be in about two minutes.'

'Window of opportunity?'

'That'll give us about three minutes to make the shot.'

'OK, then. Let's make this quick.' Major Rogers tore the message off the now silent printer and checked the first line of coded instructions against a sheet she had just ripped from a sealed envelope. 'I have a properly formatted Emergency Action Message designated NUKILL. Do you concur?' She handed it to her Weapons Officer, who held it so that the second-in-command could also see it.

The 2IC nodded to the Weapons Officer, who handed the paper back to Major Rogers. 'We concur, sir.' On a screen behind him the decrypted form of the body of the message was now coming through.

'Not heavy on detail,' Rogers observed. 'They just want us to do it, they don't care how.' She turned back to her team. 'Options?'

'The missiles are still in close formation at this point. A single Killer ought to take out the lot. Send a second to tag along in case there are any stragglers to mop up.'

Rogers considered a moment, then nodded. 'OK, then. Wind up two of the birds and let's see if they really can fly.'

The first sign of life apart from the slow revolution of the space station was a slight shudder as the lower ends of two of the missile pods split open and folded back on themselves. The movement was slow, heavy, and silent in the darkness. A moment later, the satellite's active targeting systems went from hibernation mode to full power. The effect was that Station Nine, the most secret military installation in history, changed on every satellite tracking system in the world from a tiny insignificant speck that might be a third-rate weather satellite to a brilliant blaze of laser and high-frequency radio emissions.

The missiles did not so much launch as drop. Their clamps released, first one then another slipped from its moorings and plunged towards the Earth. After a few seconds, once well clear of the station, the burners cut in and more unexpected readings scratched across printers and glowed on radarscopes around the planet.

The first of the Nuke Killers shot into the middle of the clump of nuclear missiles at over three times the speed of sound. As it flashed through the centre, the first-stage rocket system fell away and slowly toppled towards the ocean beneath. The remains, the nose cone, split up into a dozen individual smart warheads, each seeking out a target and comparing the signal ident and trajectory with its fellows to ensure there was no duplication. Only when all the available targets had been acquired did the central targeting computer, already dropping out of range with the discarded remains of the nose cone, begin to reallocate missiles.

With co-ordinates locked in, the individual rockets in Station Nine's smart nuclear warheads cut in, thrusting each at its designated target. The result was a conflagration a thousand miles above the Earth that made a particularly impressive display of the Northern Lights look like a guttering candle. A moment later there was another, smaller explosion as the backup Nuke Killer aborted, its targets already dead. Then, as suddenly as the lights had burst into brilliance, they were gone.

For an instant the library wall had been a pattern of reflected glory and colour. It was as if the whole of the power of the sun were contained inside the Philosopher's Stone, and for a split second a part of it had managed to escape.

Then it was gone.

'Where did they go?' Sam stared at the wall-screen in disbelief.

A few seconds ago the tracer lines of the missiles had been hastening towards the United States. Then there had been what looked like the flare of a flashbulb at the top of the screen, a sudden retina-etching burst of colour that was still there when Sam blinked. From that light source, as Sam, the Doctor, Silver and the others shielded their eyes, sped out a thin line of fire. It was so fast she almost missed it as it raced to intercept the missiles. Then there was another starburst. When it faded away, together with the brilliant glow that had spawned it, the screen was a blank map.

The silence was broken by Silver's explosion of laughter. Sam could hear the pent-up relief as well as exultation in the echoing sound. 'Station Nine,' he cried out between bursts of laughter. 'At last, we have it on the map.' He guffawed again. 'On everyone's map.'

'So that's what all this was about?' the Doctor called from where he sat beneath the landing. His voice was calm, curious, a sane foil to Silver's manic exuberance.

'Of course, Doctor.' Silver was slightly calmer now. His face was still contorted with humour, but his snorts of laughter had died away.

The Doctor answered Sam's unspoken question without turning his attention away from Silver. 'Obviously the Americans have some crude defensive satellite they have managed to launch into orbit.'

Silver laughed out loud again. 'You call that crude?' His finger was extended towards the main screen. 'It's brilliant. Brilliant.' His face was suddenly serious. 'And now we have it.'

'But you knew it was there,' the Doctor pointed out. 'Nobody tries a bluff like that on a whim.'

'You think I wouldn't go that far?' Silver's eyes were gleaming in the fluorescent lighting.

'I think,' the Doctor said, 'that you are not actually interested in finding out for yourself. You will correct me here, I'm sure, if I misspeak, but –' He paused, as if selecting his words carefully. 'I think the point is that everyone else in the world now knows about Station Nine.' He grinned and nodded in satisfaction.

'Why?' Sargent asked him.

The Doctor's eyes widened and his mouth opened in a sort of mild attack of horror. 'Why? Well, they'll have seen what happened just as we did. Nobody with a radar dish from the People's Republic of China to Radar Ham Harry in the Hebrides will have missed that. And they'll all draw the obvious, logical, and of course correct conclusions from it.'

Norton Silver seemed to stir into life. 'You are almost right.' He turned from the screen and stepped towards the Doctor, leaning on a desk like a patient lecturer confronted with a lazy set of students drawn from the lower end of the intellectual spectrum. 'We knew that Station Nine existed. Or at least, I had a very strong suspicion. Strong enough for this exercise to be worthwhile. But there were two objectives. One was to find out just where it is. It happens to be a satellite, which is, I admit, a possibility I had not anticipated. I had considered a bona fide US military installation as cover. A remote site secreted away somewhere in the Arizona desert was another possibility, as was a submarine or underwater base. I had even considered Area 51, which would explain much. But now we know for sure.'

'And the second objective?'

'As you surmised, Doctor. It was quite simply to smoke out the installation. To make Station Nine undeniably visible to the world.' He turned back towards the screen. 'And I'd say that the exercise was a spectacular success, wouldn't you?'

The Doctor clicked his tongue. 'And for a few moments there we thought you really did want to start another world war.'

Silver laughed, without turning from the screen. 'All in good time, Doctor. But for now I'm afraid you've been barking up the wrong tree yet again.'

The Doctor frowned. Nobody made any attempt to stop him as he typed several commands into the keyboard on the terminal in front of him. Once again the security camera shots of the paintings and the corresponding views sprang up on the screen. The Doctor stared at them for a few seconds, then nodded in quiet satisfaction. 'Of course,' he breathed. 'So that's it.' He typed in another command, and the screen blanked out again.

Silver seemed not to have noticed the Doctor's brief interlude. Nor did he seem to notice as the Doctor leapt to his feet and approached him. He hardly reacted when the Doctor observed from behind, at point-blank range, 'You still haven't answered the obvious question. Why?'

Silver laughed again, almost a cough, as he turned to face the Doctor. 'For posterity perhaps. A demonstration of the relationship between the Art and science.'

'And by the Art, I take it you mean the overwhelming interest of your predecessor and ancestor Matthew Siolfor – alchemy?'

'Of course.' There was a slight edge to Silver's voice as he answered. 'Alchemy is the basis for every action we – I – take. It is the binding principle that holds the natural world together, as we shall soon prove.'

'Well –' The Doctor seemed momentarily thrown by Silver's sudden passion. Then he shrugged, grasped Silver's hand in his own, and shook it enthusiastically. 'Good luck.' He released Silver's hand, stepped back and threw his arms open like a proud father inspecting his daughter in her bridal gown.

'The modern Pythagoras, perhaps,' the Doctor suggested. He tapped his chin, apparently taken with the analogy. 'Actually, you know, that's not a bad comparison. Pythagoras, after all, first discovered the linkage between mathematics and nature, discovered that maths is the basis of science.'

Sam watched his enthusiasm bring him meandering and proclaiming up the aisle and past the rows of desks and consoles. The black candles flickered in sympathy, a domino effect, as he passed them. Many of them guttered and died in the breeze as the Doctor swept by, his coat swirling behind him. He stared up at Sam, and gave the faintest nod. Beside him another candle snuffed out, and Sam gently opened the door.

As she slipped from the room, the main screen flipped without warning from the map it had been showing to an image of a face. The face was huge, a man in his early forties, clean-shaven with short dark hair.

'You there, Silver?' The man's voice had an American accent as it boomed from speakers either side of the screen. 'I assume you got what you wanted out of that.'

Silver answered, his voice raised for the microphones. 'Ah, Mr Kellerman. Indeed, yes. A first-rate performance from all concerned.'

The face of the screen nodded. 'Roskov and his boys did good. They're dead by the way, in case you haven't heard.'

Silver shrugged. 'To be expected.'

Sam sprinted along the passage towards the main staircase. She had left the door to the cupboard open. The light from the hallway spilled into it, reflecting off the transparent cover of the Emergency Power Off button. She pushed the cover up with one hand, and reached for the button.

She pressed the heel of her hand against it. Then she pressed the button inwards, and was momentarily horrified when nothing happened. Of course, the house was on a different ring main. Could she be sure it had worked?

The lights went out, and the screen blanked to leave only a faint phosphorescent glow. After the bright fluorescent light and the glow of the screens, the sudden switch back to just candlelight was extreme. The darkness was deeper round the Doctor since so many of the candles he had passed had blown out. Silver, Miss Allworthy, and Tanner were shouting. The Doctor was dragging Sargent after him as he raced for where he remembered – and hoped – the stairs were.

A rectangle of brighter light appeared, high up. It was the door at the top of the stairs opening. Sam was already there, waiting. The Doctor and Sargent were still running, negotiating the desks and equipment, trying not to step on each other's feet. The light gave the Doctor enough of a point of reference to adjust his bearings and quicken his pace. It also orientated Tanner and Miss Allworthy. Tanner's shotgun went off first, chunks of masonry and plaster exploding from the stairwell above the Doctor's head, showering him and Sargent with debris. Another shot, and they both instinctively ducked as it went wide.

Sam pushed Sargent through the doorway, and dived after him. The Doctor followed them and slammed the door shut.

'Come on.' He pulled her back to her feet and led the way down the corridor still running. 'No key, and no bolt,' he explained. 'They'll be after us in a minute.'

'Back to the TARDIS?' Sam suggested.

'Where?' Sargent gasped.

'The ruins on the hill,' Sam explained.

'No.' The Doctor's voice was quietly firm as they reached the front door. He held it open for them. 'I understand the paintings now. I know why poor Coulter killed himself, what he saw.' He pulled the door shut behind him, and led them at a brisk pace out into the night.

The night blackness of the basement operations room flickered in the candlelight, then sparked back into a semblance of daylight. By the thin light of the tiny torch on his car key, Silver was lighting the candles that had gone out in the Doctor's wake.

Tanner was already heading for the staircase. 'I'll get them,' he said gruffly. 'I'll drag them back here or shoot them where they stand.'

Silver's response was quick and sharp. 'You'll do no such thing. The Doctor is a distraction, nothing more. We can find him any time we choose. Let's not dilute our forces for the moment. She must have thrown the Emergency Power Off switch – it's under the stairs. You'll need the key from my study to reset it.' He called across to Miss Allworthy. 'Be ready to get the communications back on-line when the power comes back.'

A few minutes later the lights flared back on. A moment later Kellerman's face splashed across the main screen.

Silver smiled. 'Welcome back, Mr Kellerman. Normal service has been resumed.'

'Peter Kellerman is the US President's new National Security Adviser,' Sam told the Doctor as they made their brisk way through the grounds. 'I'd have thought you'd know that.'

'Would you? I've not had much time to keep up with local politics recently.'

'Hardly local,' Sargent muttered from a few paces behind.

'Hardly universal,' the Doctor snapped back.

'Wasn't he a lecturer or something?' Sargent ignored the

Doctor's comment. 'Surprise choice. It was all over the news the other day.'

'Yes. So what do you reckon, Doctor? Is the assassination something to do with all this?'

The Doctor stopped dead in his tracks. They were crossing the terrace, the moonlight streaming across them. 'His predecessor was assassinated?' Sam nodded. 'Probably that's something to do with all this.' He set off again, quickening his already brisk pace. 'Perhaps they had to get Kellerman into the right position to influence the President.'

'But why go to such lengths?' Sam asked as they started down the steps. 'Why didn't Kellerman just ask about Station Nine. In his position surely he'd know anyway, wouldn't he?'

'Good point. Interesting implications, too.'

'What implications?' Sargent asked them.

'If Kellerman didn't know or couldn't find out,' the Doctor called back from the bottom of the steps, 'that suggests that even the President didn't know about Station Nine. Hence this elaborate plan to smoke it out. And the more elaborate the plan, the greater the expected end result.'

'That sounds ominous.'

They continued on their way in silence for a while. Before long they had traversed the rose garden and passed behind the maze. Sam was able to match the Doctor's pace without much difficulty, but Sargent was falling a little behind. Now they were heading out across the meadows towards the low hill topped by Lord Meacher's Clump.

'Why aren't they following us?' Sam asked.

'Bigger fish to fry, I expect.' The Doctor paused for a moment to let Sargent catch them up. 'It was the harmonics which tipped him off, you know.' He said it as if he were continuing the previous thought, and it took Sam a few blinks to realise he had completely changed the subject.

'I'm sorry?'

'Pythagoras.' He paused until Sargent had sat down heavily on the ground. 'All ready? Good. Off we go, then.' As they walked, he continued talking. 'It was an autumn evening, a bit warmer than this one admittedly, but then it is warm down there. Very pleasant, as I recall. He was talking about triangles – he was always talking about triangles – and about how his school was going and so forth. It was a whim, really. I saw the blacksmith's forge on the other side of the dusty street, and crossed the road towards it. He seemed so caught up in his enthusiasm that I doubted if he would notice, but it seemed like it was worth a try.'

'Pythagoras, right?' Sargent was shaking his head and breathing heavily. 'I think I'll stick to the local museum after this.'

The Doctor continued undaunted. 'Anyway, we paused outside the blacksmith's, feeling the heat coming from the open door. Pythagoras had to shout to make himself heard above the ring of the hammers on anvils coming from inside.' A faraway look came into the Doctor's eyes and he paused and turned. Behind him, the first streaks of dawn were forming a half-halo around the trees on the hilltop. Lord Meacher's Clump stood tall and proud on the skyline, its distinctive shape a two-dimensional cutout. 'It was quite funny to watch, in fact. He actually stopped in mid-sentence. His ears got there before his brain did, and he looked at me as if to ask what it was that he had half realised. But I said nothing, of course. Not my place.'

The Doctor turned and resumed his trek up the hillside. 'It came to him in a flash of inspiration. I saw the realisation in his face. The hammers were ringing in our ears, several of them striking at different intervals as the blacksmiths went about their business. And whenever two of them struck in time, there was a harmony. Or a discord. In fact, there was just one hammer, and you could tell it from its sound, which did not form a harmony with any of the others. Yet several of the hammers' sounds went well together.'

Sam cleared her throat. 'Is this entirely relevant, Doctor?'

'Or even slightly?' Sargent added.

The Doctor ignored them – they might as well not have spoken. He continued, his wide smile echoing happy memories of that day long ago. 'We were there for the rest of the afternoon after that. He was rushing around, banging hammers down in time with each other, measuring them, weighing them.' The Doctor shook is head. 'Once he had the general idea he had only to ask me, of course. But no, he wanted to work it out for himself.'

'And did he?' Sam knew he would finish the story whatever she said. Her best hope was to hurry him along and hope that there was some real and useful point to be made.

'Oh yes. Forget triangles, that was the turning point for mathematics. He pretty soon worked out that the hammers that rang in harmony and produced chords were those whose weights were in a simple ratio. If one was half or a quarter the weight of another, they sounded well. But the discordant hammer's weight was no simple ratio of any of the others, so it always sounded awful. From that Pythagoras went on to realise that the different degrees of tension in the strings of a tuned lyre also formed a simple ratio. Made the tuning much easier. They did it entirely by ear until then.'

'Is there a moral to this story?' Sargent asked when they had walked on in silence for a while.

'Indeed. That was the day that Pythagoras discovered that there is a direct connection between mathematics and other sciences, between numbers and the physical world. Maths is the basis of all the sciences.'

'So?'

'So that includes perspective.'

Sam smiled, seeing some clarity at last. 'Which brings us back to the paintings.'

The Doctor nodded. 'Which brings us back to the paintings.'

They had almost reached the top of the hill now, and the night was becoming oppressive. Sam could feel the air heavy against her face, almost pushing her away. 'Can we stop for a moment?' she asked.

'Tired?'

'No. Not exactly. More, well…'

The Doctor stopped and sat down on the damp grass, waving for Sam and Sargent to join him. 'Feeling the pressure? I think we all are. Another clue.' He peered into the dim surroundings, then reached out and plucked a small flower from the grassy ground. 'Final confirmation if we'd needed it,' the Doctor said as he held up the flower. It was small and delicate, with blue petals and an orange stem. 'There are more of them around here than anywhere else on the estate that I've seen. We're getting close to the focal point.'

'Focal point of what?' Sam was feeling better now they had stopped. Just for a moment she had felt nauseous and weak.

'It was when Silver said I was "barking up the wrong tree" that I got an inkling of what's wrong with the paintings.'

'And that is?'

'Nothing. Nothing at all.'

'So what has perspective got to do with it?'

'Everything. I lined up the real world with the paintings, the representations of the same views on Silver's monitors, remember? And give or take a few differences caused by the different season and the passage of time, they match very well.' He leaned back and pointed up at the clump of trees on the top of the hill. 'That set of trees, Lord Meacher's Clump, is quite a distinctive landmark. It is depicted entirely accurately in quite a few of the pictures, and given it is a raised focal point on the horizon that's hardly surprising.'

'So why are we here?'

'Well, there are a couple of interesting things about Lord Meacher's Clump.'

'I hadn't noticed,' Sargent mumbled as he lay on the ground, one hand clasped inside his jacket pocket.

'The first is that the distinctive shape of the clump of trees, or the size of the trees, does not seem to have altered at all over the last hundred and fifty years. That in itself is odd, but not something our friend Coulter would have realised. What is rather more strange is the actual shape of the clump itself.'

'Certainly distinctive,' Sam agreed. 'It's as recognisable from here as it was from the TARDIS.'

'Yes. And that's the point, really.' The Doctor stood up and pointed across the landscape. 'Because, the TARDIS is in the ruins of the old house, which is right over there.' He turned and pointed to another area. 'One of the paintings is from over there.' He turned again. 'Another from down there. Several from closer to the house, and one is a landscape of the whole estate from a hill we can't see from here as it's right the other side of the Clump.'

'The point being?'

'The point being that Lord Meacher's Clump, with its oh-so-distinctive shape, with those two central trees standing taller and further forward than the others, looks identical in each of those paintings. And it looks identical from each of those vantage points in real life. And since the three-dimensional shape should by no means be either symmetrical or recursive, that is impossible.' He settled back on the ground, head resting in the crook of his elbow as he lay back and stared at the lightening sky. 'Coulter understood perspective probably better than either of you, and he realised something was wrong though he couldn't tell what. It isn't that any particular view is at fault, but they are all at odds with each other. It wasn't the perspective in his paintings that was wrong; it was the real world. He found that, wherever he painted it from, that clump of trees always looked exactly the same to him. And he knew that was wrong, that it was impossible.'

'And it drove him mad,' Sam observed quietly.

'Eventually, yes.' The Doctor leapt to his feet. 'It's a psychic barrier, makes you feel ill if you come too close. Probably designed to keep out inquisitive locals and suicidal painters. Feeling better yet?' He did not wait for an answer but started up the hill at a run.

Sam raced after him, aware of a tightening in her stomach and the return of her nausea. She looked back, and saw from Sargent's contorted face that he was feeling something similar. 'Come on,' she called. 'Ignore it, and come on.'

It was like diving into a cool swimming pool on a hot day. At once, as they reached the tree line, the tension in Sam's stomach eased and lifted. It was almost refreshing. At the same moment, the pressure of the heavy air abated, and the whole world seemed to shimmer for an instant, as if she had been looking at a perfect reflection in a pool of mercury and someone had now thrown in a stone. When the ripples died away, Sam realised that she had crossed through beyond the image that was thrown up on the top of the hill in the shape of a clump of trees. Lord Meacher's Clump was a single two-dimensional picture projected to hide what was really there, with the psychological barrier to deter anyone from accidentally walking through it.

Behind her, Sargent gasped in astonishment. It was almost comic, Sam thought. Like an over-rehearsed double-take. In front of her, the Doctor turned like a conjuror showing off his latest miracle.

There were no trees at all, just an overgrown, grassy landscape. The hilltop was a tangle of greenery interspersed with hundreds and thousands of the small blue flowers, so they seemed to glow through the vegetation from underneath. In the middle of the brambles and overgrowth, standing stark against the skyline on the top of the hill, was the blackened ruin of an ancient chapel. Ivy and creepers crept over it like an exoskeleton holding the ancient stonework together, or a green web of veins and arteries.

A long trench ran from the edge of the concealed area up to where the back wall of the chapel had been. But it was no longer there. The wall had been struck down by the impact, the heavy stones scattered across the landscape and all but lost in the green carpet of the ground. And half buried in the side of the chapel, jutting out like an anachronistic appendage and covered with moss and lichen, was the bulbous, shattered and decaying wreck of an alien spacecraft lying where, centuries before, it had made its final planetfall.

9
Planetfall

With the immediate crisis now over, they had adjourned to the Oval Office to discuss the longer-term implications. The emphasis had shifted from survival to credibility. And again, President Dering found himself short of options.

Together with the President in his office were his National Security Adviser, the Secretary of Defense, and the recently arrived Secretary of State, Marion Hewitt. Dering had resisted the suggestion that they be joined by the heads of the CIA and the FBI, just as he had declined the opportunity to invite his Joint Chiefs of Staff. This was a political discussion, not a military or intelligence matter. Whatever they decided could later be checked back with the others to be sure there were no obvious security ramifications that had been missed.

The only other person in the room was Dering's ever-present Secret Service agent. Everyone was a little on edge, and the presence of the agent in the room might keep tempers calm as they discussed the problem.

The problem was simple, and Dering restated it: 'So, we had an ace up our sleeve we didn't know about. But now it's out of the bag.' He waved away the mixed metaphor with a tired hand. 'Whatever.'

'You mean this Station Nine,' Marion Hewitt prompted. Her voice was as forceful as her personality and contrasted with her small frame. She was a veteran diplomat who had served for ten years at the UN. Now in her early fifties, her hair, like her personality, was severe and grey.

Dering nodded. 'After years of pretending that the Strategic

Defense Initiative – Star Wars – was a failure, we now have to explain how we got a fully functional nuclear killer space station into orbit. Quite apart from the cries of hypocrisy from the anti-nuclear lobby, we're wide open to the international community's accusations that we're in contravention of the spirit and the letter of at least three strategic-arms-limitation treaties we not only signed but actually instigated.'

'It's a mess,' Horner said. 'Not as much of a mess as it could have been, but you're right, Mr President, people will soon forget or overlook that small fact.'

'Suggestions?'

'We could deny it ever happened,' Hewitt suggested. But her tone betrayed the fact that she did not think this was really possible.

'And make matters worse still,' Kellerman pointed out. 'Everyone with a radar knows for sure what's up there now. Everyone who watches CNN knows just about as much.'

'So if we can't deny it, maybe we admit it outright.' Horner rubbed his chin thoughtfully. 'Say it was a one-off satellite that blew itself up with the missiles, a fail-safe device we put in orbit years ago and never bothered to deactivate even though it seemed its use was over.'

'I don't buy that either,' Dering said. 'What happens,' he asked, 'if we tell the world the truth?'

For long seconds no one spoke. The silence was broken by Marion Hewitt. 'That depends on how much of the truth you're advocating, Mr President.'

'All of it.'

She shook her head. 'Not good. We need to be seen as strong right now. *You* need to be seen as being in complete control. The situation in Russia and China is not as good as it might be in any case. Admitting that our military had a secret nuclear base that even you didn't know about might not help.'

Horner laughed, a short humourless bark. 'Dead right, Marion. Everyone will be wise after the event and say they knew the rumours about Station Nine were true. Not the detail, but the notion. You say you didn't know, and at best they'll think you're lying.'

'And at worst?'

Horner shrugged. 'Think of the headlines in Europe, the Middle East, former Soviet states.' He reached across and helped himself to more coffee. 'US military out of control. President played for a sucker.' He stirred a spoonful of sugar into the coffee and shook his head again. 'As Marion says, not good.'

Dering sighed, and put down his own untouched coffee. He stood up and walked over to the window, staring out across the lawn. 'You bring a fresh perspective to this, Pete.' He turned to Kellerman. 'What do you reckon?'

Kellerman seemed relaxed and at ease, at odds both with his colleagues and with the angry impulsive he had been as the missiles approached. Perhaps he was better, Dering thought, when the immediate pressure was off enough for him to think things through.

'We need to take the offensive, Mr President,' Kellerman said after a pause.

'Go on.'

'Station Nine is now a proven force. It works. And the fact that it is up there and it works and everyone knows that means that it can – and will – maintain the peace for another fifty years.' He looked round his attentive audience. 'The point to stress is that Station Nine is not, and never was, a US-only defence system. It is quite by chance that the first, and let us hope only, use of the station was to combat an attack launched against the United States. But now everyone with any nuclear aspirations at all – Gaddafi, Saddam Hussein, the

Massada Group – knows that there is a sentinel up there above us, keeping us all safe from the darkness.'

There was silence for a while as the implications settled in.

'We could no longer keep the station a US-only base,' Horner said at last. 'There would have to be some credible check and balance, otherwise it's US imperialism all over again.'

'The military would love that,' Hewitt observed.

'The military probably still think that any conflict we find ourselves caught up in is purely a question of force of arms. Any repercussions from this will be an economic war. Sanctions and tariffs. We couldn't sustain that for long.'

'So what do we do?' Dering asked. 'Throw the place open to the world and his wife?'

'In a sense, yes.' Kellerman leaned forward. 'We hand Station Nine over to the UN. Naturally US forces will continue to run it, but under UN supervision and with some observers from key players. One from each of the Security Council, for example.'

Dering nodded, liking the idea. 'We maintain effective control, and preserve our credibility. Provided,' he added, 'the gesture we make is big enough.'

'There is a Canadian army colonel called Jean-Pierre de Tannerie,' Kellerman said. 'He's highly respected within the military community and well known for his work holding the UN forces in central Africa together last year when the trouble blew up there.'

Horner agreed. 'A good man. Sharp, and politically adept.'

'He is also space-trained,' Kellerman went on. 'He flew on one of the Defense Department's secret shuttle missions over China a few months back as an observer. He's one of us, French Canadian on his father's side, but his mother was from Iowa.'

'You're suggesting he'd make a good observer?'

'Not quite, Mr President. You mentioned a big gesture to cement the credibility.' Kellerman finished his coffee and carefully set down the bone-china cup on its saucer before he finished his point. 'I think he'd make a good Station Commander.' The silence in the room was complete.

The only sound was their breathing and the scrape of their feet on the moss-covered floor. Perhaps because of the age of the building, perhaps because of the symbiotic mix of architecture and vegetation as each supported the other, perhaps because of the religious nature of the place, Sam found herself in awe. Even without the tarnished hull of the ship protruding from the end wall of the chapel, there would have been a surreal atmosphere to it all.

They made their way slowly across what had been the floor of the nave, looking up at the fragile walls poised precariously above them. The roof was long since gone, though several of the holes where the heavy beams had intersected the walls were still just visible. Ivy poured over the top of the walls, as if spilling its way in over the lip. A dark mass of sinews and fibres against the dawn sky.

The floor was surprisingly even under the matting of greenery that trailed across it. It was filthy with the dust and grime of the ages, but the flagstones had not been worried by human feet for centuries. They had entered at the west end of the chapel, and were making towards the east end. The east end was where the altar would have been, but where instead the shattered nose of the spacecraft was pushed through into the chapel. Incongruously, a doorway was set into the wall beside the ship's bulk. The rotted remains of shattered wood were just visible where they still clung to the rusted hinges. The steps that had led up to the altar and the door now seemed to be purpose-built for them to reach the ship.

At the foot of the steps, the Doctor stopped abruptly. He held his arms out to prevent Sam or Sargent passing him, then stooped down. Peering over his shoulder, Sam could see that he was carefully pulling the creepers away from something that lay buried beneath them. It was at first an indistinct shape, about four feet long, grey and dusty. As more of it was revealed, Sam could see that it was the ancient remains of a body.

'My God, what's that?' Sargent breathed.

There was barely more than a skeleton left. Its legs were hunched up, the knees drawn in to the chest, and one arm was up to protect the head. The other arm lay pointing away from the body, as if reaching out for something. It was not the fact that it was a body, lying crumpled at the foot of the steps where it had probably fallen, that had surprised Sargent. Sam assumed that as a historian he had seen skeletons before, if only in museums. But those bodies, Sam knew, would have been human.

The creature was humanoid and would have stood about four feet tall. The skull-face was a snarling mass of heavy bone that reminded Sam of the gargoyle imagery in the manor house. And looking at the rest of the body she was in no doubt that it was from this creature, and others of its race, that the imagery derived.

The Doctor seemed to have come to the same conclusion, because even as the thought struck Sam he pointed to the top of the skull and said, 'Look here, you can just make out the residual stumps of the horns. And on the shoulders are what look like wing cases. My guess is that the hands were slightly webbed, as were the feet, and I wouldn't be surprised if it had a short tail as well. Probably forked.' He straightened up and dusted his hands on his coat lapels. 'You don't seem as surprised as I might have expected,' he said to Sargent with a grin.

Sargent shrugged. 'I won't pretend this is all in a day's work,' the historian said, 'but I think I must have seen my six impossible things before breakfast.'

The Doctor laughed, and the sound echoed round the ruined chapel like a release of tension and pressure. 'Well, let's see how many more impossibilities this place holds for us, shall we?'

'The spaceship?' Sam asked.

'The spaceship.'

Age and the initial impact had done nothing for the ship. They climbed in through the main portal, which was halfway along its length. The door at the top of the short flight of steps in the chapel had brought them out alongside the rusted hull, and the black oval of the entrance was plainly visible in the gathering light. It was a steep step up, and inside was dim and gloomy. But as Sam's eyes became accustomed to the half-light she found she could easily make out the details of the damaged interior.

The craft was about forty feet long and on a single floor. The design had either been open-plan, or the bulkheads had since disintegrated or rotted away. One slightly raised area seemed to be the flight deck, with cracked and blackened consoles and the fractured ends of trailing cables hanging loose. The walls and floor were scarred with the evidence of an ancient fire, and dented from the impact.

They spent a while looking over the flight deck. Sam and Sargent picked their way carefully through the wreckage, getting increasingly confused and bored. The Doctor stayed at one of the consoles, gently teasing it back to some form of life and scrolling through data on a screen that flickered and dimmed before finally giving up the ghost completely.

'Anything useful?' Sam asked him.

'Ship's log. Quite interesting,' he said. 'It's fuelled some suspicions of mine.'

'Such as?'

'Such as let's look round a bit more, and when I'm sure I'll tell you.'

Sam sighed. 'I love it when you get all mysterious,' she said.

The front end of the craft had apparently shattered on impact with the stone wall of the chapel, and various glass jars and specimen cases lay in broken ruins across the floor. The Doctor nudged a pile of rotting material with his toe. 'This is, or rather was, a collection of spores and seeds,' he said.

'Those blue flowers?'

He nodded. 'The seeds are quite delicate. Some would have travelled on the breeze, but not very far or they wouldn't survive. So the effect is relatively local.' He turned on the spot, his foot smearing the seeds into the floor without realising, as if he were stubbing out a cigarette. 'Ah,' he said with evident satisfaction, 'life support.'

The life-support area was set into a hollow in the hull of the craft so that it was almost a separate room on its own. In the centre of the area stood a single console, rather like a lectern. Around it, set into the walls, were several cubicles, each covered with a semitransparent membrane. These membranes had been rendered more opaque by the passage of time, by decay and the build-up of dust and grime. But as she wiped at the surface of the first with the back of her sleeve and peered through the misty sheen, Sam could see quite clearly what was inside. And she was grateful that she saw through a glass darkly.

On examination, all but one of the cubicles contained a creature. They were of the same race as the skeleton in the chapel, and almost as decayed. But what was left of the sterile atmosphere inside the compartments had preserved some at least of the flesh and the leathery skin. Enough to make the rotting corpses truly hideous and vile in their appearance.

Sam turned away in disgust from the first of the cubicles as Sargent moved curiously to take her place and the Doctor examined several more. 'They're all the same,' he reported. 'I suppose we're lucky none of the screens has fractured.'

'Why's that?' Sargent asked.

'Think of the smell,' Sam told him quietly, and was pleased to see that this provoked a reaction.

'Where be your gibes now?' the Doctor asked the final compartment. Then he turned his attention to the console in the centre of the area. Sam and Sargent joined him, watching as he ran his fingers round the smooth surface of the hollow indentation set into the top of the console. There were no other controls or constructs, just the single shaped space where something might have rested as if on a plinth. Something shaped like an egg.

The Doctor nodded, and Sam could see his grim expression trying to fend off the satisfaction of his discovery. 'So, now we know,' the Doctor said. 'A Khameirian cruiser. And this is where the Essence Chamber was kept, linked to the dying force of the crew in those compartments.' He gestured at the mass of cables and wires that hung from the sides of the cubicles and ran across the floor to the console where they stood. 'Here is the life linkage, you see. And one of the crew, quite possibly the captain, managed to get the Essence Chamber into the hands of the intelligent life that would keep it safe until the essence rebuilt its strength to a critical mass. Until the energy it absorbed from the surroundings brought it to the brink of being.'

'Doctor,' Sam said, 'what are you talking about?'

He blinked at her, then grinned. 'Sit down,' he said as he settled himself cross-legged on the filthy floor. 'Sit down, and

I'll tell you what I found out from the log, and what I've pieced together about what probably happened here.

'The Khameirian cruiser,' the Doctor continued, 'was already beyond its tolerances when the Yogloth Slayer brought it down. They had been playing cat and mouse across half the galaxy, twisting, turning, running. And the cruiser was the mouse. Rounding Rigellis III, it ran out of space, time, and luck.

'The self-targeting torpedo must have torn through the drive section of the cruiser like a wolf through a rabbit. Life support would have escaped the worst of it, but the main computer and navigation systems were taken out, along with communications. Perhaps some of them died in the blast, it hardly matters. The Stone knew them.

'The systems limped on for a while, unwilling or unable to give up the fight. Some residual energy in the drive systems, maybe. But the end was inevitable. It is said that the Khameirian will to survive is unparalleled. But they had to make planetfall to have any hope at all. And there are no planets to be fallen to in the Rigellis systems. They burned across the cosmos, leaving legends and prophecies in their wake. The Slayer probably broke off after the initial hit. They're great ones for economy of effort, the Yogloths. I have seen one of their assassins turn and leave the seedy bar where he had cornered his target before the bolt was halfway down the guidance beam. Lucky for me...'

Sam and Sargent sat uncomfortably on the cold floor, hardly moving as they listened to the Doctor's words. Around them the wind moaned as it clawed its way through the broken hulk of the ship. The increasing light of the new day fought its way into the darker corners, but always the Doctor's face was in shadow.

Penelope Silver poured herself more coffee from a glass

cafetière and shivered slightly within her silk dressing gown. There was a strong breeze now.

'More coffee?' she offered. She knew her husband had not been to bed the previous night. Probably he had slept for a couple of hours in a chair or on the sofa. He often worked through the night, and she was used to it. She tended to retire early and rise early herself, and how he could keep going on so little rest always amazed her. 'Norton?' she prompted when he did not answer.

'Oh, sorry, my dear. Yes.' He did not move, standing silently in the shadows beside the house. He allowed her to take the cup to him, and sipped gently at it without comment.

'Is everything all right?' He seemed unusually quiet and distant this morning. Even more withdrawn than usual.

'Oh yes. Everything is fine. Just fine.'

The sun dipped behind a cloud, and the breeze tugged at Penelope's hair.

'We may have some guests soon,' Silver went on. 'Another conference, I'm afraid.'

Penelope reached for a piece of toast. 'It adds a bit of variety,' she said. 'Just so long as they don't expect me to do the catering.' She smiled, and was relieved to see that her husband returned the smile.

'I think they can handle most of the arrangements themselves. I'm expecting a call any time now to confirm that they're coming.'

'So,' Penelope asked him, 'just who are they?'

'The Khameirian?' The Doctor brushed some of the dust from his trousers as he stood up. 'I don't know much about them, I'm afraid. Hardly more than I've learned today, or at least over the last few days. Their homeworlds are somewhere on the outer reaches of this galaxy. In the Antares sector, I think.' He walked over to the central console in the life-support area. 'You can see as well as I what they look like now. You can deduce how they might have seemed in life. Not, of course,' he added 'that they are really dead. Only their bodies.'

'What do you mean?' Sargent's tone was slightly breathless, urgent. The first time, Sam thought, that she had seen him really rattled by events rather than just accepting or ignoring things.

'The crew of this ship were killed, either by the initial hit from the Slayer, or when they crashed here. One of them survived a few minutes more, but no longer. But for the Khameirian, the body is just a vessel, not unlike this ship was. The essence of their lives, their very force of being, can be stored inside other vessels. They need the body to walk about, to communicate properly, but they can preserve life for huge periods of time inside what they call an Essence Chamber. That was how they first experimented with deep-space flight, a sort of suspended animation if you like.'

'And you said there was an Essence Chamber on this ship,' Sam remembered. 'It was in that hollow space.' She paused, remembering the Doctor's recent description of the creature's gift to Siolfor and his followers. 'The Philosopher's Stone.'

The Doctor nodded. 'Exactly. I was puzzled by the material when I first saw it. Remember how it seems to glow from within.'

Sargent laughed. 'It's always done that. It's just the reflected light from the halogen spot that shines on it.'

Sam shook her head. 'No, the Doctor's right. It even glows in the dark. Not much, but it does.'

'It does. And that glow is I suspect stronger now than it was when the stone arrived. It indicates that the life force within is growing in strength, regaining some of its power.'

'So how does it work?'

The Doctor was standing by the stained plastic cover of one of the cubicles. When he spoke it was as if he were addressing the rotting creature within. 'The Stone does several things. It stores the life essence until such time as it can be reconstituted. Presumably it slowly absorbs background energy from the environment to this end, and eventually has enough amassed to bring a new body, or bodies, into being and liberate itself from the Stone.'

'A slow process?'

'Painfully slow, at least in this sort of low-tech environment. Normally they'd rely on some local source of suitable energy to speed the process along. But that's not always the case, so the Philosopher's Stone also channels some of the initial energy into alternative vessels. Partly as a way of influencing events to try to maximise the availability of any energy that is around, but also as a fail-safe. To prevent having all their mental eggs in one basket so to speak.' He grinned at his own allusion.

'What other vessels?' Sam asked. 'Are you saying it affected the coven?'

'I imagine it affected the first group of people who came into contact with it. Who knows whether the Khameirian were actually able to detect and home in on suitable mental candidates as they plunged towards the Earth? But whether by luck or design, Siolfor and his followers were infected with a tiny part of the Khameirian collective mind. By impulse, or so they would have believed – I doubt there was any conscious thought to it at that stage – the members of the group formed a society which interbred and guarded the great secret which they didn't really know or understand. The result is that the life force within them has strengthened rather than dissipated down the generations. It has kept focused within a relatively small group, and slowly gained power over the years.'

Sam stood up and stretched her legs. She had not realised

how uncomfortable she was until she moved. She also realised she had been biting at a fingernail. 'And we know just how the society progressed from their family tree.'

'Yes. We can trace most of them up until fairly recently. We can see how the names changed over time. Tannian became Tanner, among other things. Wyrpe became Allworthy. Ross presumably evolved to Roskov after some of them emigrated to Eastern Europe.'

'And Siolfor became Silver.'

'Indeed it did. I'll tell you something else you might find interesting.'

'Yes?'

'Yes. Kell is an Old English word.'

Sam was not impressed. 'Really?'

Sargent, by contrast, nodded enthusiastically. 'Yes, it's another word for an oven. A kiln.'

'So?'

'So this Kellerman you thought I should know all about has a name which suggests he's descended from a man who looked after a kiln, or several kilns.' The Doctor grinned again, his white teeth gleaming in the strengthening light. 'If you think back to the list, you'll recall that a chap called Thomas Kilner was one of Siolfor's initial group.'

'Right.' Sam rubbed her eyes with the heels of her hands. 'OK, let's recap, shall we? What exactly does all this mean?'

'It means that the National Security Adviser to the US President is infected with the Khameirian mentality. The Khameirian's mental energies took root in the subconscious areas of the minds of the people at that first ceremony, dissipated from and focused by the Philosopher's Stone. The Stone also powers the mental barrier round this area and the image of Lord Meacher's Clump disguising the chapel. They were lucky that it was a private chapel, ruined even then, so nobody much came here anyway except Siolfor and his cronies. The Secret Society was formed, the only members being the descendants of the original hosts. This was a way of keeping the Khameirian "mind" in contact with itself as it grew in power.'

'So it's working to some great plan? All those centuries it's been slowly executing some grand design?'

The Doctor sucked in his cheeks. 'Well, therein lies the problem. No, I don't think that's how it works at all. The power is residual – it's not conscious in any real sense. Just an impulse to keep the whole thing going, to perpetuate the status quo until such time as there is enough energy to create a new body.'

'And how long would that take?' Sargent asked.

The Doctor shrugged. 'Difficult to say. But I doubt it could be much less than half a dozen millennia. It might even be as long as a million years.'

'So if Silver and his mates do have some great plan going, and I reckon from what I've seen they do,' Sam summed up, 'it should have nothing to do with this Khameirian mind thing at all.'

'That's about the size of it, yes.'

'Hmm,' Sam said, looking out though the shattered hull of the ship at the morning sun edging up over the distant horizon. 'Spooky.' A sudden shaft of sunlight illuminated the cubicle beside her. The decaying creature inside collapsed to its disintegrating knees as if it was so fragile the light had fractured its bones.

A curtain blew angrily in the morning breeze. Inside the cabinet, the smooth milky surface of the Philosopher's Stone pulsed slightly in the morning light. Then the curtain flapped away again, and the sun obliterated the glow with the force of its own iridescence.

Outside on the terrace, Penelope Silver finished her breakfast as her husband walked to the end of the paving to look down towards the driveway. Miss Allworthy quietly and efficiently started to clear away the breakfast things as the deep sound of the engines reached them on the morning breeze.

There were three trucks, heavy and camouflaged. Their headlights were on despite the clear light of day, smearing the retina as they lumbered up the driveway, crunching to a halt on the gravel outside the main door.

Silver reached them as the soldiers leapt out of the tailgates and assembled in two rows in front of his house. The officer in charge marched over to Silver and handed him an envelope. 'A letter from the Secretary of State, sir.'

'So I see.' Silver unfolded the heavy paper and read the single sheet quickly. 'You, I take it, are the "significant security arrangements"?' he asked.

'The start of them, sir. I'm Major Hayward, in charge of the advance party. We shall secure the area immediately. The rest of the contingent should be here shortly. There is also an American force arriving, which we will be operating with jointly.'

'Well, Major, we're not up to providing breakfast for you all, but we can manage an urn of tea if you want it.'

The major declined. 'I think we'll get started, if you don't mind, sir. We shall need access to the house as well as all areas of the estate.'

'Not a problem. I have some leaflets from the last conference we hosted here, albeit with rather less security. They do show the areas we will make available and indicate the private rooms. I trust that will help. You should know that I am expecting some private guests of my own as well. I'll let you have the details.'

His last sentence was punctuated by a low guttural rumble as the first of the light tanks turned on to the main driveway. Hayward checked his watch. 'Right on schedule,' he reported. 'Good.'

'It does seem,' Silver agreed quietly, 'that everything is going according to plan.'

'The Khameirian is not, in its current state, a conscious thing,' the Doctor was saying. 'It's more a feeling or desire to do what the Khameirian wants: instinctive.'

'But Silver's up to something, all right.'

'I agree. And I don't believe in coincidence.'

'So how come? Maybe the Philosopher's Stone has more power stored up than you thought.'

The Doctor clicked his tongue. 'It would have to be a massive amount. A huge surge of energy from somewhere nearby for it to start to influence at the level where a grand plan is thought out and executed. There's no evidence of activity in the society before Silver, or even until recently. So it's happened only a short while ago, whatever it is.'

Sam laughed. 'You ought to be used to it, Doctor.'

'Used to what?'

'Stuff hitting the fan just when you turn up.'

The Doctor frowned. 'Sam,' he chided, 'that's –' He broke off, and his face cleared as if the frown lines had been rubbed out. 'That's brilliant.'

Sargent shook his head and wandered off towards the flight deck, apparently bored with the Doctor's and Sam's banter.

'You're absolutely right,' the Doctor continued, ignoring Sargent's departure. 'The power loss when we arrived – I should have seen it sooner.'

'You mean we provided the energy? The TARDIS did?'

'I'm afraid so, yes. The Philosopher's Stone detected and sucked up the Artron energy from the TARDIS when we landed close by. Such a massive infusion of power must have given it the impetus to start the final rebirth of the Khameirian. It must have given Silver and the others quite a jolt too.'

'So now it's using the TARDIS energy to tell them what to do.'

The Doctor nodded vigorously. 'Sort of. They just know what they're up to and how to proceed. Silver has the largest proportion of the Khameirian mind in his, I suspect. That's also why his family has stayed so close to the Stone. So he acts as the co-ordinator. The overall, subconscious plan was already far enough advanced to have people in places of influence. Now the immense cunning and pragmatism of the Khameirian has examined the resources at its disposal and formulated some plan to provide the huge amount of power it still needs to burst from the egg of the Philosopher's Stone and out into reality.'

Sam looked round the Khameirian cruiser. Now that it was fully light, the place looked almost like a ruined church in its own right. The chapel of the life-support area with its lectern-like console; the raised flight deck with its altar of a main control desk. Sargent stood at the control desk, his back to Sam and the Doctor. He seemed to be fiddling with something either on the desk or in his hand. Sam ignored him, and turned back to the Doctor.

If Sam had been closer, she might have been able to see that Sargent was in fact holding a cellular phone. Closer still, and she would have seen him press the buttons, glancing furtively round to check he was still unobserved.

Outside in the distant morning, a pheasant cried out and

was answered, one creature calling to another of the same kind. Over a mile away, in the study of the manor house, a phone started to ring. Another call of like to like, another transfer of information.

10
Information Received

'So, what's the plan, Doctor?' Sargent was back with them. Sam had hardly noticed his approach until he spoke.

'Ours or theirs?' the Doctor responded.

'I meant ours.'

'Ah. Well, that depends on theirs.'

'Which is?'

The Doctor raised his arms above his shoulders and let them drop back to his sides. 'Tricky to say just now.'

'Is this helpful?' hazarded Sam. 'At all?'

The Doctor slapped her on the back without warning. 'Good point, Sam. Excellent.' He nodded appreciatively. 'And your suggestion is…?'

Sam glared. 'Let's go over what we know, shall we? See if we can deduce a pattern.'

The Doctor beamed. 'Good idea. Capital, excellent.' He tapped his chin with a long finger. 'I think this Station Nine business is the key. On the face of it, Silver and Kellerman, not to mention the late Colonel Roskov, went to an awful lot of trouble to expose the existence of Station Nine.'

'Yes, but why?' Sargent asked.

There was silence for several moments.

'He's asking why, Doctor,' Sam said at last.

'Yes.' He tapped his chin, clicked his fingers, and spun on his heel. When he completed the circle and was facing Sam again, he said, 'We just don't have enough to go on. So…'

'So?'

'So our plan is to get more data.'

'And that means going back to the manor house?' Sargent asked.

'Yes. But on our terms this time.' He started towards the entrance. 'Come on, no time to lose.'

Passing through the barrier the other way was far less unsettling. The landscape beyond – the real landscape beyond – was clearly visible, and the only clue that they had indeed appeared at the other side of the false image was the faint rippling sensation and the sudden feeling of dread and nausea. It seemed, Sam decided, to be caused simply by proximity to the barrier on the one side rather than by direction of travel or intent. She looked back over her shoulder, and saw the distinctive shape of the trees of Lord Meacher's Clump rising high above her, concealing what she knew really lay beyond.

'What exactly are "our terms"?' Sam asked as they made their way down the hill.

'I'm not quite sure,' the Doctor admitted. 'But somehow we need to get information from Silver, Tanner, and Miss Allworthy. I don't think Penelope Silver is a major player, so we're equal in number now.'

'Except they have guns,' Sargent commented.

'And we have our innocence, our aspirations, and our love of beauty alone.'

'Is that supposed to make us feel better?' Sam challenged.

But the Doctor did not answer. He had stopped abruptly, and held his hand up for Sam and Sargent to stop too. 'Down, quick,' he hissed and hit the deck. Sam dived after him, leaving the bemused Sargent to crouch down behind them.

From somewhere, probably his coat pocket, the Doctor had produced a pair of field glasses. He handed them to Sam without comment and pointed down the hill towards the manor house. Sam could just make out a group of vehicles parked outside the main entrance. She raised the binoculars to her eyes, and adjusted the focus ring over her nose.

The image swam into view, and Sam could see the vehicles clearly now. There were several large army trucks and three small armoured cars. At the furthest point of the forecourt a larger tank was parked, its long gun aimed along the length of the driveway as if expecting a full frontal attack by massed hordes.

'What is it?'

Sam lowered the glasses and looked from Sargent to the Doctor. 'He's called in reinforcements. Literally. There are armoured cars, tanks, troops, the lot. What the hell is going on, Doctor?'

'I have no idea. But I'd say the odds are no longer stacked so favourably.'

'True enough. And it was a long shot to begin with.' She scanned the area again through the binoculars, watching the soldiers fanning out in two- and three-man patrols. Then she shifted her attention back to the trucks and armoured vehicles. There was something about them, something slightly odd. Then she realised. Some of the trucks were of a different design, as was one of the armoured cars. She studied the markings and insignia.

'Could this be tied in with Station Nine somehow, Doctor?'

'Maybe. You tell me.'

'It's just I think some of those vehicles are American.'

'A joint operation of some sort?' The Doctor considered. 'But what? And why here?'

'And how do we find out?' Sargent asked.

Sam handed the glasses back to the Doctor. 'I think the house is most definitely off limits, Doctor. But I do know someone who might be able to help.'

'Oh?'

'I don't know exactly what, but Captain Pickering is

something high up in Anglo-American military relations.'

The Doctor grinned and tapped her gently on the nose. 'Good notion. And I bet you have an idea where we can find him.'

Sam grinned back. 'Just an address and a phone number.' Then her grin faded as she realised. 'They're scribbled on a beer mat in my room.'

They all turned and looked back at the house. 'No chance you can remember them?'

'The address, probably. The phone number, no chance.'

The Doctor considered a moment. 'Good enough,' he decided. 'Come on.' Keeping crouched below the skyline he set off across the meadow.

'The main gate is secure,' Major Hayward told Silver. 'There's no chance these people can get out that way.'

'Good, good. They must be apprehended as soon as possible. My man is following them, but obviously he can't signal regular reports in case they spot him.'

Hayward smiled. 'No problem, sir. So long as he keeps his phone line open, we can home in on the GPS signal. My men are calibrating it now, so we'll have them in minutes.'

Silver nodded, satisfied. Now that the Doctor had left the area behind the barrier, he could use the security forces to sort him out. 'Remember, Major, they seem to be armed. I suggest your men take no chances.'

Hayward smiled. 'Don't worry about that, sir.'

'Won't the gate be guarded?' Sam asked as they jogged through a small area of woodland.

'Ah.' The Doctor held aside a branch for Sam and Sargent. 'But we're not heading for the gate.'

'Where then?'

'The TARDIS. She should have enough power restored by now to cover the few miles to London in, well, in no time at all.'

They emerged from the woodland at the bottom of the long slope up to the remains of the old house. In the distance Sam could see the outcropping ruins. At the nearest edge was the fallen gargoyle statue.

'Right, I suggest we tread carefully from here on,' the Doctor advised. 'It's open ground.'

They made their way warily up the hill, pausing frequently to look all round and to listen for any tell-tale sound that might suggest they were being followed or had been seen. There was nothing.

'Why the gargoyle motif everywhere?' Sam asked as they reached the fallen statue.

'Subconscious imagery,' the Doctor said. 'The mind throws up all kinds of mental flotsam.'

'You mean it seemed to them like a good idea at the time.'

'Something like that, yes.'

The Doctor paused again to look around. They were almost within sight of the TARDIS now. But even as the Doctor beamed, and Sam exhaled with relief, the ruined landscape in front of them came alive. It was as if the rocks and stones of the house shifted and moved, then stood upright. Just for a second. Then Sam could see that the movement was made by figures rising to their feet. They wore combat uniforms and carried an assortment of rifles and sub-machine-guns.

'You will lay down your weapons and surrender immediately.' The voice was loud, echoing round the hilltop. 'Lie face down on the ground with your hands behind your head.'

'Don't be so melodramatic,' the Doctor shouted back. 'We're not dangerous and we don't have any –'

'Now!' The sharp order cut him off.

'We'd better do as he says,' Sargent said.

The Doctor looked back at the soldiers. 'No, they won't shoot us,' he decided. 'We're in Britain.' He nodded to punctuate his argument. 'Right then –' he stretched his arms up behind his head, making it look as though he was obeying the instruction – 'when I say run…'

'I know,' Sam said, imitating his action.

'Go!' The Doctor was already haring back down the hill towards the trees. Sam charged after him, aware of Sargent close behind. The shouts of the soldiers followed them all.

'You said "go",' Sam gasped as she tried to keep up with him. 'You're not supposed to say "go", you're supposed to say "run".'

'OK,' the Doctor called over his shoulder. 'If you prefer, "run".'

They dived into the trees as the first rasp of automatic fire kicked up the ground behind them.

'You said they wouldn't shoot, too,' Sargent pointed out as he held on to a tree trunk and tried to catch his breath.

'I said they wouldn't shoot us. And they didn't. They missed.'

'I wouldn't count on them making that mistake again, though,' Sam said. 'Come on, we've got to get out of here.'

'And we still need to get to Pickering,' the Doctor said as he followed her at a run.

The voice was calm, businesslike, and clipped. It sent a shiver down Pickering's spine. The last thing he wanted was his commanding officer ringing him up at home while he was on leave. Notionally on leave.

'What can I do for you, sir?' But Pickering suspected he knew what had prompted the call, if not the details.

'You've seen the news, I take it.'

'Yes, sir.' How could he have missed it?

'Well, our cousins are in a bit of a flap about it all, as you can imagine. But they've come up with an interesting proposition.'

Pickering listened to the proposition, and to his role in it. It was indeed extremely interesting.

'Given your particular skills, Pickering, I think you're more than suited for the job. Ideal, even. Your recent training might be just the option we need in a situation like this. What do you say?'

Pickering didn't say anything. He knew he had was locked in, had no option.

'I don't think we have any choice,' Sam insisted. 'We have to scout ahead and see what's going on.'

From the ditch where they were hiding, the Doctor, Sam, and Sargent could hear the sound of engines, of orders being shouted, of dogs barking.

'All right,' the Doctor agreed. 'But be careful.'

'I'm always careful.'

'Then be extra specially careful.'

'Right.'

Sam took a deep breath and leapt out of the ditch. They were still in the wooded area to the north of the house, and there was plenty of cover. There was also plenty of opportunity to make a noise, which was both an advantage and a disadvantage. It meant that Sam could hear the troops closing in on them, but it also meant that they would hear her if she wasn't careful.

Lightly, carefully, Sam edged forward, listening, trying to get a bearing on where the soldiers were, where the dogs had got to. They had run along a shallow brook for a way, and that might have helped to throw the dogs off the scent.

Sam crouched down as she realised she was close to the edge of the wood. Through the trees she could see a line of soldiers slowly moving forward. She guessed they were part of a circle closing in on their quarry. Had she passed through the line? The field beyond seemed to be empty. Sam toyed briefly with the idea of trying to lead the soldiers away from the Doctor and Sargent. If they kept going, they would find the Doctor's hiding place pretty soon.

But even as she discarded the idea, there was a shout from behind her. A moment later a shot rang out and a piece of bark exploded from the tree to Sam's left. She swore, jumped to her feet and ran. She did not have much choice, given where she already knew the troops were, and burst through the tree line and out into the field. A hundred yards away, a hedge rose up from the grass – the back of the maze. She remembered the trouble she had had trying to break through one of the hedges before. But she hadn't had people shooting at her then. A hundred yards, twelve seconds. Or a lifetime.

Behind her Sam could hear the soldiers' boots crashing through the wooded undergrowth. Automatic fire chewed up the ground at her feet. What was the effective range of a machine pistol? Not far? Too far, probably. Her head went back as she sprinted. The wind in her ears was louder than the rattle of the guns. The roaring doubled in volume.

There was a bank to her left, a short steep slope down to the edge of the rose garden. The roar came from beyond the bank, and Sam risked a sideways glance. In time to see the motorbike launch itself over the top of the slope and crash down almost beside her. The wheels seemed to compress as the suspension absorbed the impact. The back tyre bit into the grass, slewing sideways before getting a grip and pushing the bike after Sam. The driver's head was low over the handlebars, the goggles and helmet erasing any personality that might have been there.

Sam dived out of the way as the motorbike shot past. She rolled, and was up and running again – towards the bike now as it skidded round in a circle and started back towards her. The good news – the only good news – was that the shooting had stopped. But the soldiers from the wood were fast approaching. All the biker had to do was to slow her long enough for them to catch up. If he didn't run her down first, Sam thought as she dived away again.

Just too slow. Her foot caught the edge of the front wheel, and she went spinning across the ground. She rolled to a stop at the top of the slope down to the rose garden. On an impulse she rolled again, and toppled down the length of the slope, narrowly avoiding a nasty encounter with one of the rose bushes.

There was a crazy-paved walkway through the garden, the way the bike must have come. The paving weaved and undulated through the rose beds. Sam ran along the path just as the bike skidded down the slope after her. At the far end of the garden was a low archway of climbing roses. The bike would fit underneath, just, if the rider bent low. And beyond the archway was the gate out on to the terrace. Sam could hear the engine gunning as the bike raced after her, picking up speed on the straight section of pathway. She sprinted, arms working, head back, gasping. The rose arch was redder than she remembered as she raced through. The world was redder than she remembered.

The bike was close behind her. It was increasing speed all the time, trying to kill her. Think of the bike, not the man. No personality, just helmet and goggles, that makes it easier.

It was scant feet behind her, the driver bent low to get under the rose arch, unable to see ahead while he was avoiding the roof of the archway. So the biker didn't see Sam swing herself round on the gatepost as she passed. Didn't see her hand close round the open gate. Didn't see the piercing stare of her eyes as they focused more clearly than ever before on her action.

Didn't see the effort as she swung the heavy metal gate shut behind her. Only felt the impact.

The bike hit the closing gate at almost thirty miles an hour. The front wheel buckled as it connected with the ironwork, and locked. The rider was knocked from his seat and propelled over the crumpled handlebars, landing in a clumsy heap several yards away.

Sam paused long enough to hear a groan. Then she ran on, heading towards the house. She could either circle back to the Doctor, or maybe find a telephone. Not that she was sure who she could call. Her dad? Do us a favour.

The gravel path from the rose garden up to the terrace had a croquet lawn on one side, and a hedge on the other. Behind her, Sam could hear shouts. The croquet lawn seemed deserted. But from the other side of the hedge there was an ominous rumble. It built like thunder rolling in across the sea. Then suddenly a whole section of the hedge seemed to fold down, to crumple away. A long pipe appeared over the top, camouflage webbing dripping from its length. A gun barrel.

The tank followed, crunching over the remains of the hedge. The front of the tracks crashed down on to the gravel so forcefully that Sam felt the ground shudder under the vehicle's weight. Gravel spat out from the tracks as the huge armoured monster started up the path after her. The turret turned slowly, as if it contained the tank's eyes, as if it were searching out a target.

Sam took the steps up to the terrace three at a time. The tank hardly paused, but tilted back as its tracks met the slope. It ate the ground between itself and Sam, crunching closer and closer. It turned with her, crashing through flower beds and over obstacles. But Sam was getting closer to the house, ever closer.

At last, she was there. She grabbed at the handle of the

French windows.

Locked.

Behind her the tank crunched inexorably up the slope. Sam turned back to the window. Inside she could see Penelope Silver sitting at the piano. Her head was tilted back as if she were listening, wondering where the low rumbled of the huge engine was coming from. Sam tapped urgently on the glass. But Penelope did not react. The sound of the approaching tank was so loud now that even Sam could not hear her knocking. She hammered on the wood with her fist, shouted, looked back and screamed as the muzzle of the huge gun lurched to within a yard of her. She stepped away instinctively, falling through the French windows as Penelope threw them open, gaping in disbelief.

'Can't stop. Sorry,' Sam yelled as she raced across the room and headed for the door. She half expected the tank to come crashing through the house after her, and wondered briefly how Penelope would react to that.

The house seemed empty apart from Penelope, and Sam got to the library with no interruptions. She kept going, through the broken French windows and back on to the other side of the terrace. She glanced round quickly to make sure she had not been followed and to check there were no troops in front of her. In fact, she could see soldiers running round to the other side of the house, drawn away by the reports of her pursuit.

She paused long enough to catch her breath, then set off at a jog. With luck she had drawn the soldiers well away from the Doctor and Sargent, and she would be back with them before long. If they could stay hidden, she had a good idea how they could find their way to Pickering's flat.

It took Sam only a few minutes to make her cautious way back up the hill to the wooded area where the Doctor and

Sargent were, she hoped, still concealed. But as the trees thickened and the light dimmed, she could hear the booted feet and shouted orders of the soldiers. They seemed hardly to have paused during the long minutes while she was gone. They were still closing in on the Doctor's hiding place. As if they knew already where he was, and had not been distracted by Sam's solo diversion.

Sam was faced with two problems. The first was getting through the cordon of troops without being spotted. The second was getting out again. And the longer she delayed, the closer the cordon tightened and the less room there was to slip through. She edged closer, listening to the instructions called down the line. She could see one of the soldiers quite clearly through the trees. He seemed to be in charge, shouting out orders and consulting a small instrument he held in one hand. Sam was not close enough to make out what it was, but it was clear what was happening. Somehow they had a trace on the Doctor's and Sargent's position.

Sargent was cramped and uncomfortable as he lay in the ditch. He shifted his weight and tried to stretch his legs a little.

'Shhh.' The Doctor's admonishment was close in his ear. 'They're still out there.'

'Sorry.' Sargent shifted again, rather more carefully. 'Where's Sam got to, do you reckon?' He wanted both of them to be there when the soldiers finally closed in. He felt in his jacket pocket, reassured by the warm rounded shape of his cell phone. He wanted to check it was still on, that he hadn't jostled or knocked a button and switched it off. But the Doctor was too close for that.

Suddenly there was a movement further along the ditch. At last. But it was not one of the soldiers. It was Sam. She crawled breathlessly along towards them and beckoned for them to lean close so she could whisper.

'Sorry, I got a bit diverted. The bad news is they're still closing in. I think I've found a gap we can sneak through.'

'Great.' Sargent tried to sound enthusiastic. 'Let's go.'

'There is a problem, though. They seem to have some sort of tracking equipment. I think they can trace us somehow.'

'But how?' Sargent was hoping he looked confused.

But before the Doctor or Sam could venture an opinion, the sound of the soldiers' shouts carried to them on the wind.

'Nothing this way. Moving forward again.'

'Ease out slightly to the east.'

'Nothing this way either, Sargent.'

The Doctor's brow knitted in fierce thought. 'I wonder…' he murmured. Then his face cleared. 'Of course. That's it.' He snapped his fingers in sudden excitement. The noise was like a dry stick snapping. 'Sorry.'

Sam and Sargent looked at him expectantly. 'Do you have a plan, Doctor?' Sargent asked at last.

'Yes,' he said slowly. 'Yes I do, actually.' He pointed straight at Sargent's nose. 'And it all hinges on you, Mr Sargent.'

'Me?'

'Indeed yes.'

'What do you want me to do?' He was aware of Sam watching them closely. She seemed about to speak, but the Doctor put his finger to her lips without even looking round.

'Now then, I want you to crawl further along this ditch.' The Doctor pointed along the ditch to where it turned slightly and became more overgrown. 'Get as far as you can into that undergrowth and keep a careful watch. As soon as you see anything or anyone coming close, then nip back here and tell me. But not until. Got that?'

'Yes, I think so.' Sargent was confused. 'But how will that help?'

'It gives us just the warning we need while we put the rest of my plan into operation.'

'Which is?'

'Not fully defined as yet. We'll let you know when you get back. OK?' He didn't wait for an answer but slapped Sargent painfully on the back. 'Good man. Off you go.'

Sargent considered for a moment, then decided that it probably did not matter what harebrained plan the Doctor dreamed up. So he nodded, and started crawling along the ditch. Behind him he could hear the Doctor whispering urgently to Sam. As he went further along, the ditch got slightly deeper. It also got first damp, then wet and muddy. Stagnant. The smell stuck in his nose and throat, and he tried not to cough or retch. By the time Sargent had reached the bend, his knees were deep in mud and he was drenched from the wet undergrowth he had to crawl through.

Sargent peered carefully out. Trees. Nothing but trees. He watched and waited. And waited. And after what seemed like for ever, but his watch thought was a little under five minutes, he saw the indistinct shape of one of the soldiers making his careful way forward in the direction of his hiding place. He looked round, and sure enough other soldiers were coming into sight further round.

Sargent edged back along the ditch, careful to make no noise, although it hardly mattered now. It took him a minute to crawl backward along the ditch until it was wide enough for him to turn around. He pushed himself forward and round the slight corner, slipping and falling as he did so. His face splashed into the mud and he suppressed a splutter. He wiped the dirt and stagnant water out of his eyes, and looked along the ditch.

The Doctor and Sam were nowhere to be seen.

As Sargent pondered this, and wondered what to do, a large

figure leapt down into the ditch in front of him. It was not the Doctor.

The soldier pointed his machine pistol straight at Sargent, holding it in one hand while the other pointed at him. The muzzle of the gun filled his view. The finger on the trigger was his entire life.

'Right, sunshine.' The voice was deep, almost a growl. It was not a voice to argue with. 'Hands on your head, and face down on the ground.'

Sargent looked slowly down at the thick mud at the bottom on the ditch, stirring it up with the filthy toe of his shoe.

'Now!'

Sargent shook his head slowly. 'You're joking,' he said as the soldier reached out with his free hand and grabbed him by the hair.

He wasn't joking.

Sam was right when she said it would be a problem to get through the cordon of soldiers. But as the Doctor and Sam crouched in a clump of bracken and watched the line of soldiers approach, there was a shout from behind them. The soldiers exchanged brief words with each other, then set off across the wood in the direction of the ditch the Doctor and Sam had just left.

'I think they found our friend, finally.'

'How did you know it's Sargent they're tracking?'

The Doctor stood up, stretched, and sauntered off. Sam ran to catch him up. 'I heard the soldiers shouting to each other,' the Doctor said as they reached the edge of the wood. 'Which way, do you suppose?'

Sam led the way. 'Down here. It's pretty sheltered and we're out of sight of the house. It'll take us to the perimeter wall.'

'And we can climb over.' The Doctor beamed. 'Good thought,

Sam.' Somewhere behind them were more shouts and the sound of a heavy vehicle arriving at the woodland. They kept walking, the wind in their hair and the pale sun on their backs.

'I realised when one of the soldiers called out something to the sergeant,' the Doctor went on, impervious to the noise from the wood. 'It just struck me. His name isn't really Sargent at all.'

'Oh?'

'No. It's S'Argent.' He pronounced it S-Argent so Sam could hear the difference. 'A corruption, I would guess, of Norman French imported into England with William the Conqueror and all his friends and relatives.'

Sam laughed. 'Of course, obvious when you think about it.' She slapped the Doctor heartily on the back and watched in amusement as he pretended to stumble. 'And "*argent*" is French for silver.'

'Exactly. Another of Siolfor's descendants.'

They walked on in silence for a while, crossing a patch of ground that had returned to the wild and then taking a narrow pathway through a hedge and across another area of woodland.

'So how did you find this?' The Doctor held out his arms wide and turned a full circle, knocking drops of water from the low hanging branches of nearby trees.

'Pickering showed me. We jogged round here sometimes.'

'Ah.'

'If Silver's in the middle of all this, whatever it is...' Sam started, not really to change the subject, she told herself.

'Yes?'

'Then why did he welcome us as guests? I mean, why give us house room and the facilities to research his dim and distant and shady past?'

'A good question.' The wall was visible through the trees now, and the Doctor pushed through towards it. 'Let's ask him later, shall we?' He stood at the base of the wall and knitted his fingers together to form his hands into a step. 'Now, let me give you a bunk-up.'

Sam raised an eyebrow, bit back the comment that first came to mind, and stepped up into the Doctor's hands.

Hands tight on the wheel, Steve Fisher felt in control. He liked feeling in control, and driving the Transit at speed along the narrow country lanes filled him with exhilaration. A big man with a big van. He grinned, hunched down close over the wheel and slammed the gear lever forward into third for the bend ahead. He felt the surge of power as he let the clutch up, and pushed down on the accelerator.

The van took the corner wide, leaning dangerously towards the kerb. Then it levelled out as it barrelled along the straight section of the lane ahead. Steve heard his cargo shift in the rear of the van, but he paid it no attention. Just a load of plastic garden furniture for a pub car park sale in Ealing. Nothing he could do would damage it.

Along the side of the road, slightly back from the grass verge, was a high wall. Steve had glimpsed the impressive entrance to a large estate a few miles back. He often passed this way, but today had been the first time he had seen soldiers standing on guard outside. He thought he had caught a glimpse of an armoured car on the driveway, facing out at the road. But probably he had imagined it.

As the van rounded the next bend, a figure stepped forward on the verge a short way ahead. Thumb out, waving for a lift. Fat chance. Steve rarely gave lifts. Then, as he approached, he saw the figure more clearly, and slowed to a halt beside her.

She was in her late teens or early twenties. A bit dishevelled, but then hitchhikers always were. She wore a sweat shirt and jeans, neither of which disguised her slim figure. Her hair was cut quite short so that her ears were visible, and she was grinning so much that her blue eyes were scrunched up.

'Want a ride?' Steve asked over-casually as he leaned across and slid the passenger door open.

'That's original,' she said without breaking her smile.

Steve grinned back. She was impressed – he was in with a chance here.

She tilted her head slightly to one side, an almost mocking gesture. 'How far do you go?' she asked coyly.

Steve almost bounced in his seat. 'Well, how far do you want to go?'

'London? Anywhere near a tube will do.'

Steve nodded enthusiastically. 'Yeah. No problem.' He tried wiggling his eyebrows as he grinned. 'Climb aboard.'

'Thanks.' She made to climb in, then stopped abruptly. 'Oh,' she said, 'let me introduce my friend.' Then she stepped aside, and almost before she had moved another figure popped up in the doorway and hoisted himself into the van.

The man was a tangle of long curly hair and a beaming smile. 'I'm the Doctor.' He reached across and shook Steve's hand vigorously in both his. 'I can't tell you how grateful we are, aren't we, Sam?' He didn't wait for an answer from the girl, who had now climbed in behind him. 'You know, it's the strangest thing, but I tried for ages to hitch a lift. Then Sam has a go and you stop straight away. I'd have thought I was a more prominent and distinguished figure, but it just goes to show, doesn't it?'

Steve grunted in a noncommittal manner, and put the van into gear.

'Hey, Doctor,' the girl said excitedly before they had gone a hundred yards, 'look what's in the back here.' She was pointing to the piles of garden furniture that half filled the back of the van. 'We could talk in the back without disturbing our... host.'

The man, the Doctor, looked round too. And his eyes lit up.

A mile down the road, Steve could feel one of his heads coming on. Behind him he could hear the couple talking quietly. The girl was sitting in a garden chair, leaning forward so her arms rested on the round plastic table in front of her. The man was reclining happily in a sunlounger. Whenever he turned a corner, Steve could see the parasol in the middle of the table twist into the frame of his mirror. He could do no more than steal the odd backward glance as he drove, and while the use of the furniture was a little eccentric, he could cope with that.

But where had they found the bone-china cups and saucers? And the tea?

11
Back to Work

Pickering was plainly surprised when he opened the door. He had his shoulder bag in one hand, and, when he saw Sam and the Doctor, he dropped it to the floor.

'Sam, Doctor.' He looked from one to the other. 'What are you doing here?' He shook his head, and stood aside, kicking the bag out of the doorway. 'Come in, come in. Though I'll have to be off in a few minutes.' He led the way through the short hall and into a tidy living room. It looked like it was part of a show home, Sam thought. Nothing out of place, and almost no extraneous objects. A paperback book lay on a coffee table beside the settee, but even this seemed to have been aligned with the table edges so that it looked deliberately placed. A single framed print on the largest wall was a pastel creation of straight lines and strongly delineated abstract shapes.

'Nice flat,' Sam said as she slumped down next to the Doctor of the sofa. 'Very, er…'

'Tidy?'

'Yes. Right. Tidy.'

'Habit, partly,' Pickering said. 'And partly I'm off on a tour of duty for three months or more, so I like to leave things –' he shrugged, almost apologetically – 'tidy,' he admitted at last as he sat down in the armchair.

'I thought you had some time off.'

'So did I. But not any more, apparently.'

'When do you leave?' the Doctor asked.

'Any minute.' He laughed. 'I thought you were the car, actually. You gave me quite a surprise.' There was a short silence while the Doctor sat back on the sofa and looked round the room. Sam looked at Pickering. Pickering looked at his feet. 'If this is a social call,' he said eventually, 'I can put the kettle on.'

'It's not a social call.' The Doctor's voice was serious. He seemed to realise this, and added, 'Sorry,' with a slight smile.

'Business, then?' Pickering seemed amused.

'If you like.' The Doctor leaned forward, the light from a standard lamp diffusing through his hair. 'Dark things are happening, Captain Pickering.' His voice was edged with a hint of anger. 'Evil things. And the evil must be fought.'

'We live in interesting times, that's for sure Doctor. But *evil*?' Pickering shook his head slowly. 'I'm not sure quite what you're getting at, I'm afraid.'

Sam was not at all sure this was going anywhere. 'Look,' she said, 'we didn't get chased round Silver's estate by a gang of soldiers and then hitchhike down here with the reigning Mr Social Graces just to tell you fairy-tales.'

Pickering held up his hands. 'OK, OK. But so far you haven't actually told me anything.' He frowned. 'Soldiers? Must be there for the conference, I suppose.'

'Could we stick to one topic at a time, please?' The Doctor stood up and took centre stage. 'Let me tell you a few things, Captain.'

'Please do.'

'Now some of them you may find difficult to accept. Others are facts you know to be true. Even if you only believe half of what Sam and I have to tell you, I think you'll decide to help us.'

Pickering settled back in his chair. 'If you say so. I'm certainly willing to listen.' He checked his watch. 'You have about ten minutes at the outside, then I really shall have to leave you.'

The Doctor rattled through a brief account of the major

events to have befallen himself and Sam since Pickering had left Silver's house. It took him considerably less than ten minutes, and even Sam felt shell-shocked and jet-lagged at the end of it. Pickering gaped.

'You're serious, aren't you?' he finally said. 'I wish I'd made that tea now.'

'You have to admit there's a connection between Silver and the attack on the USA,' Sam pointed out.

'Do I?'

'You were there, you saw Roskov,' the Doctor said. 'You even told us who he was. At the very least it's an amazing coincidence that a few hours after he leaves Silver, in fact, almost as soon as he arrives back at base, I would judge, he launches an unprovoked and pointless nuclear attack on the United States.'

'A stressful flight back, perhaps,' Sam offered. 'And nothing at all to do with his meeting with "Norton Silver, Mind Control a Speciality".'

'OK. Maybe, just maybe, there's a connection. But I still don't necessarily believe all the alien mumbo-jumbo.'

'Fair enough,' Sam said quickly before the Doctor could object. 'But will you help us?'

Pickering smiled. 'Depends what you want, really, doesn't it?'

'Information,' the Doctor said simply.

'By hook or by crook, no doubt.'

The Doctor looked blankly at Sam. She shrugged, having no idea what Pickering meant.

'Never mind,' he apologised, 'before your time, probably. So what can I tell you?'

'You can tell us about Station Nine, for starters. And about how the Americans are coping with world reaction to its existence.'

Pickering considered. 'All right. I'll tell you what I know.

Since I haven't been briefed properly yet, most of it is in the public domain anyway, so I'm not telling you anything secret, you understand.'

'But you are saving us an awful lot of hassle.'

'First off, world reaction to the fact that the USA has a secret military satellite capable of shooting down nuclear missiles with its very own smart nuclear weapons has been quite vociferous.'

'I can imagine,' the Doctor said. 'Go on.'

'The Yanks have dealt with it in a novel and clever way. They've said the station is a force for preserving the nuclear peace, and offered it to the United Nations. The US keeps its station and most of the crew for the moment, but the UN appoint a commander and the members of the Security Council send observers to the station. That may lead eventually, they say, to a multinational crew and complete UN control. I doubt it, though.'

'Why?' Sam asked.

'The pressure will ease up after a while, unless the Americans do something silly. Once there's been an upheaval, the new status quo gains a sort of inertia.'

The Doctor nodded. 'If it ain't broke, don't fix it.'

'Exactly. Another nugget of information for you, and this is confidential up to a point, is that the British observer on Station Nine has already been appointed.'

The Doctor grinned broadly, though Sam didn't immediately see the joke until the Doctor said, 'It's you, isn't it?'

Pickering nodded. 'That's where I'm off to in a couple of minutes. There's a special shuttle leaving from the Cape. I'm rather looking forward to it, actually. They've even commandeered a Concorde to get me there in time.'

'Good for you,' the Doctor said, raising an imaginary glass in a virtual toast.

'That's a bit quick, isn't it?' Sam said.

'Actually, Sam, yes it is. In fact, the speed at which events are moving is phenomenal.' He gave a short laugh. 'You know, it's almost as if influential people around the world were waiting for just this to happen.'

Sam glanced at the Doctor. At that moment the doorbell rang, a two-tone chime with a synthetic echo.

'I must go.' Pickering stood up. 'But you're welcome to hang around here if you want. I've cleared out the fridge, I'm afraid, but there's stuff in the freezer if you're hungry. And help yourself to the bathroom, shower, all that.' He hoisted his kitbag over his shoulder. 'Just leave everything, er, tidy,' he added with a grin.

'Anything else you can tell us?' the Doctor called after him as Pickering made for the hall.

Sam could hear Pickering talking with the man at the door, telling him he'd be right down. Then he returned and stood in the doorway. 'Only that you'd have done better to stay where you were. The UN conference to decide how Station Nine is operated starts tomorrow. And it's at Abbots Siolfor.'

'Silver's house,' Sam said quietly.

'Thank you,' the Doctor said, suddenly shaking Pickering's hand. 'You've been most helpful.'

'No problem. Look after yourselves. Sam.' He nodded to her and half waved.

'Have a good trip,' she said. 'It's great out there.'

'You sound like you've been.'

'Where there's a will, there's a way.'

Pickering nodded, slowly, as if hesitant to leave now. As if unwilling to stop smiling at Sam. Then he said, 'Be seeing you,' as if this were a joke, turned and left.

They waited until the downstairs door banged behind him before either of them said anything. Then Sam said, 'I could do with a shower,' at the same moment as the Doctor said, 'I wonder if he has a car.'

Then the Doctor said, 'There's no rush,' just as Sam said, 'Yes, an old MG.'

The Doctor put his finger to Sam's lips. Their eyes were close and their noses almost touching as he whispered, 'You have a shower, while I find his car.'

'What for?' Sam was also whispering, although she didn't know why.

'To get clean.'

'That's not what I meant, and you know it.'

The Doctor nodded with a grin. 'He won't need his car. And we do.'

'To get back to Silver's place?'

'I'm sure he'll have left the keys somewhere.' The Doctor was already on his way to the door. 'I wonder who's on the guest list,' he said. 'Still, it will take them a while to get organised, so I suggest we kip down here for the night. We can head back in the morning.'

The guest list made for interesting reading. Silver received the file, along with a draft agenda for the meeting, by secure e-mail. From outside the study window came the throbbing mechanical sound of a helicopter. He looked up from his screen and smiled.

The helicopter was more modern than the one in which Roskov had arrived a few days previously, but it landed at almost exactly the same point outside. Silver watched from his study window as the large insect-like aircraft set itself down, dust blowing up from the ground as the rotors continued to turn.

A door in the side of the huge metal beast was slid back, a man in khaki overalls and wearing earphones was briefly visible as he swung it aside to let another man step out. Silver rubbed his hands together in delight as he watched Pete Kellerman jump down from the helicopter, followed by a large man wearing a suit and sunglasses.

Silver met Kellerman in the drawing room. Miss Allworthy had already given him a drink – bourbon. The Secret Service agent was standing unobtrusively behind the sofa, hands clasped in front of him and jacket unbuttoned. He had a good view of both the door and the French windows.

Silver dismissed the housekeeper and poured himself a whisky while Kellerman went through the standard spiel, mainly for the Secret Service man. 'So,' he finished up, 'the President has asked me personally to supervise the proceedings at this end. I hope you have no objections.'

'Indeed not. No.' The ice clinked in Silver's tumbler as he held it up to inspect the straw colour of the single malt. 'If only all the people who organise conferences here were as clear on their objectives and responsibilities as you are, Mr Kellerman.'

'Good.' Kellerman drained his glass. 'I'd like to review the security arrangements with you, if I may.'

The glow was a diffusion of light from inside. It made the surface of the stone almost shimmer with its pulsing intensity. The veins and shades of the marble, if it was marble, were lost in the increasing light that spilled from within.

Sam was afraid she would be pitched out of the MG as the Doctor took it round another corner at a speed she was astounded the car was capable of. The noise of the engine was almost deafening, and she had given up trying to make heard her protests at the Doctor's driving. She remembered the Doctor saying that they were in no hurry, and there was such a thing as undue and dangerous haste.

They had left London behind their squealing tyres a while ago, soon after a late and meagre breakfast. Sam recognised some of the landmarks from the glimpses she had snatched from inside the Transit van yesterday. She had thought they were whizzing past fairly quickly the first time. Blink and you'd miss them now as they blurred by. Still, at least she felt clean after her shower. Cleaner, anyway. A quick check in Pickering's organised wardrobe had convinced her she would not find any suitable clean clothes. He did not even seem to possess a decent baggy jumper. So the relief of her shower and a good night's sleep was somewhat mitigated by the muddy jeans and old hastily rinsed and hairdryer-blown undies she was forced to give another chance.

The autumn afternoon was already drawing in by the time they reached the village. It would be almost dark when they got to Silver's estate, several miles up the road. Sam glanced at the clock on the dashboard. Almost half past three. If it were midsummer, the afternoon would hardly have started and the day would have hours still to run. Another of the tricks Time plays, she decided, and did her best to relax. The shiny covering of the bucket seat was sticky in the muggy heat. The draft from the cracks where the soft roof almost met the bodywork blew cold on her face. Her stomach protested at another long bend turned into a hairpin by the speed of the Doctor's advance on Abbots Siolfor. She glanced up at the darkening sky, wondering whether Bill Pickering's shuttle had left yet, whether he was already somewhere in the sky above them looking back down at the Earth.

They were running adjacent to the perimeter wall now, not far from where they had caught their lift, though heading in the other direction. Sam looked to see if she could pick out the exact spot where she had stood. As she peered through the small window into the gathering gloom, the car suddenly slewed sideways, pitching her into the door. Her shoulder ached and her elbow had cracked into the door handle as the car skidded to a halt on the wrong side of the road, tyres protesting. There was a vague smell of burning rubber as Sam gasped, 'My God, what is it?'

The Doctor was leaning forward over the wheel. He pointed to a tiny black dot hovering high over the wall of the estate. As Sam watched it dropped like a stone towards the earth before the bird flapped its wings again and gained height once more.

'I think it's a kestrel,' the Doctor said quietly. His voice was a combination of amusement and fascination.

'Is that all? I thought at the very least there was a roadblock or something.' Sam sighed and rubbed her elbow. 'Men with guns and dogs. Tanks. The lot.'

'No no no.' The Doctor was still staring out through the windscreen. 'I'm almost sure it's a kestrel.'

Sam gave up rubbing her elbow and put her head in her hands. She blew out a long breath, rubbed her eyes, and inspected her nails. Most of them were bitten down almost to the quick. Most of them, she reckoned, had achieved this state in the last hour.

'So,' the Doctor said as the distant bird flew off into the dusk, 'what's the plan?'

'What plan?'

He held up a finger. 'Ah, I asked first.'

Sam waited while the unsuspecting car that had just rounded the bend ahead of them managed to swerve round the MG, horn blaring. Then she said, 'If this is going to be a long discussion, shouldn't we be on our own side of the road?'

Almost grudgingly, it seemed, the Doctor put the car into gear and slowly, carefully, edged across the road. He drew up thirty feet further on, nearside wheels on the grass verge. 'Happy?'

'Ecstatic. Now, what are we talking about?'

The Doctor drew a long, obviously over-patient breath. 'The entrance to Abbots Siolfor is just around the bend,' he said. 'So we need a plan.' He smiled. 'To get in,' he added helpfully.

Sam considered this. 'Yes,' she said at last. 'Yes, you're right. We do.'

'So what is it?'

'Hey, look, who's in charge here?' The Doctor just smiled at her. 'OK. Here's the plan.' She tapped her fingers on the dashboard, hoping for a moment of inspiration that never came. 'We're here for the conference, whatever it is.' No reaction. 'And whoever we are. Whyever we're here.'

The Doctor nodded slowly, not seeming convinced. Then suddenly the car was screeching away, leaving skid marks in the grass behind them. 'Brilliant.' The Doctor seemed not to have to shout to make himself heard clearly. His voice was apparently at its normal soft volume, clear as a bell within Sam's head. 'Absolutely brilliant.' They rounded the bend at breakneck speed. The entrance gates were just ahead, closed. A soldier stood in front of them, machine gun over his shoulder, its muzzle pointing at the ground. He stared at the windscreen of the car as they turned in.

'Better stay inconspicuous, Sam,' the Doctor hissed as they drew up. 'I'm not sure you're dressed absolutely appropriately for this.' Sam looked him up and down, and made no comment.

The soldier leaned down and tapped on the driver's-side window. Another soldier had stepped forward, hand lightly but firmly on his gun, covering his colleague. Prepared for the worst. Great, thought Sam, we don't even get through the gate.

'It's OK, sir,' the soldier said as the Doctor wound down his window. He tapped the windscreen where a square sticker with an intricate and abstract design was attached. 'Your security pass is quite in order. They'll check you against the list of delegates at main reception.' He pointed out the route up to the house, then turned back with a terse smile. At this point he seemed to notice Sam for the first time, and the smile froze in position. She smiled back, hoping the state of her jeans was not too apparent in the fading light.

'Left in a hurry, did you, miss?'

'Yes, actually.' She tried to stare him down, without success. 'Short notice, no time to change.'

The soldier nodded. 'Had a couple of people say the same thing. Well, you're in plenty of time.' He peered in at her again, and Sam guessed he was wondering at the mud that spattered her jeans and shirt.

'Paintballing,' she said.

His face cleared. 'Really?' He nodded in appreciation. 'Done a bit of that myself, though it's a bit of a busman's holiday these days. I don't see any paint.'

Sam was about to answer, when the soldier straightened up and waved to his colleague. She realised he had meant it as a compliment.

The second soldier swung the gates open for them, and the Doctor drove carefully and surprisingly slowly through. There were more troops just inside the grounds, some of them setting up arc lights. Just off the driveway, so that it was hidden from the road outside, stood the impressive bulk of an armoured car. In the gathering dusk it was barely more than an angular silhouette against the grey sky. The turret and gun barrel of the silhouette tracked the MG as it passed.

The front of the house was illuminated by floodlights that Sam did not recall. Either they had been installed specially, or Silver had not bothered to use them when he merely had house guests. The harsh light made the dusk around it seem even darker, while lending the front of the house a splendour of Ionian white which Sam knew it did not in fact possess.

Inside, past two more soldiers on sentry duty, the entrance hall had been transformed into a reception area, mainly by the addition of a large table. Behind the table sat a woman with horn-rimmed spectacles. She was what Sam's dad would have described as 'of an age,' meaning somewhere in the no man's land between forty and fifty-five. She looked up as the Doctor and Sam walked in. Her grimace, Sam decided, was probably intended to serve as a welcoming smile. On the table in front of her were several rows of file boxes. Each contained a collection of envelopes. One for each of the delegates at the conference, Sam decided. Probably an agenda, a pin-on badge, and a smarmy welcome letter from someone important. Maybe she would soon find out.

'Can I help you?'

The woman's voice was like gravel set in ice. Maybe she wouldn't.

'Yes, thank you,' the Doctor said beaming as if he was being reunited with his mother for the first time in ten years. 'We're here for the conference.'

'Really.' She was obviously far from moved by the Doctor's charm. 'Do you have names?'

'One each, actually,' Sam confessed. She ignored the Doctor's stare. The woman, in her turn, ignored Sam.

'Smith,' the Doctor offered. 'John Smith. My assistant is Miss Jones, though she may not be on your list due to the late arrangements.'

The woman made no effort to check through her envelopes, or to consult a list of any sort. She just stared at them. 'And who are you with?' she asked at last.

The Doctor laughed shortly. 'Well, each other,' he said. 'Sort of.'

'I think,' Sam offered, 'she's asking which delegation we're with.'

'Ah. Of course. Yes.' The Doctor turned to Sam, apparently bored with the whole proceedings. 'You tell her,' he said helpfully.

'Thanks,' said Sam. She was still wondering how to cope with this opportunity when help came from an unexpected direction. It came from down the hallway in the shape of Penelope Silver.

Penelope greeted the Doctor and Sam as long-lost friends. When she had allowed the Doctor to kiss her hand, and Sam to kiss her cheek, she demanded of the increasingly sour-faced woman what the problem was.

The woman was contrite, at least in her manner if not her expression. She carefully hunted through the boxes of envelopes twice, then produced a printed list of names from a folder. She consulted this, too, before hazarding the suggestion that the Doctor and Sam were not expected, however well known they might be to Mrs Silver.

Penelope was at a loss. 'But they are personal friends. Close friends,' she insisted. 'If they say they are here for the conference, then they are here for the conference, and my husband will vouch for them.'

'That may not be sufficient, I'm afraid, Mrs Silver.'

'Then they can join our private group.' She turned to the Doctor. 'We've got Andrew Price from the States – do you know him? No? Charming. Well, he and several others are staying here.'

'Are they on your husband's list of private guests, then?' the woman asked sourly.

Penelope Silver looked round, as if for inspiration. She found, instead, Miss Allworthy. The housekeeper was coming down the main staircase carrying an empty silver tray in one hand. But before Penelope could enlist her help, she saw the Doctor and Sam. At once she quickened her pace, taking the stairs two at a time. Her mouth was open, shouting a warning or an instruction.

But the sound Sam heard came from right by her ear. 'Run!' the Doctor shouted to her.

She took one step further down the hallway before the Doctor's hand grabbed her round the waist and lifted her. 'Not that way.' He swung her around so she was facing the front door. 'This way. More scope for escape.' With that he grabbed the printed list from the woman behind the desk, flipped through it rapidly, then handed it back. 'Thank you, must dash.'

Sam smiled an apology to Penelope Silver, scowled at the woman behind the table, caught a glimpse of the urgency in Miss Allworthy's eyes as she approached, and followed the Doctor at a run.

The night was cold after the relative warmth of the hall. The soldiers on duty outside the door turned to watch as the Doctor and Sam ran down the steps to the gravel forecourt. Behind them, Sam could hear Miss Allworthy shouting at them to stop. Her voice was drowned out by the sound of approaching motorbikes.

'Watch out,' the Doctor called to the soldiers as they reached the bottom of the steps, 'she's got a gun.'

The two soldiers were already unshouldering their weapons and turning back to the door. Sam watched as Miss Allworthy emerged at a run, hand held out – pointing. It was an ambiguous gesture, and one of the soldiers turned his automatic rifle towards the grey-haired woman. The other dived across the doorway and knocked her flying. Miss Allworthy crashed back into the doorway with a cry.

The motorbikes swept into the forecourt. There were two of them, escorting a large black limousine. The Doctor ran up to the nearest motorbike, waving frantically to the rider, his arms windmilling quixotically. He pointed over to the doorway where Miss Allworthy was trying to disentangle herself from one of the soldiers while being simultaneously thumped by the other.

'Quick, they need help over there. The woman's possessed.'

The rider leapt off his bike and set off at a run, pulling his helmet off as he went. 'Don't worry,' Sam called after him. 'We'll look after this for you.'

The Doctor was already on the bike, hand on the throttle. Sam leapt on behind him, holding him tight round the middle. She felt the front of the bike lift slightly. Then, with a scattering of gravel, they were off. Behind them, the second motorbike soldier looked from the fight in the main entrance to the Doctor and Sam speeding away. A moment later, his bike raced after them in pursuit.

The ride was bumpy, and Sam had to cling on tight to the Doctor to avoid being flung off the bike. She had somehow expected that the Doctor would head back to the main gates, but instead he set off across the terrace and along the narrow path that lead back towards the ruined house and the TARDIS. The wind blew through Sam's hair, ruffling it, reminding her of its length. She was soon chilled to the bone, her hands numb as she tried to hold on. Her cheeks felt frozen.

She risked a look back as they bounced over another hillock, and wished she hadn't. The pursuing motorbike was a way behind them, its light bouncing along as it followed. But behind that were larger lights, higher up. As she watched, the bike was overtaken by a Range Rover, which rapidly gained on them, ignoring the uneven terrain as it bounded along. The headlights flashed as it bounced up the incline, all the time narrowing the gap between them.

The Doctor's voice was clear in her head again despite the

noise of the bike and the rush of air. 'We should just about make the TARDIS before they catch us. If we're lucky.'

'Good,' Sam shouted back. 'Anyone interesting on the guest list?' But even she could not hear her words as they were swept away.

Nonetheless, the Doctor answered. 'Yes, actually. It seemed mainly to be made up of civil servants, dignitaries, and officials. But a suspiciously large number of them have names close to the Society's founding members.' He paused to negotiate a copse of trees, weaving through them at speed. Sam hoped the gaps were too narrow for the Range Rover, and when she glanced back was pleased to see it skid to a halt before setting off on a detour to avoid the trees.

'I think,' the Doctor went on, 'that many if not most of the Society will gather from all over the world in the manor house over the next day or two. Penelope Silver mentioned that they have guests of their own. The name she said was "Price" – another Society name.'

'So why are they all here?' Sam screamed back.

'That is a very good question.'

The ground was more uneven now, and the path steeper. They were, Sam realised, nearing the ruins. Almost there. Almost home. The Doctor veered off the path and started up the final incline, the bike's engine roaring as it accelerated up the hill. They swerved violently to avoid some rubble, then the Doctor reined in the bike, and skidded it to a halt. Again, they both looked back, and saw that the lights of their pursuers were pinpricks in the distance, a long way down the hill behind them.

'I think we can walk from here.' He turned off the bike's headlight. 'No point in giving them any clues.' The Doctor waited for Sam to dismount before swinging his leg over the bike and taking her hand. He kept hold of it as they picked their way through the ruins. At last, the reassuring shape of the TARDIS loomed out of the darkness.

'There's the old girl, at last.' The Doctor already had the key in his hand, was reaching for the lock.

He froze like a rabbit in the beam of the headlights. They both turned, slowly, in time to see the soldiers leaping out of the Range Rover and throwing themselves to the ground. The light gleamed on their rifles as they trained them on the Doctor and Sam.

The Doctor sighed, and pocketed the key. 'Not again. This is the way it so often ends,' he said to nobody in particular as they were led away, 'with a whimper.'

12
Not with a Bang

'What a lovely room,' the Doctor said.

Sam did not recall ever having seen the ballroom before.

'I take it this is where it is all happening,' the Doctor continued, pausing in the doorway. Miss Allworthy, a dark bruise under one eye, nudged him with her shotgun but the Doctor remained where he was.

Silver gestured to Miss Allworthy to indulge the Doctor for a moment. 'Just one minute, Doctor. Then, when you've admired the decor, we really must be moving on.'

'Must we?' The Doctor seemed to notice the shotgun for the first time. 'Yes, I suppose we must,' he admitted.

In the few moments they had in the doorway, Sam noted the chandeliers fixed to the ceiling by hooks set into heavy plaster bosses. The room was large, so large that the delegates seemed lost in it. Tables were laid out in a chevron arrangement of rows, facing the front of the room but also angled towards each other. At the front of the room was a raised dais on which stood a lectern with microphone. Speakers stood on tall stands along the length of the room. Above the dais was a large screen. It was blank.

Sam nodded towards the screen. 'Anything good on?'

'There certainly will be,' Silver answered. 'In fact, quite soon. So let's be running along so as not to miss the show.' He smiled, it was not pleasant. 'I have arranged fireside seats for you.'

'Oh goody,' the Doctor exclaimed. 'I love a good flick.'

'I beg your pardon?'

'Oh come on, Sam. Archaic expression for a movie. A film. A cinematic experience.' He started through the door and into the ballroom. 'Let's get an aisle seat close to the ice-cream lady.'

Miss Allworthy hauled him back by the collar before he had gone three paces.

'You're the ice-cream lady?' the Doctor hazarded.

'Regrettably,' Silver sighed before his housekeeper could react to the query, 'your seats are not in the main auditorium. That said, you will have, if anything, a rather better view of events.'

The seats that Silver had arranged were in the viewing gallery of his underground control room. Miss Allworthy ushered the Doctor and Sam into the oversized fish tank at the back of the chamber, giving the Doctor a shove for good measure. There were two rows of seats inside, and the Doctor and Sam each slumped into one. Silver stood in front of them, arms slightly open, as if welcoming them to his show. He had been a stage performer, Sam remembered, and she could see something of the showman in him now.

'If you're about to thank us for coming to your little show,' the Doctor told him, 'I'll tell you what I think of it so far.'

'Wise guy,' Sam chided.

'Little show?' Silver was amused. 'High drama, I would say, Doctor. The last act, in many ways.'

The Doctor nodded slowly. 'Yes. *Act* is a good word. That's what this all is, after all. A show put on for the governments of the world, for the delegates. A bit like the show you put on for us before, us and for the US President. An act.'

'Very perspicacious of you, Doctor.'

'But there's another act, too, isn't there. You're just following a script yourself, after all. Following prescribed actions. Going through the motions. All very Stanislavsky. No improvisation, no self-will.' Silver twitched, a nerve ticking under his eye. The

224

Doctor went on, 'So why is the Khameirian keeping us alive? Do you even know?'

'I'm in control here, Doctor. I make the decisions.' There was a tremble, a cadence in Silver's voice.

'Oh yeah?' Sam challenged. 'Is that why you became a hypnotist – so you could try to regain some level of control?'

The Doctor chuckled. 'Layers of illusion. The illusion of control; the illusion of self-will.' He stood up and paced along the line of chairs. 'How much control do you actually have? Or is everything set in stone?' He emphasised the last word.

'What?' Silver was angry now.

'Stone. You know. Like a carving, an engraving.'

'A statue,' Sam offered. 'Like the one at the ruined house. The one with the horns and wings.'

'Or like the Philosopher's Stone up there in the library.'

Silver did not answer. He was looking from the Doctor to Sam, apparently both angry and confused.

'So why are you keeping us alive, then, Norton?' the Doctor asked again. 'If we assume for a moment you actually have any say in the matter. Shall I tell you what I think?' he went on without pause. 'I think you goofed. Big-time.'

Silver seemed to slump against the glass wall. He spoke quietly, as if gathering his strength. 'I was confused. The sudden awakening, the realisation. I thought for a while you might be a messenger of some sort. Might have come to explain everything. The confusion.' His face crumpled into a deep frown. He massaged a temple with his fingertips. 'The pain.'

'So you gave us access to your library. You let us try to make sense of what was happening for you.'

Silver nodded, his face betraying the pain he was suffering.

'Then I'm sorry.'

'Sorry?' Silver's voice was quiet now. Almost pathetic.

'Yes, sorry. I did you a disservice. You must indeed have had some will of your own left. Enough at least to question what was happening to you. How many of the others, I wonder, managed such a thing?' He sat down again, in the chair next to Sam this time. 'But you knew, really, didn't you? You knew we were not sent to help. That's why you had Sargent there to keep tabs on us. That's why you removed the final painting when you realised I had found it.' He leaned forward, his voice now urgent, pleading. 'Where's that self-will now?'

Silver said nothing. He was leaning heavily against the wall, his mouth slack and his face empty of expression. Miss Allworthy took a step forward, unsure what to do. The Doctor looked at Sam and raised an eyebrow.

Then, just as Sam was beginning to believe they might have achieved something, Sargent came hurrying down the steps into the main chamber. He scurried over to the gallery, oblivious to Silver's dilemma.

'It's almost time, Mr Silver,' he said breathless. 'The delegates are taking their seats for the opening address.' He exchanged a puzzled look with Allworthy. 'Mr Silver, sir?'

Silver seemed to wake up at the sound of his name. He blinked, and a nerve twitched again below his left eye. Then he pulled himself upright with an obvious effort. 'Yes,' he said, his voice still quiet. Then, with increasing vigour and conviction, 'Yes. It is nearly time. At last.' He breathed out heavily, and seemed to be his old self again. 'At long last.'

'So much for Plan A,' the Doctor murmured to Sam.

'Plan B, perhaps?' she suggested.

The Doctor nodded and winked, raising his index finger to tap the side of his nose in knowing agreement. Then he frowned. 'What was Plan B again?' he asked.

'Just improvise, Doctor,' Sam hissed back.

'Is this a private conversation?' Silver asked. 'Or may anyone venture an opinion?'

'Certainly.' The Doctor buttoned his coat, then unbuttoned it again. Then he pulled out his pocket watch, flicked it open and consulted it a moment. 'I was just wondering,' he said as he pushed it back into his pocket, 'why now? After all these years, the long centuries, why now?'

'You mean the Becoming?'

'If that's the pompous term you use for it, whatever it is, then yes. The Philosopher's Stone has been brokering the life essence of the Khameirian for centuries – why should it become more proactive now?'

'Because now is the appointed time,' Silver said. There was a renewed strength in his voice and it reverberated round the glass room. 'This is the moment that has been planned for centuries. The time foretold and designated from the beginning.'

'Really.' The Doctor whispered to Sam, 'He doesn't know about the TARDIS or the influx of energy from her.'

'Is that good?'

The Doctor's mouth curled down at the edges. 'Well, it's not bad. It means he's not in direct and complete communication with the Khameirian mind. Not yet, anyway.'

'Now is the time,' Silver was continuing, his eyes apparently fixed at a point in space somewhere over and behind the Doctor and Sam. 'This is my time. I am the instrument of the Khameirian. I, Norton Silver, am the purest of the descendants of the original group, with the most of their blood in his veins. The last of the direct family line of Siolfor.'

Sam was about to comment, to offer mock condolences, but the Doctor touched her on the arm and shook his head slightly. So she let Silver continue. Perhaps they might learn something from this, or at least delay him a little.

'The Khameirian has come back to its initial level of strength in me, undiluted by heirs or close relatives. It stops here.' He blinked again, and refocused his gaze on the Doctor. 'It was partly in the hope of getting confirmation of this, before I knew it for certain, before the power grew to the level it has now attained, that I allowed you access to some of the secret documents. I hoped that a man of your obvious learning and knowledge, Doctor, would find evidence to confirm that the Khameirian's rebirth was nigh.'

'But now you don't need any more evidence,' the Doctor pointed out. 'Now that the Khameirian have you in their complete control.' Silver nodded. 'As I said before,' the Doctor told him, 'I'm sorry.'

Silver ignored this last remark. 'Now,' he said, 'I'm afraid I must leave you.'

'Bye,' said Sam.

'But I shall not leave you for long. Or in ignorance. Once the final process is set in motion, I shall return so that you can share our moment of supreme glory.'

'Don't put yourself out on our account.'

Silver did not answer. Sargent and Allworthy followed him from the gallery. Miss Allworthy gave the Doctor and Sam a look of undisguised contempt, and closed the door behind her. She slammed the bolt home, and stood at the bottom of the steps, shotgun over the crook of her arm.

Silver and Sargent meanwhile were powering on the monitors and consoles. The huge map image sprang up once more on the main screen. The other monitors showed other views. Some showed the delegates seated expectantly in the ballroom, others showed dimly lit areas of cramped metal space not unlike the inside of a submarine. Figures in military uniform were going about their business in some of the metal rooms.

'Station Nine?' Sam suggested.

The Doctor nodded, lips pursed. 'Kellerman and his friends have somehow fixed a video link. On the whole,' he went on, 'that might have turned out better.'

'Next time, eh?'

He nodded and grinned. 'There's always a next time.'

'Unless it's the last time.'

'Must you always look on the bright side, Sam? Ah, I think something's happening.'

Another image had sprung up over the central part of the map. It was a circular emblem with a stylised eagle in the centre of it. Around the edge was an inscription. It was the seal of the President of the United States of America.

The circular presidential seal was woven into the carpet. Tom Dering stared at a point just above the eagle's head as Angela Palmer dabbed at his forehead with her powder puff. Not for the first time, he reflected that it was not so much the speeches that strained the nerves as the palaver that went with them. Make-up in particular he detested, although Angela was more than competent. She knew his feelings and did her best to keep things efficient and quick.

Angela untied the grey apron that remained, as ever, spotless, and pulled it away. Underneath, the President's suit was if anything more dishevelled than the apron had been. 'There you are, Mr President,' she said. 'Your own mother wouldn't know you.' It was what she always said. And he smiled politely and thanked her, as he always did.

Agent Summers watched carefully as Angela packed away her things into a small briefcase. The President wrinkled his face in a vain attempt to stop the powder from making his nose itch. He dared not rub it. But it would be something to take his mind off the speech. He had read it through several times, knew it almost as well as if he had written it himself.

And it would be on the autocue. He settled himself behind his desk. The top was completely clear. The powerful light beside the camera reflected off the highly polished wooden surface, and he wondered how long it would be before the video crew noticed and angled the light away.

The words of the speech were already displayed beside the camera lens. The speech would be beamed live across the world. Not to a mass audience for a change, but to just two rooms. One was the ballroom at Abbots Siolfor, where the delegates for the Global Defense Conference were waiting. The other was the main operations deck on Station Nine. He mouthed the first few words of the speech that Pete Kellerman together with his own communications office had drafted for him: 'My fellow citizens of the world…'

'You are gathered together to decide, perhaps, the fate of our entire planet. It is in your hands.'

The room was completely silent apart from the President's voice booming in stereo from a dozen pairs of speakers. His face filled the huge screen above the dais. The view through the window behind him was a larger-than-life landscape over four thousand miles away. The delegates listened, rapt, as President Dering summarised the events of the last few days. They listened just as quietly, if more cynically, as he described how Station Nine had always been intended as the ultimate deterrent, as a truly global guarantor of peace for all time.

'As I speak to you now, my words are also being relayed to the multinational force on Station Nine itself.' The President nodded, knowing that the phrasing might surprise some of the delegates.

Susan Rogers crumpled her empty Styrofoam cup and tossed it into a nearby bin. In the last hour she had been replaced as commander of Station Nine. She was prepared to listen to her President's explanation as it was relayed to the main monitor on the satellite's control deck. But she wasn't prepared to like it.

'That's right,' Dering was saying, 'multinational. Because just an hour ago the first of the UN observers arrived on the station aboard the shuttle *Inspire*. Even now, command of the station has passed to the United Nations in the form of Colonel Jean-Pierre de Tannerie of the Royal Canadian Army.'

In the ballroom, Pete Kellerman, sitting at the front of the room, wondered whether it really was called the Royal Canadian Army. Probably he should have gotten that checked out. Sounded impressive, though. And de Tannerie was certainly the man for the job.

'I wish you well in your deliberations.' The President's voice was slightly tinny through the small speakers at the back of the observation gallery. 'The future of the world, of our planet, of our children's peace, rests with you over the next few days. God bless our world.'

'He was obviously careful not to mention America,' Sam said.

'The word, not the thought,' the Doctor qualified. 'Echoes of imperialism,' he offered grandly.

'Is that a quote?'

'It is now.'

They both turned at the sound of the bolt being drawn. Silver pushed open the door and stepped into the gallery. He held a pistol in one hand – the other hand was thrust into his jacket pocket. 'Now that the speeches are over, we can get on with the main event.'

'And that is what, pray?'

'Patience, Doctor, patience.' He gestured to the main

chamber outside with his gun. 'First we have to patch through our communications.'

Even as he spoke, Sargent was typing furiously into a console in the room below them. He sat back and pointed to the main screen. The President's seal, which had replaced the man himself when his speech ended, was in turn replaced by another image. It was similar to the main map display that had filled the screen earlier and the edges of which were still visible, acting as a frame for the new picture. But this map showed the United States at the centre of the world, and it was annotated with many more symbols and legends.

'Ah, good. It seems that Kellerman's codes work.'

'Kellerman being the US National Security Adviser.'

Silver turned. 'It seems that you too are well advised, Miss Jones.'

Sam scowled. 'I hate villains who call me Miss Jones,' she told him. 'It makes me feel like a Bond girl.'

'But this,' Silver responded, 'is high theatre, as the Doctor has pointed out. Not action adventure where the dashing hero saves the day despite the insuperable odds, but rather tragedy.'

'Don't bet on it, Mr Silver.'

'That image,' the Doctor interrupted, pointing to the map now displayed on the far wall of the chamber, 'where exactly is it being relayed from?'

'From the Briefing Chamber on the third floor of the Pentagon.' Silver's reply was almost smug. 'What they see, we see.'

The Doctor's eyes narrowed. 'And what we see, they see?'

'How right you are, Doctor. How right you are.'

'Of course. That's how you get the massive influx of energy you need to complete the process.' The Doctor slumped back in his seat, his own energy seemingly drained by his terrible realisation. 'So why not kill us now? Why let us sit it out?'

'Oh,' Silver said, a smile baring his sharp teeth, 'I have a use for you yet, Doctor.'

'What is it, Doctor?' Sam was disconcerted by the Doctor's defeatist tone. 'What's going on?'

'Go on, Doctor,' Silver encouraged, the glee evident in his voice. 'Why not tell her?'

'The Khameirian needs a vast amount of energy to free itself from its human constraints, and become corporeal again. The sort of energy only released in a nuclear blast.'

'You told me that before, Doctor. So?'

'So we know that the Khameirian agents have a computer simulation that was good enough to allow Roskov to fire his missiles.'

'Something knocked up by a couple of our fellows,' Silver said with pride. 'Our influence extends even to Silicon Valley and MIT. Or did, I should say. They are of course upstairs now. Guests of mine who happened to be invited here ahead of the conference.'

'And, I imagine, all the members of the Society are here in some capacity, all the people infected with the Khameirian mind.'

'Indeed. The simulation program for Colonel Roskov was a work of art, an adaptation of one of the base's own simulations, but modified so that the simulation safety features were no longer an inhibitor.'

'And I assume you have another program. Another simulation.'

Silver nodded. 'And this one,' he said, 'is a work of theatre. Elegant in its simplicity. It merely feeds data into the Pentagon systems. Data to which those systems will respond with their own pre-programmed inevitability.' He turned to face the front wall of the gallery, taking his left hand from his pocket. He made a gesture with his left index finger, exaggerated so that

233

Sargent in the room below could see it, could interpret what he meant. The gesture was a focused stabbing motion, like the pressing of a button. A moment later, a light started flashing on one side of the map. Electronic ripples seemed to emanate from the point, like a seismic event. At the same moment a klaxon sounded.

General Kane reacted at once to the loud, insistent sound of the alarm. He swung round in his chair – the chair he had spent most of the last few days sitting in while he had debriefed his staff time and time again.

The map of the wall of the Emergency Conference Room showed the source of the alert. A tiny point of light winked on and off, concentric circles flashing in turn so they seemed to radiate from the point. Everyone in the room had the same point of focus. The klaxon seemed to scream in time to the radiating circles flashing on the map.

'Sir.' The operator leaned forward, a genuine but misguided attempt at discretion. He handed the Chairman of the Joint Chiefs of Staff a flimsy printout of the initial analysis.

Kane took one look at it, then screwed the paper into a ball. He threw it to the floor as he stood up. At the same moment a monitor at the side of the room flickered into life and President Dering's face appeared, seeming to watch Kane as he spoke.

'OK, listen up, everyone.' As if in response to his words, the klaxon faded as someone found the volume control. 'We have an unconfirmed launch in mainland China. The preliminary data is not good, and we hope to confirm real soon now.' On the map, two more points started flashing, close to the first. The radiating circles overlapped as they appeared around the focal points. 'Make that multiple unconfirmed launches,' Kane said. He turned to face the President's screen. For reasons of ergonomics, the cameras were arranged at both ends of the link so that looking at the image of a person made it appear to the person at the other end that they were being looked at.

'Mr President,' Kane said, 'these launches may be unconfirmed as yet, but may I suggest we go to DefCon-2?'

Dering nodded. 'Horner's not here yet, but we don't need to wait. Go to DefCon-2, General.' He was calmer this time, more composed. He evidently thought he knew what to expect.

'Thank you, sir. And may I suggest you have Station Nine stand by for a possible NUKILL?'

'They're already patched through to your operational data,' the President told him. 'I'm ready to release the codes.'

13
Releasing the Codes

The sound of the pager was unnaturally loud in the confined metal space. Captain William Pickering leapt from his bunk, his head colliding with the low ceiling. He cursed, grabbed his jacket, and hurried from his cabin.

Typical, he thought as he made his way to the control deck. He had been on Station Nine long enough for a quick tour of the satellite and a few minutes' rest after the shuttle flight. Now this. Whatever 'this' was.

He realised almost immediately what was happening when he arrived on deck. Colonel de Tannerie and his immediate command staff were gathered round the main terminal. Pickering and the other observers stood at the back of the group, peering the best they could over their shoulders. There were only two other observers so far on Station Nine: Zina Chreschky, a tall, thin Russian woman with severe blonde hair and an angular face, and a small Frenchman, Pierre Latour.

Pickering knew enough about the state of the art in nuclear command-and-control systems to see that there were multiple launches marked off in China. Whether these were probables or actuals, he could not tell. Most likely it was too early for them yet to be confirmed.

'It never rains but it pours,' Pickering said quietly. He heard a soft, female chuckle behind him.

'I guess, as a Brit, you'd know that, right?' It was Susan Rogers. They had met earlier, when she handed over command of the facility to Colonel de Tannerie, who had been on the same shuttle flight as Pickering and the other observers. She had done her duty in the overpolite and efficient manner of someone who resents it. Pickering could quite understand why. She had done the job perfectly, executing her orders to the letter under extreme circumstances and proving the capabilities of her command. And her reward had been to be replaced. Worse than that, after years of living with the secret of Station Nine, of keeping the knowledge within a small group that had become almost an extended family, she had handed over control to a complete outsider. Different army, different country, even a different first language.

'You do seem to be kept busy,' Pickering told her. He led her to the back of the room. Nothing would happen now for several minutes, until they got confirmation of the launch. 'Tell me,' Pickering asked, 'how does the system work? I mean the release-and-control system.'

'We can't fire our weapons without the control key. Only the President can authorise a launch, in which case he sends us the key and the target information. It's quite straightforward.'

'So what's to stop you reusing the key he sent you last time?'

She smiled. 'This isn't the Dark Ages, you know. We're not still reliant on two people opening a safe when they agree they've been properly ordered to and taking out a printed set of codes. Technology has moved on.'

'So what happens?'

'There are two identical computer chips, each using the same program to generate random numbers at regular intervals. Every three minutes, in fact.'

'From the same seed?' Pickering asked. He was beginning to see how it worked.

'Exactly. The chips generate exactly the same number, randomly, at exactly the same time. One of the chips is in the President's Doomsday Box. The other is here, embedded at the heart of our control systems. The President has a PIN, a number only he knows. Well, the Vice-President and the Chairman of the JCS have it too, of course.'

'And that PIN, typed into a keypad attached to the other chip, tells him what the current random number is?'

Rogers nodded. 'It also tells him when it will expire and be replaced by another. So he may choose to wait, if there's less than, say, a minute, and signal the next number in the sequence.'

'So, you receive the number – the trigger code – together with the target package. And you program them both into your systems.'

'Right. The trigger code both authenticates and authorises. It authorises us to prime the system for the window of time that the code lasts until the next number is generated. We can fire at any time, but the target package must be loaded during that interval. If the code matches ours, then we know it can only have come from a legitimate source. Equally, we couldn't fire without the legitimate authorisation.' She started back towards the terminal. 'It's all quite fail-safe,' she said as her parting shot.

Pickering watched her rejoin her new commanding officer. 'Nothing is quite fail-safe,' he said quietly to himself. 'It's all dependent on the President's decision, for one thing.'

The President had already made up his mind. He was well aware that his hesitation during the last crisis, his reluctance to release the trigger codes when his military advisers wanted them, had been justified only by the existence of Station Nine. By all the measures he could possibly have been aware of at the time, his decision to delay had been wrong. He had agonised over it in his dreams – both sleeping and waking nightmares. He would not make the same mistake again.

There was a sense of *déjà vu* coupled with a general depression in the White House Situation Room – a feeling that events were somehow getting out of control. Vice-President Michaels had gone straight to Andrews Air Force Base this time, as if the previous crisis had been a sort of dress rehearsal. Kellerman was at the UN conference in England. Both attended the session by video link. Defense Secretary Horner and President Dering sat together. The Bag Man was a few seats away, impassive as stone.

Station Nine also made a difference. Its very existence, and the fact that it had proved so effective against the Krejikistan missiles, lent an added layer of unreality to the proceedings. If the Chinese had launched an attack, they had done it knowing how deadly and efficient the response would be. Unless they somehow hoped the UN involvement would water down that response, or add a level of confusion that would mitigate or remove the role of the satellite.

'I'm inclined,' Dering said as the waiting seconds dragged into minutes and there was still no firm confirmation of an actual launch, 'to release the trigger codes to Station Nine now.'

'That involves a certain...' Horner paused, seeking a diplomatic phrase. He settled on 'loss of control'.

Kellerman, however, disagreed. The video link across the Atlantic was far from ideal, his movements seeming choppy and disjointed as the satellite communications struggled to achieve an adequate frame rate. 'It seems a prudent move to me, Mr President. Once we get confirmation, there may be little time for the formality of code authentication. And there is the political angle.'

Dering considered this. 'You mean, if I release the codes now, make it clear that this is a transfer of authority to the station commander, then the decision to destroy the missiles is a UN decision, not ours alone.'

'That's exactly what I mean, sir.'

'What if this Canadian colonel decides not to shoot them down?' Horner asked. His tone betrayed his opposition to the idea of early release.

But Kellerman had an answer. 'If he decides not to shoot them, that's what he decides. When he gets the codes makes no difference. In fact, the longer he has the codes, the less excuse he has for failing to make the kill.'

Dering turned to the monitor linking the White House to the Pentagon. 'What's your opinion, General Kane?'

Kane's answer was immediate. 'I do share Secretary Horner's reservations, Mr President. But that is mainly because I don't know Colonel de Tannerie. I haven't looked him in the eye, or seen the sweat on his brow. From a purely military perspective, the longer you have to prepare for an engagement, any sort of engagement, the better – the more chance of a successful outcome. That said, you have to recognise that this is primarily a political decision, Mr President.'

Dering stared at the table in front of him. Every line of the wood grain below the polish was suddenly starkly visible. The lines were intricate and unique, like a fingerprint. Like the nerves thrown in patterns by a magic lantern. When the President looked up, it was to the Emergency War Officer, the Bag Man, that he turned. 'Give me the card,' he said.

'Yes, Mr President.' The officer dialled in a combination on each of the locks on the briefcase in front of him. Then he held out his free hand, the one that was not chained to the case, and took the small key the President held out to him. He unlocked the case, and opened it.

Inside the case, held securely in place by the foam packaging, was a row of thin cards. Each card slot was labelled, with the exception of the bottom right card. The Bag

Man removed the card from the unlabelled slot. It was slightly larger than a credit card, and on its face were ten touch-sensitive buttons bearing the digits 0 to 9. Above these was an LED readout line. The officer took the card carefully from the case, and handed it to the President.

Dering looked at the card he held in his hand. So small, so powerful. 'Ready, General?'

'The Emergency Action Message is ready, Mr President. We just need the code.'

Dering tapped in his personal identification number on the buttons. It was an eight-digit number, and it changed every month. But he knew it off by heart, knew it as if all the lives in his care depended on it. As he tapped the last digit, the readout changed from the number he had typed to another number. It filled the readout, all twenty-four digits. A bar of colour down the left of the readout indicated for how much longer the trigger code was valid. It had almost expired, and Dering waited several seconds until the bar of colour faded to nothing. At once it filled up again as the code number changed.

The President of the United States took a deep breath and read out the number on the Station Nine trigger card. When he had finished, he leaned back in his chair and closed his eyes.

Over four thousand miles away, Kellerman cut the video link and got to his feet. He was in Silver's control room. Silver, Sargent, and Miss Allworthy had all watched the deliberations, but from out of the view of the video camera.

'Won't they be suspicious that you cut the link?' Sargent asked.

It was Silver who answered. 'It doesn't matter now. De Tannerie has the codes.' He turned to Kellerman. 'Well done.'

'Thank you,' Kellerman said. 'Now I guess it's time we invited a few more people to the party.' He looked up at the observation gallery, where the Doctor and Sam sat staring out. Both had their chins cradled in their cupped hands, elbows resting on their knees.

Pickering looked bored. But Susan Rogers knew that in fact he was paying close attention to everything that was happening. She had seen the keen black points of his pupils as his eyes darted about, watching everything. She saw him frown slightly as Colonel de Tannerie programmed in the target instructions himself. His back was to them so they could not see precisely what he was doing.

'It's a holding instruction,' Rogers told Pickering. 'Dummy co-ordinates, probably out in space somewhere. The instructions can be altered later, once we have an actual target. But we have to enter something now to use the trigger code.'

'I thought you couldn't change the target package once it was entered with the correct trigger code.'

So, he had been paying attention. And, more impressively, he had understood and remembered what she had told him. 'That's true, under normal circumstances. In this case we have a target package that in effect defers the entry of the actual target. It authorises the entry of the real data at a later time.'

'Pre-authentication.'

'If you like.'

'Not much,' Pickering said. 'Difficult to keep control.'

'Meaning what?'

'Meaning Colonel de Tannerie could be entering anything he likes.'

Susan Rogers looked back at de Tannerie. Not for the first time she reflected that she knew next to nothing about him, except that he had an impressive record. But so far he had done everything by the book.

De Tannerie turned and looked round the assembled officers. 'You all know the situation,' he said. His French-Canadian accent was noticeable, but not intrusive. 'We have been authorised to launch a counter-offensive against a suspected Chinese nuclear attack on the United States. The final operational decision has now, with the release of the trigger codes, passed to this station's command. To me.' He paused. 'We cannot afford anything or anyone to influence our impartiality in making that decision. That is why I am now taking this station to silent running.'

Rogers gasped. Everything by the book. Until now. 'Sir,' she called out across the room, 'I must object. We don't have the surveillance or intelligence capabilities on our own to –'

De Tannerie cut her off. 'This is not a suggestion,' he shouted. 'It is an order from your commanding officer.' He waited a moment to see if she responded to this. But Susan Rogers just shook her head slightly, and looked at the floor. De Tannerie went on, 'From this point until the crisis is resolved, there will be no external communication either into or out of Station Nine.'

'We're on our own,' Geoff Harrison said quietly to Janet Timms, 'at last.' She laughed.

Harrison was a tall thin Texan with an angular face and not an ounce of surplus fat anywhere on his body. He was in his late forties, and he knew Timms from Anglo-American backroom discussion sessions at the UN. They were old sparring partners.

Janet Timms was slightly younger, a well-preserved forty-three who could pass for thirty-five. She was considerably shorter than Harrison. 'I'd hardly call this "alone",' she said, looking round the ballroom. Her slightly nasal, public-school tone contrasted with Harrison's careless drawl. There did seem, however, to be rather fewer people about than there had been before the emergency. Most of the others were probably on the phone or frantically checking their e-mail for advice and information. Of the fifty delegates at the conference, there were perhaps fifteen left in the ballroom.

They both turned in surprise as the main doors crashed open. Around the room other faces turned too, to see Norton Silver step into the ballroom. There was a sudden silence after the loud noise, like the embarrassed pause as a stranger walks into a local pub on a stormy night. It was broken by Silver.

'Take them below,' he said. His face was a mask that mixed contempt with a suggestion of indifference.

'Now just a minute,' Harrison called out as Silver turned on his heel and left the room again. 'What do you mean –' He did not finish.

Tanner, Sargent, and Miss Allworthy, together with several of the delegates, were standing in the doorway. Each was holding a machine pistol. They fanned out into the room, pushing the remaining delegates back towards the door, where other armed accomplices waited to herd them away. Harrison saw Manuel Estavez pull Helene Buchier roughly aside, grabbing her by the elbow. Estavez's face was set, impassive. His eyes were dead holes. Harrison had no time to comment or react before he and Janet Timms were also forced towards the main doors.

Startled and nervous, the delegates allowed themselves to be escorted through the house. Harrison gasped in surprise as he was prodded through yet another door at gunpoint. They were in what looked like a home-built version of Cape Canaveral. Everywhere he could see, black candles flickered, ragged and bizarre wax shapes spilling down their sides and distorting their form. A huge map display covered one wall, and, even as Harrison noticed a cluster of flashing lights over a corner of China, they winked out of existence and the screen darkened.

'What happened?' Dering stared at the screen. It took him a moment even to work out what had changed. Then he realised that something had vanished from the display rather than been added to it.

Kane was still visible on a monitor, though Kellerman's link seemed to have gone down. The general was talking urgently to an operative. He held his hand up, asking his President to wait a moment, while he finished the hushed conversation. When he turned back to the camera, his expression was ambivalent.

'Well?' President Dering asked. 'What's happening?'

'It would appear that we have a negative confirmation of the launch, Mr President.'

'What?'

'There has been no launch. The Chinese deny there has been any military activity in the area we identified. It seems they were telling the truth. Even the satellite that raised the alarm now has no record of a rocket plume.'

'How can that be?' Horner asked with the trace of a nervous laugh.

Kane drew a deep breath. 'Frankly, sir, we have no idea. Rogue data from somewhere. Somehow.'

'OK, General, let's worry about that later.' Dering rubbed his eyes. 'Signal Station Nine to stand down.'

Kane coughed. 'Er, that's the other thing, Mr President.' Suddenly he looked embarrassed. 'We are unable to make contact with Station Nine.'

'You mean you can't raise them?'

'I mean, sir, that they have instigated a complete

communications blackout.' He shrugged, almost apologetically. 'It's real quiet up there.'

The room was in darkness. Silver picked his way carefully across towards the bed. He moved extremely quietly for such a big man. But even so, his wife stirred, turned over in bed, seeming to sense his presence.

'How's it going, darling?' she asked, her voice heavy with sleep. She was so tired these days. So tired.

'It's going well,' Silver said softly. He reached out, allowed his hand the brush her cheek. 'Very well.'

She took his hand, and held it against her face. 'Are you coming to bed?'

'Not yet. Things are still happening.'

'I don't know how you do it,' she sighed. 'I'd be asleep by now even normally. Don't be too long. You need your sleep too.' Her voice faded with her grip on his hand. She was drifting back into sleep.

Silver looked down at Penelope, her form outlined by the duvet, her long hair spread over the pillow and cascading over the side of the bed. A sound came from his throat, a sound which might have been a stifled cough or an intake of breath. Or a suppressed sob. 'I just came to say good night,' he said. He reached out towards his wife, made to stroke her hair. But his hand stopped short. 'Good night,' he whispered again. Then he leaned over, and kissed her for the last time.

'For the last time,' Sam said to Geoff Harrison, 'they are not terrorists.'

The Observation Gallery was noisy. It was by no means full, but there were fifteen UN delegates all talking loudly and nervously to each other in an enclosed space. Sam was arguing with Geoff Harrison and Janet Timms. The Doctor sat between them, his hands over his ears, watching what was happening in the main control room outside.

After the initial silence of disbelief, Sam had introduced herself and the Doctor to Harrison, who just happened to be the nearest person. The Doctor had nodded a sympathetic welcome and muttered something about having been seconded to a UN body a while back for scientific and military work. Now fright and nerves had set people talking loudly to each other.

'Then what are they?' Timms asked, shouting to make herself heard.

'Misguided,' the Doctor said. His voice was surprisingly soft. 'Afflicted.' Yet it seemed to carry across the room. 'Desperate.' As he spoke, so the other conversations seemed to quieten until the ambient level of sound was down to a reasonable volume. 'Good,' the Doctor said. 'Now you can hear me think.'

'And what do you think?' Sam asked.

'I think I know what's going on.'

'Then perhaps you would care to enlighten us,' Timms suggested.

'Certainly,' the Doctor agreed with a grin. 'But you'd never believe me.'

'There are a lot of things we'd never believe,' Harrison replied. 'I'd never believe Manuel Estavez would get mixed up in something like this for one. To say nothing of the rest of them.'

Timms was shaking her head. 'Norton Silver, too. What the hell is going on here?'

'I'm afraid we don't have time to go into all the details, all the ins and outs. But suffice it to say it's in the blood. Breeding.'

'And that's your great revelation, is it?'

'Why don't you shut up for a minute if you really want to

hear what he has to say?' Sam was angry. Partly she was angry with Harrison, but she was also frustrated that there seemed to be nothing they could do.

'So what's Silver up to, Doctor?' Timms asked.

'By now, I would think he has control of Station Nine.'

'How?'

The Doctor looked surprised. 'It doesn't matter how, but that's his objective.'

'To what end?' Timms asked.

'Oh that's quite simple. Silver wants Station Nine to launch its nuclear missiles at a location on the Earth's surface. I imagine this farce,' he gestured at the map at the far end of the room, 'is something to do with getting the trigger codes released.'

Harrison and Timms exchanged glances. 'I'm not sure I buy it,' Harrison said at length. 'But let's take it as a straw man for now. That just leaves one obvious question. Two, if you ask why he's doing this at all.'

'The obvious question I'd like answered,' Sam told him, 'is what is a straw man?'

'It's a proposal,' Janet Timms said. 'Usually one made just to get discussions going. One you expect to be knocked down.'

'Crikey,' Sam said. 'What a language.'

'You'd prefer Latin?' the Doctor asked with a slight smile.

'The question I had,' Harrison interrupted, 'is where is he going to aim the missiles?'

'Oh that's an easy one.' The Doctor tapped his foot on the floor. 'Here.'

'Here?'

'Well, give or take a half-mile.' He looked from Sam to Harrison to Timms. His eyes had a deep intensity now as he spoke, an urgency echoed in his voice. 'I said you wouldn't believe me, and we don't have time to go through all the proof. But Silver aims to destroy this house together with the people he's managed to gather inside as a result of revealing the existence of Station Nine, and only incidentally will he wipe out about half of Britain. The force of the explosion will release the Khameirian life essence from the people who carry it within them and from the Philosopher's Stone. The energy will be sufficient to re-create the Khameirian and revitalise their spaceship in the grounds outside. And the reason he hasn't killed us, and hasn't killed me in particular, I suspect, is that he wants our minds to be absorbed by the Khameirian at the moment of their re-creation.'

'You're right,' Harrison drawled after a suitable pause. 'I don't believe you.' He gave a short laugh. 'Hell, I don't even understand you.'

'Not,' Timms said, 'that you have a better explanation.'

'True enough. But it's academic anyway. Station Nine will never fire its missiles, that much is certain.'

'Oh?' said Sam. 'What makes you so sure?'

Harrison rounded on her. 'Because those of us who have known anything at all about Station Nine also know that for each installation – including this one – there are fail-safe cutouts that can be operated from Cheyenne Mountain. Those fail-safes will defuse the missiles and turn them into lumps of harmless metal that will at worst survive re-entry and crash into a field somewhere.'

'You could be right, actually.' The Doctor was peering at one of the monitors in the room below. He pointed it out to Harrison and the others. 'Silver has several video links of his own. He has one to Station Nine, despite their communications blackout. Probably put in place by de Tannerie.' The Doctor pointed to a monitor at the front of the room. A group of people were standing round on the Station Nine control deck. Sam could just make out Colonel de Tannerie at what seemed to be the main console. 'He also has a link directly to the Pentagon systems,' the Doctor went on. 'See.'

On the screen the Doctor indicated, the words FAIL-SAFE PROCEDURES ACTIVATED had appeared. Sargent waved to Silver and Kellerman, and they joined him in front of the terminal, blocking off the view of the screen from the gallery. As Sam watched, Silver turned away, rubbing his hands together and laughing. Kellerman shook his head, and followed Silver.

'They don't seem very concerned,' Sam pointed out.

As Kellerman followed Silver, so the screen was visible again. Across the FAIL-SAFE PROCEDURES ACTIVATED message was flashing TRANSMISSION FAILURE.

Dering stared at the screen in disbelief. Before he could comment, Kane's voice came from the monitor beside him. It sounded slightly squeaky, partly because of the quality of the speakers, and partly through anxiety.

'Mr President, at the same time that they blanked out their communications, they also removed the ability for us to send the fail-safe signal. We cannot disarm the weapons by remote control.'

'And now they have the codes,' Horner said, thinking aloud, 'they can fire those missiles at any target they choose.'

'Only the three missiles we released, thirty-six warheads in all. But yes, sir, they can.'

Dering's fist slammed down on the table in front of him. Further along, a coffee cup bounced in its saucer. 'What are they doing up there?' he hissed.

'What is he doing?' Pickering whispered. He was standing beside Susan Rogers on the control deck. Colonel de Tannerie was still at the main console, seemingly oblivious to anyone or anything else. Rogers was sitting at an ancillary terminal.

Pickering had one hand on the back of her chair, the other on the top of the desk.

'I don't know,' Rogers admitted. She pointed to the status report on the screen. 'He's cut off all communications in and out. But why…' She threw her hands up in confusion. As if in response a message flashed up on the screen. They both read it. 'My God,' Rogers breathed. 'He's getting ready to launch.'

'Have we had confirmation of the Chinese launch?'

'Who knows? I can't tell from here. But what else is he going to launch at?'

'Can I see the original Emergency Action Message that released the trigger codes and authorised their use?'

Rogers turned to look at Pickering. His voice had sounded suddenly more distant, detached. There was a deep, faraway look in his eyes. 'Of course,' she said, and reached for the keyboard. She read through the message again while Pickering examined it on the screen. It was brief and to the point. Exactly what she would have expected.

'Is this it?' His voice was still odd. Strained.

'Yep.'

'There's nothing else?' There was an urgency now too. 'No other communications from the White House or the Pentagon?'

'Nothing.'

She felt his hand close tightly on her shoulder. 'Are you sure? Nothing?'

She pulled away, shook her shoulder free. 'Yes, of course I'm sure.' She stood up and faced him across the keyboard. 'What's got into you.'

Pickering blinked. 'I'm sorry,' he said. 'I… I had to know.' He shrugged. 'I'm sorry,' he said again, and she sensed he was apologising for something more than his insistence.

* * *

'So much for technology,' Janet Timms said. 'And for the special relationship.'

'How do you mean?'

'Come on, Geoff. How neutral can Station Nine be if you have a fail-safe override? Even if it doesn't actually work.'

Harrison looked down at the floor without comment.

Timms continued her attack. 'And what about the agreements with NATO to consult before taking precipitate action? Did Dering get authorisation from Downing Street before he passed on the trigger codes? This time or the last?'

Harrison laughed. 'You're kidding? Why should you Brits have any say in our self-defence?'

Timms was angry at that. 'Because we have an agreement. That's why.'

Harrison was shouting too. 'But this is war. Nobody in their right mind would allow another power or group of powers control of a weapon like this.'

Sam stepped between them, hands held up for silence. 'Excuse me, but I think we have rather more immediate problems than some petty diplomatic squabble.'

'It's not petty,' Timms argued, her voice low and hard. 'It's to do with who really controls the release of nuclear weapons.'

'Is it? Well Norton Silver does at the moment. So just can it, will you?'

Timms laughed. 'No he doesn't. He might think he does, but that's different.'

'Janet,' Harrison said quietly, 'the fail-safes had no effect. You just saw that.'

Before Timms could answer, the Doctor intervened. 'I rather think there might be another fail-safe.'

'Another one?'

The Doctor nodded. 'Yes, yes.' He took Janet Timms by the elbow and leaned forward conspiratorially. 'Isn't that what you're telling us?'

She looked at the Doctor, then at Harrison and Sam. 'All right,' she said after considering. 'Yes, there is another fail-safe. Geoff is right, you know. Nobody in their right mind would be prepared to let another power have complete control of a weapon like this.' She looked directly at Harrison. 'Any more than we are prepared to let you control Station Nine's weapons.'

Harrison was gaping. 'You're telling me you have your own fail-safe systems installed on Station Nine? The most secret military installation in the history of warfare, and you have an override?'

'Yes,' she said simply. 'Now that we know about it, yes we do.'

'What override? How does it work?'

'I can't tell you that. But I can tell you that unless the release of weapons was accompanied by a particular code phrase, one we would have added to the Emergency Action Message once we agreed with the release order, those weapons will not be fired.'

Harrison's eyebrows knitted together as he frowned. 'You're bluffing,' he said at last.

'Is she?' Sam asked the Doctor.

The Doctor shrugged. 'I don't know,' he said. 'But we shall find out soon enough.' He pointed down into the control room again. 'The Americans have reorientated a spy satellite. Silver's intercepting its transmissions as well. Look.' On the main screen the map had been replaced by another image. It showed a large satellite, a space station built round a central axis, revolving slowly against a backdrop of stars. Limbs stretched out from the central structure, and from these limbs hung heavy, blunt-nosed pods.

As they watched, the ends of three of the pods broke open and swung away.

* * *

'My God,' Secretary Horner said as they watched the pods open, 'he's really going to do it.'

Dering said nothing. He sat transfixed, watching the nightmare unfold on the screen in front of him. The silo doors hinged away, revealing the tips of the missiles sheathed inside.

'He's opened the doors,' Rogers said. 'All safety features are off.'

She looked round, and saw that Pickering was no longer behind her. Across the room, Colonel de Tannerie was leaning forward, his finger pointing at the firing button on the main console. On the wall behind, his enlarged shadow went through the same slow-motion sequence. Finger closing on button. And from where Susan Rogers sat, it seemed as if the curl of the shadow's finger was a long-nailed talon, reaching down. A claw.

Then, just as the finger reached the button, the shadow was gone in a sudden intense burst of light.

The marble egg of the Philosopher's Stone seemed to be about to crack open, to burst under the strain of its internal luminance. Its shape could no longer be discerned, the glow was so fierce. And with every moment it grew stronger; with every second the rebirth of the Khameirian – the Becoming – edged closer.

14
Becoming

Silver had called it 'theatre', Sam remembered. As she watched it on the big screen, she felt it was more like cinema in presentation. But the involvement she felt was very real, not the vicarious thrill of someone else's imagined danger. The inability to take part in the events that were actually taking place was more frustrating than when she had watched, helpless, as Roskov fired his missiles. This time she could see the people involved, could imagine all too easily what they might be thinking and feeling. One in particular.

'The lambs to the slaughter,' she murmured, and heard Janet Timms gasp.

'How did you know?' Timms demanded, grabbing Sam roughly by the shoulder. 'How did you know the code phrase?'

Sam shook off her grip, did not look from the screen, did not think what it might mean that the phrase had risen unbidden in her mind. Made no connection.

The camera afforded a good view of the control deck of Station Nine. In the foreground at the left edge of the frame, a woman was rising slowly to her feet and turning towards Colonel de Tannerie. He was centre stage, further away. But Sam could clearly see his finger pointing down towards the console, towards what she imagined must be a large red button. A point of no return. The officers and crew grouped around the console seemed oblivious to what was happening, with the exception perhaps of the woman still turning in slow motion, dreamlike. On the wall behind de Tannerie, the red-tinged lighting threw a grotesque caricature of a shadow, an image formed as if by a distorting mirror. Three points of movement only: de Tannerie's finger; the woman, turning; and Bill Pickering.

Pickering was on the right of the frame. He was the only one who seemed to be moving in real time, although probably it was the sudden speed of his actions that seemed to slow the others. His right arm extended, his hand flat as it chopped into the throat of the armed guard by the door. Before the guard had fully reacted, Pickering already had his machine pistol, had ripped the strap from his shoulder, swung the weapon in an arc as he lowered it and brought his left hand up to steady the stock.

The woman on the left of the picture flinched at the muzzle flash. Or perhaps at the noise, though, since Sam could hear nothing, she had no way of knowing how loud it might be. Silent movie.

Despite the speed, the burst of fire seemed well aimed. De Tannerie's finger was within an inch of the firing button when the bullets ripped into his chest. His hand jerked away as his body was lifted off the floor and slammed over the top of the console. He crashed into the wall behind, hanging for a moment in defiance of the artificial gravity. Then the base commander smeared his way down the wall before toppling forward on to his face.

Sam heard herself cry out, a quick gasp of escaping sound. She felt an arm round her shoulders, pulling her close in a hug, and knew it was the Doctor. She felt her cheek meet the material of his shirt. The vision in one eye was slightly obscured now, but she could not look away. Not yet. On the big screen Pickering was herding everyone out of the room, past the camera, off stage.

The woman who stood on the left of the shot was the last one to leave the room. She spoke soundlessly to Pickering, and he kept the gun lowered. Everyone else he had threatened. After a short exchange, the woman left, too. She paused as she passed Pickering, touched him lightly, delicately almost, on the arm. Sam looked away, feeling the sob welling up in her chest, and the pang of jealousy rising with it in her throat as she buried her face in the Doctor's chest.

A moment later, Sam felt herself being gently lowered into one of the seats. She wiped her eyes and looked round blearily. Most of the conference delegates in the observation gallery were also sitting down. There were several muffled conversations, but most people were just staring at the images on the main screen, too stunned and surprised to move or speak.

Sam forced herself to look back as the screen, wishing the silent movie were also in black and white. The red smear on the wall was a ragged line breaking down the very centre of the picture. The size of the image meant that the edges of the stain were rough and pixellated. The colour balance was slightly maladjusted, so the blood seemed to glow both on the wall and on the floor where it formed a pool and ran off in narrow rivulets.

'Now is the moment,' the Doctor whispered close to Sam's ear. 'Now might I do it, pat, while they're distracted.'

'I'm Sam, not Pat,' she managed to say. Even she could hear the break in her voice.

The Doctor frowned at her. 'No no no no no no no.' The sonic screwdriver was in his hand and he waved it at her in admonishment. 'It's Shakespeare.'

'Pat Shakespeare?' She knew he was doing this deliberately. Setting her up. She was grateful for it.

'I despair of you sometimes.'

Sam smiled. A weak, thin gesture, but a smile nonetheless.

The Doctor grinned back, and slapped the sonic screwdriver

into the palm of his hand. It made a heavy, distinctly metallic sound. 'Not very often,' he admitted, 'but sometimes.'

'So what's the plan?' In the room below them Sam could see that Silver and his colleagues were totally absorbed by the image on the main screen. They milled around, talking to each other, desperately operating controls on the consoles to no apparent avail while Pickering sat at the main console in the sealed control deck on Station Nine. He seemed to stare back at them, gun across his lap, totally still. Action and inaction.

Apart from Sam, only Timms and Harrison seemed at all interested in what the Doctor was up to as he crouched at the foot of the door. The door was made of the same transparent material as the rest of the gallery. The bolt was clearly visible on the other side, and it was clearly not moving.

'Not very good with bolts,' the Doctor admitted as he adjusted the screwdriver. 'I'll try to turn this into a powerful electromagnet.'

'I suggest you hurry up,' Timms told him.

'I suggest you accept that posting in Washington,' the Doctor retorted without looking up. 'When it arrives, that is. I know it's an upheaval and the children are at a critical point at school, but they'll do well in the long run.' There was a low scraping sound as the bolt started slowly to move. 'Malcolm in particular will get a lot out of it, I'm sure,' the Doctor finished.

Like the Doctor, Sam was crouched down, concentrating almost all her attention on the bolt as it started to slide back in its socket. She heard Janet Timms struggle to form an answer to the Doctor's comments, and she could imagine the confusion and bewilderment on her face. But before she could turn and see it for real, there was the tapping sound.

From his expression, the Doctor was also confused by the noise. It was definitely coming from the door, but it did not seem to be the bolt making the noise. The Doctor looked at

Sam. She shrugged. He looked back at the bolt. They both leaned closer. It was still moving, almost out of the socket now. Just a few more seconds…

They both seemed to realise at the same moment that the tapping was from higher up the door. The Doctor and Sam exchanged glances again. Behind them, Harrison cleared his throat, obviously trying to get their attention. Sam looked up, aware that the Doctor was doing the same beside her.

On the other side of the door, standing on the small landing at the top of the steps up from the main control room, was Norton Silver. He was knocking gently on the door with his forefinger, his manicured nail hitting the glass with a regular tapping sound. He was smiling.

The bolt finally slid fully back. Silver pulled the door open. Behind him stood Kellerman, holding a pistol.

'Thank you, Doctor.' Silver's voice echoed slightly in the enclosed chamber. 'My friends and I have had a little discussion about the latest turn of events.'

'I can imagine,' the Doctor said pulling himself to his feet and dusting at his knees. The sonic screwdriver had already disappeared into a pocket somewhere. 'Things not going quite according to plan, are they?'

'Sadly, no. Which is why I need to get to Station Nine. Rather urgently.'

'Bon voyage,' Sam told him.

'It looks as if I shall have to go to Station Nine and fire the missiles myself. Sadly, I shall also have to destroy the station, of course, in order to release that portion of the Khameirian life essence within my own mind. And the most expedient means of transport, Doctor,' Silver said, 'would seem to be your TARDIS.'

The Doctor's face clouded over. 'How do you know about that?' he demanded, his voice a low, harsh whisper.

'I know all sorts of things about you, Doctor. You may soon discover the source of my information.'

'The Khameirian mind?'

Silver snorted with amusement. 'Doctor, you may know something about the Khameirian. But please don't be so naive or egotistic as to assume that they would know anything about you.' He shook his head, like a disapproving headmaster. 'We're wasting time.'

Silver stepped back, allowing Kellerman to enter the gallery. He reached out. Sam tried to duck, to twist away, but she was too slow. Kellerman grabbed her by the hair and pulled her violently towards him. The pistol jammed into her cheek. Maybe growing her hair had been a bad move. Maybe if he pulled a little harder, she wouldn't have to worry about her hair any more.

'Like Mr Silver said,' Kellerman drawled, 'we're wasting time.' He jerked his head to indicate that the Doctor should follow Silver out of the gallery.

The Doctor scowled, buttoned his coat, and started down the stairs. Kellerman released his grip on Sam, and pushed her after him.

They made their way through the house in silence. Kellerman had put the pistol in his jacket pocket, and he kept his hand in his pocket too. The jutting bulge from the jacket left Sam in no doubt that he was keeping a constant hold on the gun. She also knew that he would use it if she or the Doctor tried to run. The Doctor could give them a free ride to Station Nine, but if they had to kill him it would just mean waiting around until they got another chance to blow themselves up. Since they had already, in effect, waited for centuries, Sam didn't think this would deter Kellerman from shooting the Doctor. She was certain it wouldn't stop him shooting her.

The soldiers guarding the main entrance stood aside deferentially as they left the house. One of them asked Silver how things were going.

'Oh, quite well, thank you.'

'A couple of minor setbacks,' the Doctor added.

'But nothing we can't handle,' Kellerman said. 'Just getting some air. We have an early start tomorrow. Need a clear head.'

Silver's Range Rover was parked at the side of the forecourt. Kellerman bundled Sam into the back, drawing the pistol and holding it tight into her side.

'I can't put my seat belt on with that there,' she told him.

He jabbed it harder into her ribs. 'You don't need to buckle up. But I'm glad you're concerned about your safety.'

Sam grabbed the seat belt and pushed the buckle past the gun anyway. 'I can tell you've never accepted a lift from the Doctor.' She jammed it into its socket and heard a reassuring click. Kellerman gave a short laugh.

Silver sat in the passenger seat. 'I assume you know where we're going, Doctor.'

The Doctor climbed in behind the wheel. As he put the Range Rover into gear and skidded off the forecourt on to the lawn, Kellerman grabbed for his own seat belt. Sam tried not to laugh. The pistol still dug into her side and any movement was painful. She was unsure whether she was more worried about Kellerman's pistol or the Doctor's driving.

Pickering sat straight and still, hardly even breathing. The machine pistol lay across his lap. From the corridor outside he could just heard the sounds of people shouting, of something heavy being slammed into the door. Then after a while it went quiet.

Pickering was impassive, waiting. He did not know what he was waiting for – he had no instructions beyond preventing the launch. He just waited.

The soldiers were standing on guard by the TARDIS. There were four of them, not sure what the blue box was that they had found, but protecting it nonetheless.

Silver and Kellerman seemed undeterred by their presence. Kellerman went to speak with them, leaving Silver in the Range Rover with the Doctor, Sam, and the gun. They watched as Kellerman spoke with the soldiers, pointing across the ruins of the old house out into the darkness. After a short while he led them away from the TARDIS and out into the night.

'Right,' Silver said as soon as Kellerman and the soldiers were lost in the darkness, 'off we go.' He held the door open for Sam and she hauled herself out of the high vehicle and jumped down to the ground.

The Doctor was already waiting by the driver's door. Silver waved the gun, motioning for them to head for the TARDIS. The beam from the headlights cut through the night, splashing over the textured surface of the police box and pooling on the ground in front of it. The Doctor stepped into the beam, his shadow thrown across the front of the TARDIS, shrinking as he approached until it was the size of a man. He unlocked the door and pushed it open, allowing Sam to enter first. He followed her, leaving Silver to bring up the rear.

A moment later the stillness of the night was broken by a sudden rasp of sound, grating and rhythmic. The light from the Range Rover cut through the darkness, illuminating the broken walls of the ruined house and falling at last on the grotesque, weathered features of a gargoyle. A slight wind ruffled the trees, the sound like a distant groan.

The sound built slowly. It was rhythmic, pulsing, grating, and seemed to tear the fabric of the very air. It was as if it came from the walls of the room, out of the air, from no one discernible point in space but from everywhere. Pickering slowly stood up, looking round for the source of the sound and failing to find it. A patch of dark on the wall caught his attention. At first it was the barest hint, the intimation of a shadow. Then as Pickering watched, the shadow slowly solidified, pulsing darker in time to the grating sound.

He checked the machine pistol, and took cover behind one of the consoles as the shadow solidified, became a dark blue. In a moment it had taken on the form of an obsolete police telephone box, the light on the top flashing in time with the unearthly noise.

Then, with a thump as solid as the police box had become, the noise ceased. The light went out and the door opened.

If Silver had been either surprised or impressed by the interior of the TARDIS, he had disguised the fact completely. His check of the scanner screen had been cursory, enough to satisfy himself that Pickering was no longer in the room.

'Job done, so it would seem that our friend has left.' Silver waved the Doctor and Sam forward.

Sam glanced at the Doctor, who raised an eyebrow. Then he made for the main doors. Sam followed him out into Station Nine, aware of Silver close behind her.

The room seemed empty. The Doctor quickly checked de Tannerie's body, though it was obvious even to Sam that he was beyond help.

Silver stood behind them, pistol in hand. 'Let's not waste time on the dead, Doctor,' he said. 'Our business, I think, is over here.' He turned towards the main console. The top surface was dusted with blood from where de Tannerie had been shot. 'Now, then, where is the launch control, do you suppose?' Silver surveyed the controls, and Sam could see the fire in his eyes as he anticipated the final moment. She looked at the Doctor, and saw that his face was grim. He caught her eye, and nodded slightly. Now, Sam thought, while he's distracted, while he thinks he's won. Now is the time to strike. She braced herself, about to launch her body across the space to Silver, hoping to knock the gun from his hand or at least surprise him enough for the Doctor to complete the task.

But before she could move, while she was still coiled tight, Pickering rose from behind the console. The butt of his machine pistol stabbed forward into Silver's gun hand. Silver yelped, and dropped the pistol. It clattered to the floor, and Pickering kicked it away into a corner where it spun to a stop on the polished metal floor.

'I should have guessed it would be you,' Pickering said. 'Somehow the police box seems appropriate.' He pushed Silver away from the console with one hand, the other holding the gun poised. Then he stepped towards the Doctor and Sam.

'You trust us?' Sam asked him.

Pickering did not take his eyes off Silver. 'I think so, yes.' He gestured at Silver with the gun. 'I certainly don't trust him. I can't let you complete the firing sequence, Silver. You know I can't. You know why I can't, why my mind won't let me.'

'But why do you trust us?'

'Instinct, partly.'

'Good. And?'

'And he had a gun on you,' Pickering added. 'Which suggests his goals and yours may well be rather different.'

'You bet.'

Silver coughed politely. He was still nursing his injured hand, but otherwise seemed to have regained all his composure and calm. 'May I say something?'

'If you must,' Pickering answered.

'Thank you.' His voice was quiet and reasonable. 'I shall fire those missiles. My whole life has been a rehearsal for this moment, so I'm not going to let you prevent me, I'm afraid.'

The Doctor spoke for the first time: 'I don't think it would help you, though, would it?'

'How do you mean?'

'There is a large portion of the Khameirian in your own mind still. There has to be for it to maintain control.'

Silver laughed. The sound echoed round the metal room. It was not pleasant. 'You think that if I destroy the host minds on Earth, that will be insufficient, that the Khameirian will not achieve the level of mental mass necessary to *become* again?'

'I do.'

Silver snorted in derision. 'But distance is nothing to us. We found Siolfor and his pathetic cronies across the trackless wastes of space, heard their minds crying out in the wilderness.'

'Waste of space is about right,' Sam muttered. But nobody seemed to hear her.

'The controls here are simple, and the trigger codes allow for a target override,' Silver continued. 'I don't need all the missiles that President Dering has kindly made available in order to release the Khameirian trapped in the minds on Earth.'

'Of course.' The Doctor snapped his fingers in realisation. 'You'll use one of its own missiles to destroy this station. To destroy yourself.'

Silver nodded. 'Provided the energy is all released at the same moment, more or less, it can cry out to itself, combine and become whole.'

'Aren't you overlooking something?' Pickering asked, punctuating his question with a jab of the machine pistol. 'You have to be alive to retarget the missiles and complete the sequence. And I can't let you do it.' He smiled. 'You of all people should know that it's against my programming.' He lingered on the last word, sneering as if he resented having to use it.

Silver nodded. 'Oh, I think I know more about your *programming* than you do, Captain.' He took a few paces sideways, thoughtfully tapping his chin. Pickering's gun immediately tracked his movements. 'Did you know that I have a few fail-safes of my own? No?' He stopped, turned, and paced back the other way.

'You mean mental fail-safes?' the Doctor asked. 'Mind locks?'

'The captain's programming is a conditioned response to a trigger phrase – oh, I do apologise for the term under the present circumstances. He is literally unable to take a decision as it has already been taken for him. No choices. An option lock. It is a simple enough technique, and one that has the advantage of staying hidden, buried deep in the mind until activated. It is so useful, in fact, that as a fail-safe I instil such behaviour into everyone that I work with.'

'I don't believe you.' Pickering's aim did not waver or hesitate.

Silver shrugged. 'I don't really care one way or the other. You know…' He switched direction again, pacing the floor like a caged animal. Except that he seemed to think he was in control. 'You know, your programming is a little different. It wasn't just a simple trigger phrase, but also the absence of a predetermined phrase under certain circumstances. I had to go quite deep for that, although I did not know the purpose, the application, when I inserted the behaviour into you mind. It had to be so deep that you could not reveal the significance of the phrase any more than you could ever forget it. Where were you to be posted?' he asked suddenly. 'Nobody knew about Station Nine when I programmed you.'

'The suggestion was that I would act as liaison officer on

board a nuclear submarine or perhaps at the Pentagon. There would be others.'

Silver clapped his hands together. 'So the British Empire keeps control after all. I like it. I like it.'

The Doctor tapped his foot on the floor. 'This is fascinating, but it isn't actually telling us anything new. I suggest we all go back into the TARDIS and away from the temptation out here. Then we can work out what to do next.' He glanced slightly nervously at Pickering, at the gun tracking Silver's movements.

'Good idea, seconded,' Sam said. 'All those for raise your hands. Anyone against?'

Silver continued as if neither of them had said anything. He was speaking directly to Pickering now. 'But there was more to your programming than that. I wonder how much you yourself know, how much you remember or have been briefed on.' Pickering did not answer, so Silver continued. 'No matter. Suffice it to say there is also a control phrase embedded in your mind, a phrase that will precipitate another course of action. I had fun testing it that night in the fountain. I would guess that the course of action it prescribes is the inverse of the other trigger phrase. In other words, the firing of the missiles.' He stopped, turned to face Pickering, his hands open at his sides. 'The irony, of course,' he said with a smile, 'is that while I prepared your mind for that phrase, I have no idea what that phrase might be. I merely made your mind responsive, provided the key, as it were. What happened next is between you and your commanding officers. A pity.'

'So much for your mind lock, then,' Sam remarked, not without a feeling of relief.

'Ah, yes.' Silver rubbed his hands together, and Sam could see the sweat glistening on his palms. This was evidently the moment of truth, his last shot. He licked his lips. His voice was flat, calm, emotionless, as he said in clear tones, 'The lion and the lamb will lie down together.'

Silence. For a moment nobody spoke. Then, as if through a fog, Sam heard Pickering laugh. 'But the lamb won't get much sleep,' he said. 'If you thought your phrase would work, I've got some bad news for you, Silver.'

Somewhere at the back of Sam's mind a memory flared, burning its way to the front of her brain.

The library was shot through with lightning as the energy crackled round the Philosopher's Stone. The intensity of the light built still further, the Stone glowing a brilliant yellow within its display case.

It was like a calm before the storm. Except that nothing had happened. The Doctor watched Pickering closely, saw that Silver's words had no effect on the captain, and breathed a sigh of relief.

'The problem may be that you yourself programmed Pickering to be immune to mind control,' the Doctor pointed out.

Silver's rebuke was abrupt. 'Don't be naive, Doctor,' he sneered. 'I expected more of you.'

The movement came out of the corner of his eye. He blinked at the speed of it, threw his hand up in front of his face instinctively as Sam launched herself at Pickering. Her shoulder cannoned into his chest, catching him completely off guard. He dropped the machine pistol, though it clung to his arm by the shoulder strap as he sprawled on the floor. Sam's punch slammed into his jaw, crunching his face sideways as she tore the gun from him.

It took only a few seconds, then Sam was standing beside Silver, behind the main console. The body of Colonel de Tannerie lay just behind her, his blood pooling at her feet.

Sam's eyes looked slightly glassy, as if she were trying not to cry. But the gun was steady in her grip.

'Good,' breathed Silver. 'In fact, excellent, Miss Jones.' He walked over to the main console. 'Now perhaps you will be good enough to stay where you are under Miss Jones's watchful gun while I sort out these targeting instructions. It stops here, Doctor,' he said. 'I am the last of the true Siolfor line. The culmination of the life essence of the Khameirian. It stops here.'

The Doctor helped Pickering to his feet. 'We were talking about Pythagoras,' he said keeping his voice calm, loud enough for Sam to hear clearly, 'weren't we, Sam?'

'I don't think she can hear you, Doctor,' Pickering told him as he rubbed his jaw and winced.

'We talked about science and maths,' the Doctor went on, 'you remember? About that day at the blacksmith's. You would think from that anecdote that Pythagoras had an open mind, wouldn't you? That he could appreciate, assimilate, even welcome new ideas.' He fixed his stare on Sam, aware that his words seemed to be having no effect, aware that in all probability they would continue to have no effect. But at least he could talk and think at the same time. 'He was burned to death, you know. In his school.' The Doctor forced a laugh and nudged Pickering playfully in the ribs. 'Another parallel with our current situation, actually.' He broke off his laugh as he caught sight of Pickering's expression. 'You're not amused. Oh well.' He sucked in his cheeks. 'Perhaps he deserved it after all. Pythagoras, I mean.'

'Doctor,' Pickering said quietly, 'what are you talking about?'

'Who knows?' the Doctor admitted in a whisper that he hoped only Pickering could make out. 'But if I can distract her even for a second...' He left the thought unfinished, but he could see that Pickering caught its meaning. Silver, working at the console, seemed not to have noticed the exchange while Sam stood immobile and emotionless.

'Yes,' the Doctor went on, his voice back at its former volume, 'there's the rub. He was working in his study one day – I don't know what he was working on but it hardly matters – when one of his students came to Pythagoras with the early draft of a paper he was writing. It was in fact a theory of irrational numbers. Now,' he went on, 'you thought that Euclid discovered irrational numbers, didn't you?'

'Absolutely.' Pickering's voice was laden with sarcasm. 'I was certain of it.'

The Doctor continued undeterred. 'And of course you are quite right. But long before that, a student of Pythagoras went to his master, his mentor, with in effect the theory of irrational numbers. So what happened?' When nobody ventured an opinion, the Doctor answered his own question. 'I'll tell you. Pythagoras, the great thinker, the philosopher with the open mind, could not accept it. He was unable to see past the integer and simple fractions. Well, the student persisted. He had a point and he knew it. "OK," he said to Pythagoras, only in ancient Greek, of course, "OK, so what's the square root of two, expressed as an integer or a simple fraction?"'

The Doctor leaned forward slightly, stared deep into Sam's eyes. Was there a flicker of interest there? The merest hint that she was listening? If there was, he could not see it. 'The old man's response was pretty extreme,' the Doctor said slowly. 'A little unexpected, but he won the argument. At least on his terms. Another analogy, perhaps.' The Doctor exhaled slowly. Now or never. He took in a deep breath, remembering the events as he described them, remembering the numbing shock he had felt at the time and hoping to reproduce just a fraction of it in Sam's brain. If she could hear him. 'Pythagoras, the great man, the teacher, the philosopher, the father of modern mathematics,' he said slowly, 'when presented with this new and different theory, had the student taken out and drowned.'

Sam blinked. Not much of a reaction, but it was enough. Pickering hurled himself at her. The sound of the gun was amplified by the metal walls, floor and ceiling. The chatter of gunfire was a riot of echoing reports. The bullets tore into Pickering's shoulder, ripped down across his side as he was in mid-air. His momentum carried him forward and he smashed into Sam, knocking the gun aside. The next burst of fire rattled harmlessly off the armour plate of the ceiling.

Sam was knocked backward, her feet skidding on the sticky pool at her feet, sliding on the new blood that spattered from Pickering's shoulder and side. She crashed to the floor, her head connecting heavily with the metal. Her eyes opened suddenly very wide, and she screamed. She was still screaming as she knelt up, staring down at her hands, the gore dripping scarlet from them.

Pickering groaned, coughed, pulled the machine pistol across the floor towards him.

Silver leapt towards Pickering, but he was too late. The gun swung up to cover him.

The Doctor pulled Sam up into his arms, pressed his cheek against the sticky mess on her face, tried to turn her away and protect her from the sight. Her voice was muffled by his coat, and after a while she stopped screaming. She sobbed into his shirt and he ran his fingers through her hair, held her tight, hugged her to him desperately.

Silver took a step backward, towards the console.

'Don't even think about it,' Pickering coughed. The blood was heavy in his throat, but the gun held steady. 'If the Doctor's right, I can kill you now, and this thing stops here.'

'That's right,' the Doctor said quietly. 'He has no descendants.

If he dies, it dies with him. And there is not enough of the Khameirian left in the other minds to survive without him. It will slowly seep away. Harmless.' He pushed Sam gently away from him and looked into her eyes. They focused back on his own, and he smiled. 'Take Captain Pickering into the TARDIS, Sam,' he said softly. Then he stepped forward and flicked a couple of switches on the main console. Somewhere in the distance, outside the sealed room, a klaxon sounded.

She frowned, her blood- and tear-stained face crumpling. 'What about you? And Silver?'

'It stops here,' he said sadly. 'I can see no other way.'

'What are you saying?'

'I've sounded an evacuation alarm to warn the rest of the crew out there to abandon the station.' The Doctor's hands were moving like lightning now over the various control systems. 'Right, that's the two missiles targeted at Abbots Siolfor disabled.'

'And the other one?' Pickering asked huskily.

'The other one I shall need.' He turned to Sam. 'Please go,' he said quietly.

She shook her head. 'What are you going to do?'

'There's no other way, Sam. Even shooting him might not actually release the Khameirian. It might find a route from his mind back to the others. It has to stop here.'

'You're going to blow up the station. And yourself and Silver.'

'It's the only way to be sure that it stops here. The major part of the Khameirian in Silver's mind can't survive without the release of the rest of the Khameirian essence. And when it is destroyed, utterly destroyed, the human hosts on Earth will be free. It will dissipate, become nothing, and they will return to their normal selves. There's no way I can see to set a timer without launching the missile, and once launched its own inbuilt safety features won't permit it to detonate within range of the station. Believe me, Sam, if there were another way…'

'There is.' Pickering's voice was a rasp of pain. 'I'm dying, Doctor. I can explode the missiles.'

The Doctor shook his head sadly. 'This is my responsibility,' he said. 'You've already saved the world twice today.'

Pickering laughed, the sound a fluid rumble in his chest. 'Why do I get the impression you do that before breakfast most days?'

A movement off to the left. Pickering was slow, coughing again, swinging the gun round just too late. Silver had dived across the floor, and came up with his pistol, recovered from the corner where it had lain since Pickering had kicked it away a lifetime ago. The shot caught Pickering in the forearm, sending a fresh plume of blood across the floor.

Pickering coughed again, a trickle of blood dribbling down from his mouth and lipping under his chin. The gun slipped from his grasp and clattered to the floor beside him.

Silver was already back at the console. 'I won't kill you, Doctor,' he snarled. 'Not yet. I want you to see this, or as close as you get. I want you to know you've failed.'

'You'll have to work out how to retarget the missiles, first.'

Silver snorted with rage, and turned his attention to the console. The pistol was firm in his grip, and he glanced back at the Doctor and Sam as he fumbled with the controls. 'I can do it,' he hissed. 'I can do it.'

'Sam.' Pickering's voice was barely more than a whisper. 'Sam…'

The Doctor took Sam's arm, gently pushing her towards Pickering. She knelt beside him, tears in her eyes. 'I'm sorry. God, I'm so sorry,' she sobbed.

Pickering shook his head. 'No. Not your fault. You had no option. Believe me, I know. You weren't responsible.' He coughed, more blood erupting from his mouth. 'But we do make our own destinies, despite what we may have to do.' He grabbed her hand, gripped it hard. His voice was barely more than a whisper now. Sam bent closer to hear him, his bloody mouth close to her ear. 'Tell me,' he croaked, 'tell me that free will is not an illusion.' He stared up at her, eyes large, pleading. 'I have to know.'

Sam looked from Pickering to the Doctor. The Doctor kept his face impassive, expressionless. It had to be her decision.

'It's not.' Her voice was choked. 'We decide our own actions and destinies.'

'Tell me.' His grip tightened on her hand.

Sam bit back a sob. 'Free will is not an illusion,' she said. And even as she completed the sentence, she realised what he had done.

Pickering's eyes glazed over as he hauled himself painfully to his feet. He coughed, retched, then seemed to gather himself.

'No,' Sam sobbed. The Doctor pressed his hands to the sides of her shoulders, turned her gently and led her quickly towards the TARDIS. She kept her head turned, watched Pickering and Silver all the way.

Pickering staggered towards Silver. His confidence seemed to increase with each step. Silver saw him, raised the pistol, shouted at him to stand still.

But Pickering kept coming.

The first bullet tore into his chest, knocked him back a step. But he stumbled forwards again, increasing his speed so that his shuffle became a walk.

Silver screamed in rage. The second bullet slammed into Pickering's shoulder, twisted him sideways. His walk was almost a run now.

Silver fired twice more. The first shot caught Pickering in the upper leg so that he crumpled to one side. But still he kept on. The last shot caught him under the chin as he was almost at the console. His head snapped back, but his momentum carried him forward. He fell across the console, arms outstretched. One hand closed on Silver's throat. The other curled into a claw and inched painfully towards the firing control.

'No!' Silver screamed. 'I haven't reset the co-ordinates!'

Pickering's finger connected with the button.

The TARDIS doors slammed shut, cutting off Sam's view.

Station Nine hung in space like a giant metal spider. Somewhere along one of the limbs, the legs, a tiny bloom of fire grew and blossomed. It was followed by another, and another. Then the whole station was ripped apart by the sudden burst of white light. The fireball spread soundlessly in all directions, buffeting the two tiny shuttles that were racing for the upper atmosphere of Earth.

In a moment the light faded. There was no debris, no hint that the station had ever been there. Just the blackness of space, the tiny pinprick lights of the stars, and a battered old police telephone box floating in the stillness of the void. On its top, a light flashed briefly. Then it faded, and the box too was gone. Darkness.

The library was in darkness. The faint glow from the Philosopher's Stone faded finally to nothing.

Below, in the control room, the conference delegates and Silver's guests sank dizzily to their knees or slumped into chairs, suddenly disorientated.

Half a mile away, Lord Meacher's Clump and the decaying chapel and alien craft it concealed were ripped apart by the awful brilliance of a huge explosion. Lines of fire stabbed up into the night sky and debris rained down heavily over the estate.

Somewhere in the grounds of Abbots Siolfor, near the ruins of the old house, a soldier grabbed Peter Kellerman to prevent him from collapsing in the middle of a lecture.

Upstairs in the house, Penelope Silver stirred. Her arm reached out, flopped across the pillow beside her, feeling sleepily for the husband who wasn't there. Her cheek was damp against the sheets, and she realised she had been crying in her sleep.

Dark Waters

In the years since I had last been there, it hadn't changed a bit. But since it was only a month later, this wasn't really surprising. It was an impulse, I suppose. Dangerous thing, impulse. But enough time had passed, for me if not for anyone else.

My feet crunched through the snow and into the gravel as I approached the house. Images flashed through my mind, mainly of myself running like hell in the dark of night. It was strange, disorientating, being back there and knowing so much had changed. So much was as it had seemed to be when we first arrived, all those years ago. The previous month.

Miss Allworthy answered the door. She was the epitome of the English housekeeper, polite, refined, proper – whatever that means. She recognised me, I could tell. But she was too polite to say anything. I said I'd wait in the Library, and she told me that she would see if Mrs Silver was at home today. Which meant, of course, that she was.

There was one of Coulter's pictures on the wall. I had seen it before, but now I looked at it knowing more than the unfortunate painter about the eccentricities of the landscape and its tricks of perspective. I also saw a sadness, a premonition of disaster in the line of the trees, as though even then, even as he started into his work, his final moments had already been captured on the canvas of the universe. I guess you get like that when you travel with the Doctor.

Maybe it was a catharsis of some sort. You tell yourself it's OK, that you've recovered. But I went to Abbots Siolfor and met a man who I killed. Actually, I didn't kill him. But turn the coin over, look at it another way and you could say *I killed him twice*. And however you turn it, whichever perspective you use, a part of me died with him on Station Nine.

The Philosopher's Stone was exactly where it had been before, framed in a glass display case on the wall. The bright light from the spotlight illuminated the mottled veins of pattern on the stone's surface. In my mood of winter dread, I stared at the patterns and saw shapes that – just perhaps – weren't there. So if the darker patches of the textured surface appeared fragile, frail, foetal, it was surely my imagination.

And if the stone seemed to glow incandescently, as if lit from within, it was surely a trick of the light reflecting off the glass and the polished surface of the egglike stone.

And however hard I stared, on that cold winter's afternoon, I was almost certain that nothing moved or rippled darkly beneath the surface of the Philosopher's Stone.

'Sam?'

As I turned, I caught a glimpse of my reflection in the glass of the display case. Caught my own eye. And I wondered again what she must think when she saw me.

'Hello, Penelope.'

'Is it really you?' She lowered herself carefully into a chair, feeling for it behind her as she stared at me transfixed. She looked tired, but otherwise in good health. Her long auburn hair cascaded over her shoulders in a perfect symmetry. In fact, she looked more striking than I had remembered. Glowing, almost. Radiant.

'Yeah. It's me.' I grinned, embarrassed. 'It's been a long time. For me, anyway.'

She nodded, as if she understood.

It was difficult at first, getting over the appearance. How do you explain the years you've gained in a month? But we got through the small talk and she stared at me less obviously as the conversation progressed. She asked me whether I was still with the Doctor, hoping, I think, for a more interesting answer than the one I was prepared to give. She asked me if I knew about her husband, obviously assuming that I did. She didn't cry when she told me about the terrorist attack on the house that night, while she slept, about the explosion that destroyed Lord Meacher's Clump and left her husband dead. Not quite.

And I didn't tell her what really happened, what everyone else who had been there had fought hard to cover up and hide from her. Not quite.

'Do you miss him?' It was a stupid question, and I guess I was asking it selfishly – for myself, about someone else. I guess she knew that.

'Of course I do. There isn't a day when I don't think about him. Sometimes,' she said, 'I hear his voice, or see him across a crowded room or in town. But when I go there or look again, it isn't him. There is an emptiness that it will be difficult to fill.'

'You'll manage,' I told her. 'You'll think of him less as the memories fade. There'll be odd reminders now and again. A recollected event, a familiar turn of phrase. But it fades.'

She smiled. 'No,' she said quietly. 'I don't think it will. You see, I shall have a more constant reminder of him soon.' And she told me her news.

I went cold. It was the sudden, dreaded cold of getting out of your warm bed on a winter's morning when you know the cold will hit you, when you feel that you spend your whole life caught at this moment of decision. Between the warm and the chill. Between the day ahead and the nightmares. The chill rippled down my spine and a lump formed in my throat. I sat down heavily, hoping my face did not betray my fear.

'It's just so sad Norton can't be here with us,' she said. 'He so wanted a child.' And this time she did cry.

Beyond her, on the snowy bank outside, I could see a mass of the tiny cobalt-blue-petalled flowers. They were waving gently on their orange stalks in the winter's breeze.

The Doctor and Sam are caught up in events that
will change their relationship for ever in

LONGEST DAY
by Michael Collier
(available March 1998)

Their adventures continue in

LEGACY OF THE DALEKS
by John Peel
(April 1998)

DREAMSTONE MOON
by Paul Leonard
(May 1998)

SEEING I
by Jonathan Blum and Kate Orman
(June 1998)